a sharp intake of breath

a sharp intake of breath

{a novel}

JOHN MILLER

SIMON & PIERRE FICTION
A MEMBER OF THE DUNDURN GROUP
TORONTO

Editor: Barry Jowett
Copy-editor: Jennifer Gallant
Design: Alison Carr
Printer: Webcom

Library and Archives Canada Cataloguing in Publication

Library and Archives Canada Cataloguing in Publication

Miller, John, 1968-
    A sharp intake of breath / John Miller.

ISBN-13: 978-1-55002-607-8
ISBN-10: 1-55002-607-0

    I. Title.

PS8576.I53885S53 2007   C813'.6   C2006-904259-4

1 2 3 4 5   10 09 08 07 06

Conseil des Arts du Canada   Canada Council for the Arts   Canada

ONTARIO ARTS COUNCIL
CONSEIL DES ARTS DE L'ONTARIO

We acknowledge the support of the **Canada Council for the Arts** and the **Ontario Arts Council** for our publishing program. We also acknowledge the financial support of the **Government of Canada** through the **Book Publishing Industry Development Program** and **The Association for the Export of Canadian Books**, and the **Government of Ontario** through the **Ontario Book Publishers Tax Credit program** and the **Ontario Media Development Corporation.**

Care has been taken to trace the ownership of copyright material used in this book. The author and the publisher welcome any information enabling them to rectify any references or credits in subsequent editions.
J. Kirk Howard, President

Printed and bound in Canada
Printed on recycled paper
www.dundurn.com

Dundurn Press
3 Church Street, Suite 500
Toronto, Ontario, Canada
M5E 1M2

Gazelle Book Services Limited
White Cross Mills
High Town, Lancaster, England
LA1 4XS

Dundurn Press
2250 Military Road
Tonawanda, NY
U.S.A. 14150

for my parents

acknowledgements

It has been said many times that all novelists are thieves. And, since this novel deals in part with guilt and confession, I must get something off my chest: While doing my research, I discovered early life experiences of two late friends of my grandparents, and found their stories to be irresistible. One friend, a jovial, respectable old man I had known at my grandmother's Passover table, spent ten years in Kingston Penitentiary in the 1930s for a mistake made as an eighteen-year-old boy. Another, shy, quiet Molly Ackerman, a talented textile artist, was Emma Goldman's secretary in the 1930s, when Goldman lived in Toronto. Molly is mentioned briefly in *Living My Life*, and a letter to her from Goldman can be found in the Berkeley archives. (Thanks also to Molly's daughter Nancy Ackerman for sharing her memories.)

I was lucky to interview the following people whose recollections of Toronto in the 1930s contributed to important contextual material: retired labour organizer Ernie Arnold; retired accountant Albert Friedman; Warren and Joyce Soloman; labour activist and former comrade of Emma Goldman's, Marie Tiboldo; and dear family friends Dorothy and Harry Stone and Edith Pike.

Paula Klaiman, speech/language pathologist, and Dr. Bill Lindsay, retired cleft lip and palate surgeon, both from the Hospital for Sick Children in Toronto, helped provide valuable knowledge on the surgical procedures and speech therapy used with cleft lip and palate children in Toronto in the 1920s. Dr. Coleman Romalis of York University helped provide insight into Goldman's Toronto years.

For assistance with research into Emma Goldman's and Sidonie Colette's lives in the South of France, many thanks go to the following residents of St-Tropez: Marius Astézan, the town's *cépoun*; Laurent Pavlidis and Simone Carrat of the Heritage Society; Marie-Ange Raboutet, town archivist; David Singleton of the Tourism Board; the notaries in the firm of Maître Bortolotti and Maître Malafosse-Bortolotti. It must be emphasized that although my research did in fact lead to the discovery of the location of Bon Esprit, the reader should not presume that the Tropéziens depicted in this novel are in fact the individuals mentioned above. And, although there is no evidence that Goldman and Colette ever met while living in St-Tropez during the same period, the passion with which the Tropéziens spoke of Colette was infectious. I couldn't resist imagining how such a meeting might have transpired.

I also owe thanks to social worker Ruth Goodman for her insight into geriatrics and life at Baycrest Centre for Geriatric Care and The Terrace, and to Bob Kellermann for his advice on the Canadian legal system.

For detailed critical feedback on early and later drafts, I'm indebted to my mother, Ruth Miller (wordsmith extraordinaire), to my agent Beverley Slopen, to my editor Barry Jowett, and especially to talented novelists Elizabeth Ruth and Sally Cooper, with whom I've had the privilege of being in a writing group these past four years. For their general support, I thank the rest of my family — my father, Eric, Tony, Daniel, Joanne, Michele, and Donna — and many friends and colleagues. For specific input and encouragement, I thank Patty Barclay, Craig Mills, Pam Shime, Hilary Trapp, and Dubravka Zarkov. Most of all, I'm grateful for the unwavering encouragement and counsel of my dear friends Vanessa Russell and Debra Shime. Thanks also to copy editor Jennifer Gallant and designer Alison Carr.

Bibliographic and video sources used include the Hon. Mr. Justice Joseph Archambault's 1938 *Report of the Royal Commission to Investigate the Penal System of Canada*; Baycrest Terrace Memoirs Group's *From Our Lives*; CBC Television's special program *Inside Canada's Prisons*; Jean Cochrane's *Kensington*; Colette's *Break of Day*; numerous letters from the University of California, Berkeley's Emma Goldman Archives (Candace Falk, editor); Ruth Frager's *Sweatshop Strife*; Jules Henry's *On Sham, Vulnerability & Other Forms of Self-Destruction*; Kyle Joliffe's *Penitentiary Medical Services 1835-1983*; Alix Kates Shulman's *Red Emma Speaks*; John Kidman's *The Canadian Prison: The Story of a Tragedy*; Paula Klaiman et al's video *Step by Step: Speech Therapy Techniques for Cleft Palate Speech*; Emma Goldman's *Living My Life* and *Anarchism & Other Essays*; Compton Mackenzie's *On Moral Courage*; Albert Meltzer's *Anarchism: Arguments For & Against*; Ken Moffat's *A Poetics of Social Work*; Teresa & Albert Moritz's *The Most Dangerous Woman in the World: A New Biography of Emma Goldman*; Thomas Nisters's *Aristotle on Courage*; Erna Paris's *Jews: An Account of Their Experience in Canada*; Stanley J. Rachman's *Fear and Courage*; Coleman Romalis's video *The Anarchist Guest*; John Sebert's *The "Nabes": Toronto's Wonderful Neighbourhood Movie Houses*; Stephen A. Speisman's *Jews in Toronto*; Stephen Tudor's *Compassion and Remorse: Acknowledging the Suffering of Others*; and Douglas Walton's *Courage: A Philosophical Investigation*.

fault

small sculptures

My first word was the subject of spirited debate; the cleft in my palate made it hard to make out. Aside from my sister Lil, who was too little to care, each relative was certain I'd said something different. My father, whose hearing wasn't good, thought I'd said "coat." My mother declared I was saying "Ma!", and she stood her ground, hopefully. A cousin was sure I wanted "up" to her eager, childless arms, and my grandmother, always critical of Ma's housekeeping, insisted I was pointing to the mop.

My other sister, Bessie, was only seven, but she was already looking out for me. She said I was asking for help.

FOR A LONG TIME, A SIMPLE BREATH could pack terror into the spongy expanse of my lungs, because I couldn't hold it forever, and so much depended on what happened next. They said that cleft lip and cleft palate didn't always afflict the same child, but I had the bad luck to be born with a split that wasn't satisfied remaining either outside or in — it ran down my upper lip and all the way to the back of my mouth's roof.

If I simply exhaled, if I allowed that breath to flow freely, barely a sound was made. That was the perilous decision I had to make as a boy: having no voice or using the one I was given. If, on the other hand, the air I exhaled passed by the vocal cords, and if those cords were allowed to vibrate, voicing was produced.

Voice isn't really what I'm talking about, of course, except metaphorically. Voicing is animalistic, feral, instinctive. It's what chimpanzees, or hyenas, or even small infants do: they groan, they screech, they cry. It's saying "ahhhh" when the doctor prods with his tongue depressor.

Speech, on the other hand, is a phenomenon not as much produced as it is shaped. Each word is a small sculpture.

Any person can squish a lump of clay through his fingers (provided he has fingers to begin with) and produce a random form, determined only by grunting pressure, how much or how little, and what oozes out here and there. Fashioning that shape into something recognizable or useful requires more than a haphazard neural impulse and a contraction of the muscles.

When a word is spoken, air first travels up the vocal tract, but then it must be directed, through either the nose or the mouth, depending on the action of the soft palate and the velopharyngeal valve. By the time the word reaches our ears, many instruments have had their chance with it: cords, valves, palates, tongue, teeth, lips. Obviously then, having good tools is essential to proper enunciation. I can work soft clay free of the spinning wheel if I apply strength and temper that force with measured restraint, but it'll take me time, and in the process of dislodging, I'll squash the bowl I've worked on. A wire passed underneath will do it swiftly and cleanly each time.

Problem was, I was handed defective tools.

Hare-lip (hæɹlɪp) n.
1. *A separation of the skin of the upper lip running right up to the nose, making the child's face look like a bunny rabbit. Meant to be adorable. Mildly offensive.*

I had only a partial separation of the skin, slightly to the right of centre as you took in my face, and the nostril on that side was a little flattened and askew. In that respect, I was luckier than some, who had a double cleft, or whose deformity was bad enough that their nose was a piece of cauliflower. In my case, "hare" didn't really fit me. I had an indent rather than a split, making my upper lip a bracket tipped over. A pointed, grammatical bracket calling attention to the tip of my tongue, which just sat there because I hadn't grown teeth yet and my tongue had nowhere to hide:

Here! Just down here is the tip of Herman's tongue!

A neighbour told my mother that if there was any animal to compare me to, it might be a serpent. She said she hoped for my sake that my teeth grew in properly because everyone knew from the story of Adam and Eve that a serpent wasn't to be trusted.

Serpent-tongue (sɜɹpn̩tʌŋ) n.

1. *The child's tongue, resting there in the opening of the malformed mouth, appearing ready to dart out at any moment and test the air to see if the climate is right for treachery.*

When I was six years old, Ma decided I needed speech lessons. Toronto's Hospital for Sick Children had one therapist then, but her time was stretched thin and she worked mostly with kids who had lisps or stutters. There was a long waiting list and my parents were advised that time was slipping by. Fearing that if I didn't soon have lessons, I might never speak properly, they hired an elocutionist who had experience with cleft palate children.

She had a body that was thin and extremely long from bottom to top, which is how I first took her in. Our house consisted of a kitchen, a stockroom at the back of the store, and a dining room stuck on the rump end of the living room. Also, there were three bedrooms and the bathroom above. I was chasing after Lil, playing a game of tag, and we'd just thundered down the wooden stairs and turned the corner through the dining room/living room. Lil had darted past the new obstacle, but as I rounded the corner into the kitchen, I ran smack into it, right into its long, scratchy wool skirt. I stared up. The lady's perfume made my nostrils twitch, and her face reminded me of a prune. Did people make fun of her too? Did she have older sisters who teased her, called her prune-face when her mother wasn't looking?

"Hello," she said. Lil bolted outside, eager to avoid the company, and I made a move to follow her, but Ma came back into the kitchen from hanging the lady's coat near the back door and thwarted my escape with a scoop of her arm. She stilled my kicking legs by putting me down in front of the prune-lady.

"This is Mrs. Debardeleben, darling. She's going to help you learn to speak normally."

Debardeleben. I couldn't believe it. Two sets of alternating *d*s and *b*s — it was a cruel joke. The measure of a successful student must have been one who could finally pronounce her name.

Mrs. Debardeleben said, "I need a pitcher of water, a glass, and a wash basin," and when Ma produced these for her, she took me into the living room. She moved the lamp onto the floor and placed the pitcher, glass, and basin on the small table beside us. I glanced to see if Ma was watching, but she'd returned to the kitchen. You rearranged furniture at your peril.

Mrs. Debardeleben sat in Pop's wingback chair and propped me upright on the ottoman. She poured a glass of water and said, "Gargle for thirty seconds and then spit into the basin. This will exercise the throat muscles."

I took the water into my mouth and tried to gargle, but it wouldn't stay in the back of my throat. Some of it dribbled out my nose and the rest of it seeped back down my air passages. I started coughing and choking until I hacked and spewed into the basin and onto Mrs. Debardeleben's scratchy skirt. Her lips pursed.

After a few attempts that produced much the same result, she declared, "We will leave that exercise for now. Next, I want you to concentrate on the back of your throat and make it move without making any sound at all."

This was a feat I could no more do than wiggle my ears. Neither Lil nor I could wiggle our ears, but Bessie could. I thought if Bessie had a cleft palate, she would manage it better. That was the first time I remember questioning why I'd been born the way I was. It was also the first time I wished that my sisters had been born that way instead of me. This thought came with surprisingly little guilt and even carried a syrupy satisfaction that coated my tongue. I imagined what it might be like to tease Bessie, who fooled Ma and Pop into thinking she was a goody two-shoes, or Lil, who was hot and cold, one minute my best buddy, the next my tormentor.

After a few weeks, Mrs. Debardeleben decided we'd try different exercises.

"Place your fingers in your mouth to stretch the muscles of your palate."

I tried, but when it was clear my fingers were too short to reach far enough back, she drew from her bag a scary metal instrument that she said should do the trick. She prodded it into my big, gaping maw.

Those were the words she used. "Open up, now. I want to see a big, gaping maw!"

The first time she said it, I stared at her goggle-eyed until she explained that my maw was not the same thing as my mother.

"A maw — m-a-w — is an animal's mouth," she said, with a slight smile. "Learning to speak like a proper human being is what distinguishes us from the animals." The implication was clear, even to a six-year-old. Which was I, though: a hare or a serpent? Maybe it depended on my mood.

She gave me breathing exercises to ensure air would be expelled through the proper channels and with appropriate force. These I was good at, as long as I didn't get distracted by Mrs. Debardeleben when she exercised along with me. She was a gaunt woman of advanced age, and when she pronounced an *o*, all the lines on her prune-face travelled from every direction towards the edges of her mouth, stopping cold at her lipstick. A few times, I couldn't keep a laugh from escaping.

"Stop it!" she would shout. "Focus and pay attention!"

Of course, she also had me repeat sentences, giving me drills in what she called "the sounds of the body's own alphabet" — *b* and *d* (for these she used her own name: "Debra Debardeleben deliberated daily!"), and also *s*, *k*, *g*, and *ch*.

"Give Gary the chocolate cake!" she'd say, adopting a scolding tone I felt wasn't entirely make-believe. It was as though she could see into my heart and knew that, had I really been in possession of chocolate cake, and had there actually been a Gary, I wouldn't have given him squat.

"Ib 'ary the 'oclate 'ake!" is how it came out when I tried. I can't even approximate what I made of "Debra Debardeleben," but it was unrecognizable to her, and she made no bones about telling me so.

My improvement was slow, and I could tell she was frustrated.

"It's Susie, not Oozie! You must listen! And you must force yourself to stop grimacing every time. Practise in the mirror when I'm not here — you look like an ape."

I'd been wrong, then, about which animal.

Ape-cheeks (eɪptʃiks) n.

 1. *The child's lips curling outwards, causing his cheeks to bunch up around the nostrils in an attempt to form a word, making his maw appear ready to emit a simian screech, and giving him the appearance of being a retard.*

I stood in front of the mirror and practised — "Five frogs flipped and flopped!" — but I couldn't control my cheeks, no matter how hard I tried.

After several weeks of gargling and poking and breathing and repetition, Mrs. Debardeleben brought out the last weapon in her arsenal. It was yet another scary instrument, but this one she gave a name: the obturator.

The obturator was a rubber device to be inserted and pressed flat against the roof of my mouth, with a tail-piece that extended back farther, against the soft palate. Even though, by then, my palate had been surgically closed, it was still too short and didn't quite block the air at the back. Like the metal instrument she'd used earlier, this contraption was to help train and exercise my disobedient muscles, but this one was also designed to prevent the air from escaping into my nose. I had to concentrate in order not to choke on the obturator and I was nervous.

"Let's call him *Ozzie* Obturator! Think of Ozzie as your friend!"

"My friend?" I scowled, taking in Ozzie's full malevolence.

"Yes, or like a friendly houseguest who helps you with your chores," Mrs. Debardeleben crowed, with a strained smile, "and stays for afternoon tea," she added, puzzlingly. Who had time for tea in the middle of the afternoon? Certainly not families who ran a store.

I looked at the device and felt a panic I didn't understand until Ma came in briefly and said, "You'll get used to it, darling. It's a bit like the special bottle I used when you were little." Many cleft palate babies die because the gap in the roof of their mouth prevents them from building up the suction needed to get enough milk down their throat. Their mother's breasts become squishy annoyances, milk-engorged menaces that clog the air passages. Ma's midwife was able to find her an ingenious nipple for the top of the bottle. It had a special flange that she inserted into my misshapen mouth and held firm against its roof.

Like any good houseguest, Ozzie didn't overstay his welcome. A few days after giving him to me, Mrs. Debardeleben asked me where he'd gone.

"Home," I said, which earned me a slap across the face.

After that, Mrs. Debardeleben didn't overstay her welcome, either. Ma had witnessed the slap, and even though she later cuffed me herself for losing Ozzie, she didn't take kindly to others hitting her children. Besides, I'd improved a bit, and any lingering speech impediments were characterized by Mrs. Debardeleben as wilful failure on my part, an obstinacy out of which I might or might not grow.

For losing Ozzie, I had to sit in the store with Ma for a whole week on a chair by the cash register while the other kids were outside playing. I concentrated on my bottom lip, the more reliable of the two, and tried to make it quiver every time she looked my way.

Ozzie's new home was a secret hiding place behind Mr. Rothbart's International Pharmacy. Ma had trusted Mr. Rothbart implicitly ever since the influenza epidemic of 1918, when he'd slept above his store to dole out capsules, emulsions, decoctions, and infusions in the middle of the night to distressed customers. Ma had gone to him several times to try to save my sister Fannie, born just after me. Fannie died anyway, but the herbs he prepared seemed to help Pop and Lil pull through.

A row of red brick buildings formed a defensive line on the north side of St. Patrick Street, blocking access to the Ward everywhere except beside Mr. Rothbart's front door, where there was a narrow laneway. Lil and I first discovered this lane one day, the year before, when Ma was picking up eardrops for an infection Bessie was whimpering about at home in bed. I'd never had an ear infection, but I couldn't imagine it hurt more than the operation I'd just had five months back to repair the cleft in my palate. Ma told us to play outside until she picked up the medication. As soon as the door closed behind her, Lil said, "C'mon," and pulled me past the garbage can that blocked the opening of the lane.

We ran the length of the building towards a small back-yard filled with clutter, dragging our hands all the way along the wall, saying "aaaaaaaaaaah" as our fingers bounced against the knobbly brick. Lil's ponytail flopped about in front of me.

At the end of the alley, there was a fence. We could've easily climbed it, except that we were intrigued by the discarded old chairs and crates with strange writing on the sides.

"That's Chinese," said Lil.

"Chinese?" I didn't even wonder how, at six years old, she might know this. She was my older sister, and it didn't occur to me that she might make things up.

She soon lost interest in the supposedly Chinese writing and moved on to one of several piles of wet sawdust beside the crates. "Let's look for treasure!" She dropped to her knees, and I started into a pile beside hers, my heart pounding with the awesome possibilities.

Lil found two bottle caps and three pennies: a fortune to us. When I plunged both hands into the damp lumpiness, it felt like the mixture of ground almonds, flour, and egg for making *mandelbroyt* cookies. My pinky grazed something slender and pointy. I pulled it out. A fountain pen! This was much better than bottle caps, even better than pennies, and Lil knew it.

"Lemme see that. It looks expensive. I bet it belongs to Mr. Rothbart and he threw it out by accident."

"Too bad, it's mine," I said. I knew what she was up to.

"Itsh mine! Itsh mine!" she taunted, making an ugly face. In addition to my muddy-sounding *d*s and *b*s, I couldn't do *s*s at all. "You don't even know how to write — what are you gonna do with it?"

"Shut up!"

"Okay, I'm serious, I really am." Now she made her best adult-giving-a-lecture voice. "If Ma finds you with that, she'll take it away and give it back to Mr. Rothbart. So the best thing is to give it here."

"No way." I squinted. I held the pen more tightly in my fist and put my hands behind my back.

"Suit yourself. I'm tired of this game, anyway," she said, and started back along the wall. She'd hardly gone more than a foot when she paused and crouched down to look closely at one of the bricks.

"What?"

"This one's loose." She pushed with one finger and it sank slightly in. She turned and announced, slowly, like I was an idiot, "I'm going ... to try ... to pull it out." She often talked to me like that. Pretty much everyone did, and not just because I was five.

She picked at it with her fingernails, gingerly, but they weren't long enough. She pulled two barrettes from her hair and inserted them into the crevices — it worked. She dropped the brick on the ground, then stuck her hand inside. "It's perfect!" she said. "This can be our secret hiding place. Only you and me will know about it. Swear not to tell. Cross your heart, hope to die, stick a needle in your eye."

"I swear," I said, full of wonder and excitement, not only at the hiding place, but also at a shared secret.

She placed her found pennies and bottle caps in there, and then stuck her hand out. "Gimme the pen."

"No! I wanna take it home and show Bessie!"

"You can't show it to *her* — she'll tell."

Just then, we heard our names called from the street.

Lil put the brick back and grabbed my hand, pulling me up the lane to where Ma was waiting, arms crossed, expression stern.

"What have you two been up to back there?"

"Nothing, just looking around," said Lil.

"And what've you got behind your back, young man?"

"My barrette," said Lil, before I could think of an answer. "I've been trying to get him to give it back, but he won't." Lil grabbed the pen, smothering it with her hand so Ma didn't see it, and she stuffed it in her dress pocket. "He got cooties all over it — I have to clean it off at home."

I frowned at Lil. She'd gotten her way, again, and managed to make me look bad too. I wished I were as smart as she was. How did she think of things so quickly? As we walked home, she whispered, "I just did you a favour. I told you Ma would've taken it away."

I wasn't sure about Lil's true motivation. I hardly ever was. Had she been helping me or just seizing an opportunity? She did give the pen back, but only a few days later, and only briefly once we'd returned to the alley behind Rothbart's. Then Lil took it again and put it in our new secret hiding place, where she would have access to it whenever she wanted.

From then on, the wall behind the pharmacy harboured all sorts of found objects Lil and I didn't want our parents to know about — an extra stash of marbles, a shiny gold crucifix we discovered behind a church and would never have dared to bring home, a box of matches, and countless stray pennies we saved up to buy ribbon candy.

The next year, when Mrs. Debardeleben was torturing me with the obturator, I went to Lil for help. One morning after my therapy session, we grabbed Ozzie and took off early to St. Patrick Street. We scanned the sidewalks as we always did, to see if anyone was watching, then ran to the end of the alley. Lil counted ten columns in from the back and five rows up. She picked at the brick, worked it out, and stuck her arm in the hole to pull out our accumulated loot. We sat with legs splayed in front of us, scattered the treasure, and started counting. When Lil declared that nothing was missing, she popped everything back and I crammed Ozzie in last. Lil placed the brick into its slot and off we shot, out of the alley and home again.

IF A CHILD IS BORN WITH BOTH a cleft lip and a cleft palate, most parents are so distraught about the lip that they choose that operation first, even though it's less pressing from a medical perspective. The goal for the lip is to stitch it seamlessly, until it's as pretty and perfect as Cupid's bow. That's the shape the textbooks tell surgeons to aim for: Cupid's bow. They know the power a smile has to shoot love's arrow straight and sure.

Ma, however, was of the opinion that vanity was an indulgence, and since they weren't able to save enough money to fix both the lip and the palate, they made a choice. Besides, since I had a partial cleft, the doctors advised my parents to consider that scarring from the operation might be more severe than the deformity itself. What a laugh. In choosing not to pursue the lip operation, my parents made the sensible decision, the one that ensured my survival, but they didn't consider how disfigurement might make survival a capricious gift. They couldn't know what it would feel like to have a warped bow, one that would cause the arrow to miss its target nearly every time. Ma frowned on vanity, but can a beautiful person, or even someone who is merely plain, truly understand what it means to be ugly?

Not just ugly. Different enough to draw attention to it.

Hare, serpent, ape.

Nowadays, comparisons with the animal kingdom are rarer. Ma didn't like them, even then. She declared, when I was born, that my notch was like a pinch of dough, raised up too high by the fingers, making a point where there should only have been a slight lilt. She said it made my mouth triangular, like *hamentashen*, the pocket pastries named after King Hamen's hat and eaten at the holiday of Purim. The tip of my tongue, showing there in the gap, was like the poppy seed filling, only the wrong colour. I don't think they filled them with cherry in those days.

She started calling me her little Hermantashen, a humiliating term of endearment only someone who loved you would inflict. Eventually, everyone used this nickname — except Pop, who said it was ridiculous — and in no time at all, it evolved into 'Tashen, and then finally just Toshy. Doctors, teachers, prison guards, my late wife ... for seventy-seven years, people have called me Toshy, a childhood nickname that still follows me.

§

I've always thought it'd be easier to be led to the gallows than to be brought handcuffed into a police station in front of your family. At least when they hanged you, they had the courtesy of putting a bag over your head.

When they brought me in for questioning, the desk clerk sneered, as if to say he knew he'd see me eventually; all he had to do was sit back and wait for me to screw things up. Bessie sat on a bench in the corridor; on either side of her were my parents. But Lil was missing. Ma had one hand over her mouth; the other reached out. My chest tightened. The look on Bessie's face I can only describe as wild confusion mixed with intense grief, as though trying to make sense of what was happening was causing a firestorm in her head. Though my mother was the one with the outstretched hand, I felt it was Bessie whose expression was calling out to me, more to ask for help than to give it. Pop just looked deeply sad, and shook his head almost imperceptibly as I was led past. He was sitting on his hands, his palms flat on the bench as though he had to stuff them there in order not to leap up towards me — in love or anger, I didn't know which one it would be. Perhaps they'd told him to be still; it didn't matter, the effect was a pupil waiting to be pulled into the principal's office.

I smiled weakly, hoping they'd believe that I'd be okay, even though I wasn't sure of anything. I wondered how or why they'd managed to get my family to the station so quickly. It didn't occur to me then that they might question them too.

They brought me into an interrogation room and left me there for the better part of an hour. The room was claustrophobic, the air thick, and contained only a small table with a chair on either side. Finally, a plainclothes detective entered. He was tall and had a bushy moustache that hung down over his top lip, the kind I wished I could grow myself. His overcoat stank of cigar smoke. I'd never seen him before; he was the sort of man you wouldn't spot as a police officer, either because he wasn't in uniform or maybe because he came out of the station only to investigate crime scenes. I'd never stuck around once I'd created one.

He paced a few times in front of me, his hands behind his back, and then he said, "All right. Now suppose you tell me how the hell you thought you were going to get away with stealing that diamond."

It was an odd question. I'd expected him to stick to facts, not strategy, and I was unprepared. I couldn't think of a thing to say. Adrenaline made my mind race, sharpen, and yet fog over all at once.

"I don't know..."

"I guess not," he said, and sat down across from me. He brought a cigar out of his breast pocket and lit up, puffing huge clouds in my direction. "So you stole your sister's key, did ya?"

"Uh-huh."

"Now suppose you tell me what was going through your mind when ya threw that diamond out the window." Another strange thing to ask. What could it matter to him what I was thinking?

"I guess I thought I could get it after I jumped."

"It was pitch black. The house backs on a ravine. How'd ya think ya'd find it? I've had three men lookin' for it for the past two hours and they still haven't turned it up."

"I dunno."

"You don't know much, do ya. You slow or somethin'?"

I paused before answering. "Ya," I said. "Why else would I throw it?"

He tilted his head and squinted at me, probably to see if I was bullshitting. "I think maybe because you're a little dumb-ass shit and you thought, if I can't have it nobody else can either."

"Okay. Whatever you say," I answered, not so much because I was defeated or trying to give him any lip, but because I was still figuring out if it was better to appear stupid or spiteful, since he'd presented me with both options.

He leaned over the table and grabbed my throat. His hand was so enormous that his fingers nearly met at the back of my neck. His cigar was bitten between his teeth, and as he spoke, he blew smoke in my face. "What I *say*, is that you'd better give me some straight answers, and fast, and stop playing me for a chump."

He stared into my eyes, and I tried to hold his gaze, but I began to tear up from the cigar. I coughed and tried to suck in air, and then all of a sudden he let me go, and we both fell into our respective chairs.

Spiteful. For now, I decided on spiteful.

An hour later, after he'd asked me each question in a half-dozen different ways, slapped me around a little, and choked me a few more times, I was led back into the hallway. My family was still there, but now Bessie's eyes were puffy, and her boyfriend, Abe, had arrived. He had his arm around her. Lil was now with them too, and just before we reached their bench, the detective handed me over to a uniformed officer and said, "Miss Wolfman, please come with me."

As we passed in the hall, Lil searched my eyes. Not the way Bessie had, in desperation. Lil was trying to divine some clue from my expression. She wanted to know how much I'd given away. The one time in my life I've actually *wanted* to open my lips to speak, I couldn't say a word.

st-tropez

My life has been long, with ups and downs that I probably deserved, each one of them. But after everything, I didn't deserve to be warehoused somewhere waiting to die. Waiting for them to serve lunch, waiting for the damned Sabbath elevator, waiting for my cancer to come back.

Bessie's son, Warren, and his wife, Susan, said that moving here was for the best, but Glendale Manors was just fine. The five years I spent there after Ellen died were decent ones. I'd been alone long enough before meeting her that reacquainting myself with solitude came easily. I was independent at Glendale. I could come and go as I pleased without anyone taking notice. If I felt like having chopped liver, there were delis nearby. The Health Bread Bakery was a block away, if I felt like a nice caraway rye. The Jerusalem Restaurant was just down the street, and not far, the Holy Blossom Temple. I barely ever attended services, but when I did, I could go and then walk home afterwards. And in my lobby, every spring, they'd have a strawberry social and name one of the ladies Strawberry Queen. That was before the bout of prostate cancer, in remission now. Once that scare surfaced, investigations were done and preparations were made for the move.

Warren designated his son Ari to help. He was back for the summer from McGill, where he was doing a PhD on the famous anarchist Emma Goldman, researching her from an angle I wasn't sure I completely understood. Ari was a patient child and grew up to be very well-suited to academics, to all that plodding, meticulous research and to the penetration of their nonsense lingo. Well-suited to help a nostalgic old uncle uproot his life, yet again.

For instance, Ari's thesis title was *Emma Goldman: Character, Courage and (Con)text — An Examination of Radical Resistance and Ethical Action in Historical Perspective.* He had to write it out to show me the crazy drivel with the brackets, and then he explained that it was the latest thing in the academic world — brackets in the middle of a word to give it a double, often contradictory, meaning.

I said, "Kind of like a pun, but not as funny, right?"

He stared at me blankly for a few seconds and said, "Yeah, I guess, kind of."

It would be just like academics to invent a new gimmick for an age-old concept and then pat themselves on the back. I imagined the average person, to understand what Ari was studying, would have to furrow his brow and set his mind deeply into the words, just as I did, but this was something that came easily to him. Still, I could tell that helping me move had tested the limits of his patience, especially when I started through my old photographs. He only perked up when I told him there might be a picture of Emma Goldman and my late sister Lil in there somewhere, but then when we couldn't find one, he was crestfallen and fell silent.

That boy was far too introspective for any person just out of his teens. Over-analyzed everything, and barely ever made a fuss or a peep. There were times I wanted to shake him and say, "Rebel! Act out! What's wrong with you, kid?" I was amazed that he and I could be related at all, so different his boyhood had been from mine. His personality was in part a reaction to loud, formerly hippie parents. Bessie's Warren had married Susan in 1970 and they named their son after Woody Guthrie's boy Arlo, who they claimed had a Jewish mother. Warren was a Bay Street lawyer now and

Susan a big-shot journalist, but on weekends, they sometimes pretended it was the old days and lit up a joint.

I couldn't imagine Ari ever trying marijuana. He was
intrigued by rebellion and protest, but only as ideas to be
studied. He was obsessed with Emma Goldman and had
been ever since he was a child and Lil told him about when
she and Emma were comrades right here in Toronto. I could
understand the appeal; I knew Emma too, and she was a
formidable woman. She cut a deep swath through our lives,
and the brush still hadn't grown back two generations later.
She was tethered to us even in her grave. Ari's studies had
revived her as a name to be spoken aloud, but I had my own
reasons to toss her around, privately, during my quietest
moments, when I imagined I might have the courage to
finally make things right, after all these years. Now that time
might be running out, those quiet moments had become
more frequent.

Every day for a week before the movers came, Ari showed
up at my old apartment and helped me fold clothing, pack
dishware, and pick through tchotchkes. He helped me, for
the second time in five years, make a lifetime of memories
contract ever further. It wasn't fair. They said old people's
minds discarded memories on their own; why not let us be
until then? I went from a stuffed house to a decent-sized one-
bedroom, and now to a tiny bachelor with a closet not even
big enough to hide a burglar.

I shouldn't complain — I didn't really have that many
clothes, and who had those kinds of closets anyway? They
were almost a myth: you saw them in movies and cartoons,
bandits standing upright, behind the door between two over-
coats, knife poised. From my own unfortunate experience, I
knew that even the wealthiest society folk, with their fancy
Rosedale homes, might have closets with built-in shelves, or
be too overstuffed with clothes to fit a person inside.

It was ridiculous to be thinking of such things. This was
how I measured the worth of an apartment? That it should

have a closet a burglar could fit into? Never mind that, in this scenario, I was the burglar. It was all sick, sick, sick. That was just my mind hitting the same detour sign, pointing back, and back, and back once more, in a continuous loop. The critical thing was that Ari had helped me stuff my belongings into this apartment and its tiny, burglarproof closet, and I appreciated the effort. Today, as I crossed the parking lot to visit Bessie at Baycrest, I made a mental note to remind Ari that he should think about which of the things we'd put in storage he wanted to take to Montreal.

He'd called yesterday to ask if we could talk after he visited his grandma Bessie, as if I were busy enough that I'd need to fit him in. After the move, I'd been certain I wouldn't hear from him for months, but everyone was making a fuss now. I got more calls from Warren and Susan than I'd had in years, and suddenly Lil's girls were phoning all the time from the States too. They were all worried for me, worried I was sad and lonely and scared.

They had no idea. I'd been all those things, and I was done with them. Breathing in didn't worry me anymore. Exhaling no longer filled me with dread. And as for speech, well, I'd said mostly all I had to say. I'd mastered the words, those small sculptures, but all works of representational art had their limits.

In the end, people saw and heard just exactly what they wanted.

BESSIE HAD A PRIVATE ROOM at the end of the hall, and as I started towards it, the smell of disinfectant assaulted me. The walls were painted beige, and the doors to the residents' rooms, a light peach. A large woman sat on a chair in the hall, her eyes closed, head slumped. One would have thought her asleep had she not been rubbing her wrinkled hands together and muttering something too low to hear. Her skin was ghostly and spider-webbed, and her age wasn't fully to blame. Old age homes badly need regular lighting. Instead, fluorescent lamps cruelly accentuate our frailty, poor circulation, and peaked skin tone.

A thick-bodied nurse came out of her station across from the elevators and helped a very short man back into his narrow room. I heard a moan from behind the walls. As I approached Bessie's door, the sound of the television reached me, and for one blessed moment I thought my sister was alone. But no. Pearl Feffer was sitting on a chair beside the bed.

Pearl, Bessie's annoying sentry.

We'd known each other most of our lives, but for many reasons, we'd not gotten on so well. She and Bessie had fallen out of touch for some thirty years, while Pearl lived out west, but a few weeks before I took my own apartment in The Terrace, Pearl had moved in a floor below me. Bossy like you wouldn't believe, and honest to God, she was getting on my very last nerve. Every time I went across the way to Baycrest, no matter what the time of day, she'd be there already visiting my sister and reading aloud from the newspaper or some novel. Bessie, poor thing, was trapped in her bed and semi-dazed from pain medication for her own battle with cancer, so I couldn't even tell if she enjoyed the visits.

As if that weren't bad enough, Pearl always gave me a kind of look — judgemental — as if to suggest I should be the one reading instead of her. She never actually said it, but she snorted at me a lot. I'd practised in my mind what I'd say to her if she could be direct enough to confront me. I'd say, maybe I'd visit more often if you weren't here. Or, mind your own business, ya busy-body.

Today they were watching the Parliamentary Channel. Pearl had the converter clutched in one hand, pointed to the set. Bessie was propped against the headboard, her bathrobe wrapped tightly under her crossed arms, her short permed curls damp and slicked back behind the ears. Pearl had given Bessie a home dye job and now her hair was a slightly lighter shade of purple than the bathrobe.

"Toshy, sweetheart, come here, pull up a chair. They're televising the Sue Rodriguez case at the Supreme Court." Bessie pointed to the screen. It was nice to see that her face had colour to it, and it surprised me, given what she was watching.

Pearl uncrossed her legs, stood up, and pulled over a chair for me to sit beside her, but I went to lean against the wall near the entrance. The last place in the room I'd choose to be would be in a chair beside Pearl. She fussed with her silver hair, immaculately groomed so that bangs more or less covered the birthmark on her forehead.

On television, a lawyer argued his case.

"That's counsel for Sue Rodriguez," said Pearl. "I *think* he's just wrapping up."

"Did I tell you my daughter-in-law Susan interviewed her last night?" Bessie said to Pearl, her voice full of pride. Susan was the co-anchor of *Searchlight*, the prominent CBC news magazine, and an occasional replacement for their lead news anchor.

"How can you be watching this?" I asked.

"Because it's historic, that's how," said Pearl, butting in. "I'm surprised at you. This is amazing, really, that they broadcast these things nowadays. Can you imagine if we'd had television sixty, seventy years ago? Think about what it would have been like to watch them argue if women should get the vote."

"I'll see it on the six o'clock news after all the yabbering is done. Bessie, it's a nice day. Are you sure you don't want to be sitting in the room down the hall?"

"That poor woman," Pearl continued, ignoring me. "She should be allowed to end her life if she wants, and by the time they hand down their decision, it might be too late for her. I honestly don't know what I'd do if I had such a terrible illness. Imagine, being trapped in your body, miserable, and not being able to even take a bottle of pills on your own. I say bravo to that Svend Robinson for standing beside her all the way. When do we ever see members of Parliament taking risks like that? He may be light in the loafers, but that man has guts."

Bessie nodded her head but her face was taut. Pearl was touching on sensitive topics and didn't even know it. For one thing, she didn't know that Bessie had a gay grandson. My sister didn't like to talk about it. She'd accepted the fact and loved Ari regardless, but she'd learned only recently that he was gay and still grieved the end of the family name. Which was interesting, since Ari carried her late husband Abe's family name, not ours.

Her grief for the end of the Kagan line was really grief for Abe, whom she thanked for saving her from a terrible mistake he knew nothing about. This mistake was a secret she'd shared only with Lil and me. It wasn't exactly accurate to say that Abe had saved her, either. Lil and I had done the saving and then Abe helped her recover afterwards. We'd fixed things, ensuring Bessie could be safe in his loving arms. The price was eleven years of my life.

The phone rang and Bessie answered it. She said, "I don't think so, dear, but I've got visitors. Let me ask your uncle Toshy and my friend Pearl." She covered the receiver. "It's Ari, down in the lobby. He wants to know if he can get us bagels from across the street. I'm not hungry, are you?"

Pearl shook her head.

"Tell him not to bother," I said. "I'm coming down to discuss what stuff he's bringing back to Montreal and I wouldn't want it to disturb your cheery television program."

"You just got here," Bessie protested.

"I'll come back later. You and Ari should have time alone." I glanced at Pearl, who stood up.

"I should go too, Bessie. I can meet your grandson another time. I have to call my daughter anyway."

"Wait, Toshy, I have a newspaper clipping I thought you'd want to see. It's over by the television." She relayed my message to Ari while gesturing to Pearl to get it. Pearl, who'd stood up to leave, passed it to me, and as I unfolded it, I was aware she was craning her neck to read along with me.

Its headline said, "Nurse and poverty activist Dorothy Fister gets Order of Ontario." The article mentioned she was raising money to support a group of homeless people setting up a shantytown near the Queen Elizabeth Way.

"Fister? Bessie, do you think…"

"It's her granddaughter. I just thought you'd want to know."

"Whose granddaughter?" said Pearl.

"Nobody. Just a very kind woman we knew when we were young," said Bessie. I folded the paper and put it in my shirt pocket.

Pearl must've sensed she shouldn't press further. I followed her to the elevator, and as we waited, I considered my reaction to the clipping, why it had set my heart pounding so. I could easily have found this woman a long time ago, had I set my mind to it. Or her father, before he died. Fact was, I hadn't, and now that Bessie had brought it up, it took on a new urgency.

I became aware of Pearl smiling at me again.

"This is taking forever. I'm gonna take the stairs."

"Good idea," she said, just to be completely maddening, and followed me.

When we reached the ground floor, I said, "Goodbye, Pearl," and hurried away before there was another opportunity for interaction.

Ari was sitting at a small table in the atrium, clutching a cup in one hand. The day had started cool but Baycrest was always overheated and I could tell he was suffering for it, because he clawed at the collar of his turtleneck. He was tapping a thick-soled boot against the base of the table, probably from too much caffeine. He'd become a serious addict ever since he'd moved to Montreal and decided that coffee served in bowls was a sign of urban sophistication. In Toronto, where we were sensible enough to know that coffee wasn't soup, he had to settle for one of those café whatchamahoozits, topped with nutmeg or chocolate sprinkles or God knows what. Whatever happened to a simple cuppa joe made with a Melita filter?

He stood up and hugged me, towering at six feet. He thrust a paper bag into my hands. "I lied to Grandma. I'd already gotten the bagels. You can take them back to your room."

"Thanks," I said, and sat at the table with him. "How's your research coming along?"

"Pretty good, actually. You know that grant application I told you about? It came through yesterday, so, guess what? I'm going to St-Tropez to try to find Bon Esprit, the house Emma lived in there."

"You are? When?"

"In a few weeks, so it doesn't give me much time to get ready. I found some journal references this morning, but I still need your help researching Goldman's years in France. I didn't want to bother you when you were moving, but I know you found a box of your old letters. I remember a few years ago you said there were some letters that Goldman sent to Aunt Lil. Can we take a look in your locker and see if you can find them?"

"There's no point; I gave them away."

He dropped his jaw for dramatic effect.

"Don't look at me like that. I didn't know you'd be doing this research. And it's not like I gave them to a passing stranger. A few years ago, I read they were starting an archive in California, so I donated Lil's letters."

"I know those archives; they're at Berkeley."

"Then you should be able to get a hold of copies if you want. That's the whole point of the archives."

"I know…" he said. "I've been meaning to call them. I suppose I should get on that this aft."

"Don't despair. I think I have something that might help: letters your aunt Lil sent me when I was in prison.

Emma was in France for part of the time I was locked up, and I think Lil mentions her and that house. Also, I still remember a few things my sister told me when she visited. When you're in prison, news from the outside world sticks with you. Also, Lil once went to work for Emma in France."

"I never knew that."

"She made the trip in secret. Our family thought she was in Montreal on a medical internship."

I walked back to The Terrace, leaving Ari to his visit with Bessie, and went down to my storage locker. While I did, an idea formed, and I turned it over and over. It was one I'd long ago given up on, but today's events had given it new life.

I searched for the letters from Lil, but I didn't need to find them to recall the words. A lot from those prison days had stuck with me, and not just news. Things I wished I could forget but couldn't. The curse of a photographic memory was that I saw everything, and closing my eyes only made the image glare brighter.

the orange sunset

To trace the moment, the very first moment when my life was set upon a different course, that was impossible. Too many factors, too many decisions, too much being determined by whim and personality and random untraceable influence. Still, if I tried to pick a little, like dragging a thumbnail across a roll of tape, I could snag a beginning of sorts, even if it wasn't really the beginning, even if it was only the remnant of a previous tear that had settled back and now clung to the rest of a sticky, tightly wound past.

There was a day that I remembered, a day when Lil's fascination with Emma Goldman began, that set in motion a chain of events that would affect us all. It was in November of 1926, and I was only ten. I remembered that day for two reasons, and the first had nothing to do with Emma.

The day started with all of us at the kitchen table, as it always did. We were a family who sat and ate breakfast together no matter what, because other things — jobs, the store, political meetings — might interfere and separate us for lunch or supper.

My parents were avid readers of the morning newspaper. One newspaper, the *Toronto Mail and Empire*, they read to keep track of their class enemies. Others, they read because of political interest or because the writers spoke to our community. The communist weekly *Vochenblatt* and the daily *Yidisher Zshurnal* — the Hebrew Journal — were in this category, though I believe they also read these two to see who was the latest person to be denounced. The Yiddish press was vicious and retributive and heaven help you if you were on the other side of their graces. Reading those papers satisfied a ghoulish fascination: who would be torn to shreds *this* week? Whose character would be assassinated ruthlessly? My parents read these denunciations, clucked, and shook their heads, but they kept going back for more.

Our father, Saul Wolfman, had emigrated, along with his parents, from Russia. They settled in the Ward, the neighbourhood in Toronto mainly populated by Jewish immigrants, bordered by College and Queen on the north and south, and Yonge and University on the east and west. Our mother was born in New Liskeard, of all places: a small, bilingual farming community near the Quebec border in northeastern Ontario, where her Galician peasant parents had settled. There, isolated from any other Jews, they eked out a livelihood. But farm life proved difficult, and in 1908, after too many harsh winters, they moved to Toronto, where they opened a second-hand clothing store with money borrowed from a cousin.

My parents' families attended different synagogues — in those days they were organized along ethnic lines — but Ma and Pop met at a secular community dance one weekend. The next year, they married at the Holy Blossom Temple, which upset their families, but it upset them equally, which was the important thing. By 1910, the Holy Blossom had become notorious for its more liberal congregants, some of whom didn't even wear head coverings when they prayed.

Maybe it was there my parents first became interested in politics. Not that they needed the Holy Blossom. If a person was working class in Toronto in the early 1900s, the rising proletarian movement in Russia was an irresistible draw to one of the city's numerous labour organizations. My parents chose the *Arbeiter Ring* — the Workmen's Circle, a local organization of mostly Jewish workers in the *shmata* trade.

Much later, in '27, they joined a more left-leaning faction that broke off and became known as the Labour League. By that time, the Russian Revolution had fired their imagination, and, choosing from an ever-lengthening menu on the spectrum of the political left, my parents identified themselves with the Russian Mensheviks, though they were proud to remain officially unaffiliated.

We grew up with a steady diet of Menshevik ideology and promotion of Labour League activities. I use the word *diet* in the sense of a regimen, or the modern American sense that connotes near starvation with nutritional value coming a distant second. Political thought in the Wolfman family was doled out in spare but regular allotments at the table, like dessert. To us children, it was an uninteresting dessert, much like stewed prunes or an apple. None of us joined the Labour League, much to our parents' chagrin. Bessie was not interested in politics in any way, Lil became involved with an anarchist branch of the Workmen's Circle, and me? Well, I just got in trouble and went to jail.

At breakfast that morning in November of 1926, Ma was flipping through the pages of the *Mail and Empire*, and she came across a small piece in the middle of the society section.

"My, my! Have you ever *seen* such a diamond? It's enormous!" She flashed the page at us. I caught its headline, "Lady Fister stuns socialites with Orange Sunset," but didn't get a good look at the picture. Besides, I was ten years old, only cared about the Tarzan comic strip, and had no reason to concern myself with society folk.

She spotted me spooning absent-mindedly at my porridge. "Toshy, eat up and don't slouch." Then, her eyes back on the page: "This woman looks familiar."

I considered my gruel. Ma always salted it too much.

"Can I see?" said Bessie, who was sitting across from me, with perfect posture. She'd already finished her entire bowl.

Ma passed her the newspaper. "That woman's diamond brooch was a wedding gift from her husband," she said.

"I know how to read, Ma," said Bessie, squinting at the text.

Lil was sitting beside her and snatched the paper.

"Hey! I wasn't finished." Bessie pulled it back, leaving a ripped corner in Lil's hands.

"You take too long."

"Girls, stop it. Bessie, read us what it says."

"It saaaaays," she glared at Lil, who was leaning in to read over her shoulder, "'Lady Fister makes a rare showing of the Orange Sunset, a thirty-six car-AT diamond...' What's a car-AT, Ma?"

"It's pronounced 'carrot' and it's a measurement for how much a diamond weighs. Thirty-six carats is very, very big."

"'...a thirty-six carat diamond that her husband purchased in South Africa after fighting in the Boer War. The diamond is an unusual amber colour, bezel-set in a gold brooch, and surrounded by twelve emeralds. After settling in Toronto, Lord Fister built a successful import-export business and he and Lady Fister had a son early in their marriage. Sources say the diamond is worth a small fortune."

I'd been pretending not to listen but I picked my eyes up from my porridge. "A fortune? Read what it says about that, Bessie."

"Hold your horses. I'm getting to that. It says, 'Lady Fister almost never wears her wedding gift, and though some say it is because she is afraid of theft, those who know her well say that she finds it too ostentatious to wear in public.'"

"Where else would she wear it?" said Pop. "In the bathtub?"

We all laughed. I reached across the table. "Lemme see."

Bessie passed me the paper, but in a wide arc to avoid Lil's clawing hands.

I saw the photograph. There was a middle-aged couple, the woman sporting an enormous diamond on the breast of her gown. She was stout, much shorter than her husband,

and though she wore a fur coat, a hat, and glasses, I knew her immediately.

"That's Nurse Grace!"

"Who?" said Pop.

"Nurse Grace, who took care of me when I was in the hospital."

"Nonsense," said Ma. "That woman is rich. Rich men's wives don't work as nurses. Besides, you can't possibly remember that; you were just little."

"I remember her. She was nice to me."

Ma got up from her chair and came around behind me. "My God, Saul, he might be right. She must have a very progressively minded husband."

"She said her husband gave her permission because she loved being a nurse. And she also told me about the diamond."

My parents' faces showed their skepticism.

"I remember!"

And I did.

When Ma brought me to Dr. Grover, I was almost five years old. It was early 1921, a bright, cold day in January, and we walked for an hour through the unplowed Toronto streets to make our appointment. Occasionally, we'd find one narrow track in the middle of a wide boulevard and follow it, the snow on either side of me reaching to above my knees. Ma carried me as much as she could, but I had to walk most of the way, complaining that she was tugging too much on my arm. She told me we would be late, that my legs were sinking too deep and that if she didn't pull me along, I might get stuck. She brought a bag full of money to the hospital. Dr. Grover gently pushed it back across the desk and told her she should keep it until afterwards, and then send a bank draft.

When I was a newborn, my parents had decided to wait even to have my palate fixed. The operations were expensive and Pop had heard from friends about the humiliating process they'd have to go through before the hospital determined it would pay. Pop was a proud man and decided they'd save for the operations themselves. They spent five years at it, putting aside a portion of the meagre proceeds of their silk and cotton retail store on St. Patrick Street. Without telling Pop, Ma went with her hand out to the Toronto Hebrew Benevolent Society, and since she kept the books, she was able to conceal the donation as business profits.

My mother, if I may say so, was a dogged and intelligent woman. She was impressed with modern medicine but she was also skeptical and inquisitive. She sought to educate herself rather than rely solely on what the doctors told her. She read voraciously whatever she came across — critically, laughing at advice she found preposterous and mocking it to anyone who would listen. One day, years later, I found a booklet in her house called "Your Baby Has a Cleft Palate?" Ma had underlined the following passages: "His condition may have been a shock to you. Stop blaming yourself ... and stop regarding your husband with questioning eyes. No one knows as yet why this developmental failure occurs and until science discovers the reason, you should stop worrying about it."

She had scribbled "What nonsense!!!" in the margin. I wondered which part she felt was three-exclamation-mark nonsense: that parents actually blamed themselves for the condition, that somehow a husband's indiscretion might be responsible for a birth defect, or that saying she shouldn't worry would be enough to allay her fears.

With Dr. Grover, however, Ma's criticism drained away, as though it were light rainfall, and his smile, the porous earth into which it seeped. Even though Dr. Grover had embarrassed her by refusing her bag of money, she spoke of him with reverence. A young, single man helping sick babies, she said. He knew all of the latest methods. Maybe it was better, she rationalized, that they had to wait five years. When I was born, Dr. Grover was away treating wounded soldiers in France, just shipped off to help in the field hospitals of Verdun. The doctor who would have operated in his absence might have been older and perhaps not well versed in modern medical techniques, Ma speculated. Dr. Grover, on the other hand, had studied at Yale University. He was handsome and kind. If only he'd been Jewish, she would've surely introduced him to a single friend.

I mostly remember a big man with round glasses, a wide forehead, and a wild tousle of auburn hair who had halitosis and who made me tilt my head back too far while he breathed into my open mouth. I remember his nurse much better, and more fondly: a stout Englishwoman who said to me, "Here at the hospital they call me Nurse Fister, but you can call me Nurse Grace."

She had limpid blue eyes, sat with me when my parents couldn't be there, and said "there, there," a lot. She made me feel safe by stroking my cheek.

Before giving me a needle she said, "Grip your mother's index finger, as tight as you can." I squeezed hard, until my hand hurt so much I didn't notice the needle at all.

One afternoon, about a month after we first met Dr. Grover and Nurse Grace, the doctor stitched together the roof of my mouth, applying an aluminium splint to keep it together and to prevent me from sucking at the horsehair stitches. Nowadays, children born like me have better treatment, and it's free. Back then there were specialists just as there are today, and the surgeons did the best they could, but the methods were less refined. The instruments appeared medieval, with hooks and barbs in places that couldn't possibly have been for anything but show. To fix a lip, for instance, they'd jab needles from one side of the cleft to the other and draw the sides together with sutures wrapped around the needles in figure eights, like tying a boat to butterfly moorings. Crude methods that did the trick but aesthetically weren't very satisfying. Even fifteen years later, when I had that operation, the techniques hadn't significantly improved.

Nurse Grace fussed over me during my recovery. When Ma and Pop weren't there, she told me stories of England, of her husband's exploits in South Africa, and of a beautiful amber diamond called the Orange Sunset, which he brought back for her as a wedding present.

Nurse Grace stroked my hair when I complained about the pain. Her voice was a soothing balm. I listened to her lilting tones while I stared at ceiling tiles or at a tiny spider spinning her web in the corner of the room, or considered the gurgling radiator in the background, a counterpoint to the gurgling in my throat.

Eight days later, they removed the splint, and I was home. I remember a marked increase in toys, and being doted on by Ma and my sisters and various relatives and neighbours. Even by Pop.

MY PARENTS HAD NEVER SAID IT ALOUD, but they believed I was slow. It didn't help that the doctors *told* them I might be, that Mrs. Debardeleben had confirmed it. It didn't help that I barely spoke, so afraid was I of what would come out. It was in this context that at breakfast that morning, my memory of Nurse Grace had made an impression.

It made a bigger one, a few months later, when the neighbours had a small fire in their shop. It was quickly extinguished, but all of our merchandise had to be removed from the shelves and triaged: aired out, washed, or thrown away. When it was time to put the salvaged stock back, I told Pop he'd gotten the order of the silk bolts wrong when he'd rehung them.

"They go blue-red-pink-beige-white, not red-blue-pink-white-beige," I said.

"You can't possibly remember that."

"You should listen to him," said Bessie. "He remembers things he sees."

Years later, I'd be told that scientists didn't believe in photographic memory. All I knew was that I had an ability others didn't have to remember things I saw — the location and sequence of objects and the placement of words on a page. When I spoke, my words sometimes came out unformed and escaped here and there, but every word I read, every image I saw got ensnared, as if in a sticky web, waiting to be retrieved.

Pop stood back and took direction from me as I reassembled the merchandise, placing rainbows of fabric in exactly the right order on the display tables. When I saw how pleased he was, I became excited and told him I knew our whole inventory off by heart. Then, my parents were impressed. They were relying on me for something.

My excitement was short-lived.

Rather than deciding I was smart, they pigeon-holed me. I was still a freakish, deformed idiot, but now I was an idiot *savant* who could briefly be relieved from his plodding stupidity to do parlour tricks or menial tasks. Bessie knew that I remembered things I saw, but she hadn't told my parents before then because to do so would have been to relay information that would have blown her cover as the perfect daughter. Even though Lil probably would've gotten in much more trouble, and she could've had the pleasure of taking Lil down with her, Bessie resisted the temptation. I didn't fully understand, until then, how much my parents' approval meant to her.

Until they discovered my special gift, Ma had delegated the keeping of the inventory solely to Bessie, who had shown some promise in arithmetic at school. It was the only subject she excelled in, and our parents wanted to encourage her. I used to follow Bessie around when she did her duties, looking at the lists she made and noting the monthly changes, how she reconciled them with the sales records. It was hard to account for a few yards of cloth — the fabric our parents sold was kept on large bolts and sold by the foot or the yard, so to be precise in the inventory would have meant unravelling and measuring, and who had the time or space for that? Another method was weighing the bolts, but we didn't have a scale.

Consequently, we counted the layers at the top of a bolt and estimated roughly that two layers was one yard. In addition, Ma asked Bessie to make a list of the number of ends — the bolts with fewer than four yards on them — and to note which colour and type of material they were.

One day, I saw Bessie checking and re-checking the list, wearing her eraser to the nub, and going back into the storefront three times to start over.

"What's wrong?" I kept asking, following behind as she ignored me and became more frantic.

"Ma's gonna kill me," she eventually muttered, walking and counting with her fingers. "I think I messed up the ends count — again. There are fifteen fewer this month, but I can only account for fourteen when I look at the sales record. I think I might've counted wrong again. This is the third month it's happened. I thought there were twenty-four last month, but maybe there were only twenty-three. Promise you won't tell Ma; she'll have my head."

"I promise," I said. Then, after a minute or two, "You didn't count wrong, you know. There were twenty-four last month. You wanna know which colours?"

"Don't bother me right now, Toshy. This is important."

"I'm telling you, I know the colours."

She stared at me and folded her arms. "You remember the colours. Sure. I'd have to look at my notebook to know that."

"I just remember. I'll show you." I proceeded to walk the perimeter of the store, pointing out the precise locations where those fifteen bolts had been and also naming their colours, including the missing one, and ignoring this month's new ends. Bessie followed me and checked off the ones I called out against her list. "And the missing one was a kind of blue."

"How did you do that?" She scrutinized me like you would a magician if you were trying to see where up his sleeve he'd hidden the rabbit.

"I just remember things when I see them."

"What kind of things?"

"All kinds of things…" I searched for an example. "Oh! Like the Tarzan comic!"

"Well, that's not too hard. It has four panels at most, and you just read it an hour ago."

"No. I mean I remember the words from every one of them. Every day." I was crazy about Tarzan. I loved how strong he could be without ever speaking a word. I loved that people didn't mock him for being like the animals. They thought he was mysterious. I would've cut out the comic strip if Ma hadn't wanted the paper intact, in case she needed to wrap things. It didn't matter; I could retrieve the images any time I wanted.

"Prove it."

"Okay." I closed my eyes and chose a day from December, the last day of school before the holidays. An image flashed in my mind, and I started reciting the words in the dialogue bubbles. I made the sound effects too, waved my arms like the gorillas, and jumped up on the tables in the store to act it all out. Bessie laughed. I retrieved the next image, and so on. I played all the parts, Tarzan, Jane, the animals, and stray hunters and villains that entered the storyline, until Bessie said, "Okay, stop it! I believe you. Holy smokes, that's really weird."

"It is?" Great, I thought, just great. Another weird thing about me. That was exactly what I needed.

"In any case, this doesn't help me figure out what happened to those extra bolts."

"Did you count the ones Lil takes into the backyard?"

"Excuse me?"

"Sometimes I see her taking an end and giving it to a man she meets in the backyard."

Bessie's eyebrows lifted. "No. No, I did not count those ones. Thanks, Toshy." She patted me on the head. I was proud that I'd solved the mystery. "I think I'm going to have to have a little chat with our sister when she comes home."

There was a sharpness to Bessie's voice. Later, I overheard my sisters arguing in their bedroom. With an ear pressed to the door, I couldn't make out everything, but I did catch the crucial bits.

Bessie said, "I don't care who needs clothes, Lil. You can't save the whole world, especially not by *stealing* from Ma and Pop!" Then Lil said, "They wouldn't even notice," and Bessie said, "*I* noticed." Then Lil: "I promise I won't do it again, but if you tell Ma and Pop, I'll tell them you've already been to second base." There was a silence, then Bessie hissed, "I trusted you!" After that, all I heard was angry mumbling.

Bessie didn't tell. At first, I thought she sympathized with Lil's generosity, but then I thought no, she just didn't want to explain to Ma why she'd gone three months without telling her she'd screwed up the count. It had to be that, because why would our parents care if she played baseball?

The next month, everything checked out perfectly.

As I BEGAN TO EXPLAIN, telling my family that I remembered Nurse Grace's stories about the Orange Sunset had one consequence worth noting: it convinced my parents it might not be a complete waste of time to bring me on the planned outing that evening. Emma Goldman was in Toronto on tour, and everyone was going to hear her. Emma Goldman, the most dangerous woman in the world! By then, people already called her that, and I was curious to see what could be so scary. I didn't know or even care she never preached violence, that people who called her dangerous didn't know a damn thing about her.

Normally, Emma lectured on controversial progressive subjects such as free love, by which she didn't mean promiscuity — though she wasn't opposed to that — but rather the freedom to love whomever you wished. In those days, when marriages were arranged contracts trapping either loveless couples or people for whom love had blossomed but then wilted, it was a radical notion to choose and change partners at will, just to follow the heart. In the early 1900s, she was also speaking out in favour of birth control, sexual and personal emancipation for women, and even, Ari has recently told me, homosexual rights.

In Toronto's Jewish community, to go to hear her speak you didn't need to be an anarchist sympathizer. She was a Jew and an infamous international celebrity. Besides, that night, her lecture topic was to be the playwright Henrik Ibsen and the modern drama, and what harm could there be in that? My parents packed us into the streetcar on that cold night in 1926 and took us to Hygeia Hall. We took seats near the back of the auditorium, near the police who were lined up and scribbling things in their notebooks.

Although I heard the lecture first-hand, it was a story Lil would tell and retell, always as if the talk had been the night before. It was hard, even for someone like me, to sift out what was authentically my memory from what was hers. Once, years later when Ari was only nine, we were over at Bessie and Abe's, eating hors d'oeuvres in their living room, and Lil was telling the story. She took the opportunity, as she often did, to tease our older sister.

"Your grandma Bessie sat through the whole lecture with her arms crossed," she said. "Everyone around her, including our father, was on the edge of his seat, but your grandma just sat there with a sour puss. Even your uncle Toshy appeared to be interested and he was only your age, Ari."

Bessie dismissed Lil with a wave of the hand. "It was winter. It was cold in that hall, and the woman was preaching nonsense, as she always did."

Lil shrugged. "That's your opinion," she said, and then Bessie said, "Yes it is," and they both shrank into their corner of the sofa. There was a chilly silence until Susan changed the subject.

It was true that Emma was a magnificent speaker. Her voice was stern and commanding that night, and her eyes, through those spectacles, appeared to bore through you as they passed in your direction. Lil said her words came at her in waves: huge, powerful breakers soaked with significance. Emma spoke that night about Nora's enlightenment in *The Doll's House*. Nora left her husband, she explained, not because she was tired of wifely duty or because she was making a stand for women's rights. She left because she'd lived for eight years with a stranger, borne him children, even, and what could be more humiliating than realizing that the person with whom you live in close proximity hasn't the slightest interest in you?

The hall was packed and noisy, the air smoky, the crowd boisterous, and they challenged Emma's ideas during the question period. Men and women pointed fingers and gesticulated wildly, standing on chairs to be heard. Emma's responses were witty, quick, and playful, and she ultimately had us all entranced, even Bessie, though she would never admit it. Even me, though I was disappointed she hadn't talked about blowing up buildings.

This tiny force of nature with round glasses and thick jowls was telling women they could be anything they wanted, that they had a right to be thought of as individuals, and this, Lil had never before considered.

"By her very example," Lil would say, when she told the story, "by her hand slapping the lectern to emphasize the importance of her message, she was showing us that the key to liberation was to first free one's mind." Her eyes were still wide with wonder, all those years later.

I can only imagine what it must've been like for her after that night, to watch the women in our family, our mother and sister, and see only captives, chained to a predictable future and uninspired dreams. As Lil grew up and began to excel in school, it was inevitable that a chasm would open between them. Our parents were proud of her scholastic accomplishments, but they worried about her ambition.

They were concerned by her impatience with injustice. Bessie tried to be an older sister the only way she knew how, to protect her and give advice, but Lil wasn't receptive to Bessie's conservatism and wasn't good at hiding her feelings. Those feelings, a mixture of pity and superiority, were the perfect recipe for condescension.

§

When I arrived at Kingston Pen in July of 1935, I was stripped of my belongings and clothes, given a uniform, and taken into a small room that was painted green and had a long table against the far wall, a simple wooden chair in the centre, and four hanging lamps evenly spaced. Six people sat behind the table shuffling paper, barely acknowledging me as I was seated in front of them. The guard had told me before going in that this was the Classification Board, where they would be assessing my educational and occupational record and testing me for my mental stability and my physique. Also, they would try to determine if I was a recidivist.

I didn't know the word *recidivist* then but the guard explained it meant you would return to your life of crime and sinfulness. How they'd be able to tell that from meeting someone for the first time and asking him a few questions, I didn't know. I pictured a person cracking under the pressure, finally shouting, "Yes! Yes, I'd do it again. Again! Over and over again, I tell you!" and then throwing his head back with a maniacal laugh.

I sat down on my hands, hugging my arms close to my sides. The cotton uniform they'd given me was stiff and itchy and the room smelled of damp sweat and mould. The men behind the table introduced themselves one by one. The first was the warden for both Kingston and Collins Bay penitentiaries, Lieutenant Colonel Craig. He was a thin man of about fifty who scrunched a monocle in one eye. He had a friendly smile and didn't look at all like a lieutenant colonel. Next to him was Mr. Fowler, a Brit with a bushy grey moustache who was the deputy warden. He was stockier than his boss, and he mostly stared at his notepad, even when it was his turn to ask me questions.

Next in line was the chief keeper of Collins Bay, a few miles down the road. Collins Bay was, in those days, a new prison, still under construction, though they had started to move inmates in already. The chief keeper's name was Frank Flaherty, and his eyes set on me like hooks trying to rip out secrets. Flaherty had a scar running from his bulbous, ruddy nose, down over his left cheekbone, ending near a sharp chin. Beside him were the prison medical officer, Dr. Platt; the industrial overseer, Mr. Jagninski; and at the end of the table, Father MacDonald, the chaplain. These last three men were remarkably alike in their features — dull and symmetrical — and their hairstyles — short hair, middle parts, slicked back over the ears. They were all in their forties, I guessed. They wore different uniforms, though — the doctor, a white lab coat; the overseer, a dark blue shirt buttoned to the neck; and the chaplain, a black shirt and stiff clerical collar. The doctor wore round glasses and fiddled with the rims.

It occurred to me that if I were ever transferred to Collins Bay, the two people with whom I might have the most contact were Overseer Jagninski and Chief Keeper Flaherty, two people with names almost as challenging as *Debra Debardeleben*. I hoped it would be possible to get away with calling them "sir."

Each person had a different way of interrogating me. The doctor, for instance, had a habit, whenever he spoke, of taking off his glasses and rubbing his eyes with the thumb or forefinger, nearly scooping out his eyeballs each time. He would heave a sigh as he did it, just before he posed a question, and it gave the impression that he was weary of having to ask it at all, that you were the umpteenth person he'd examined that morning, and that you might help him by answering quickly and by not going on and on.

Sigh. "Any history of lung disease-polio-influenza-measles-scarlet fever?" he asked, jabbing his thumb into his eye socket.

"No, sir. I had a baby sister who died of the influenza."

He then turned to the warden and said, as though I weren't there, "I see the judge indicated there is likely mental retardation. If you'd like me to do an assessment, I'll need to see him separately, and we may need to call in Dr. Sherman."

"No, that's fine," said Warden Craig. "He understands our questions and can answer them readily enough. Can't you, son?" He peered at me through his monocle.

"Yes, sir. If I may, sir, I just have trouble speaking. I was born with a split palate."

Sigh. "Mental retardation often goes hand in hand with that," said Dr. Platt. Then he wrote a whole paragraph down in his notebook. I was going to mention my lip but stopped myself for fear he would write several pages. I'm sure he noticed the deformity anyway. The notch was only slightly covered by my wispy attempt at a moustache.

Dr. Platt finally stopped scribbling and asked me to stand with my hands clasped on the top of my head and my chest puffed out, chin up, legs apart. He examined my physique. It'd been a long day; I hadn't been allowed to shower yet and I was embarrassed by my body odour. He circled, inspected me up and down, then took my pulse and listened to my heartbeat. I was grateful for his strong cologne. A scratchy tongue depressor was shoved in my mouth, and when I said "Ahhh," he murmured, "Yes, I see. I see." After the examination, he declared to the others that I was healthy enough to participate in the construction project (meaning Collins Bay Penitentiary) or in any other activity Overseer Jagninski saw fit.

Jagninski asked me questions leaning back in his chair, twirling his pen with his fingers and tapping his foot against the table leg.

"Ever done any carpentry, son?"

"No, sir, but I could learn."

"Any farming?"

"No, sir. I'm from Toronto."

He checked his notes to confirm that I wasn't lying. "Oh yes, I see that now. Well, we also have a smithy, we do masonry and stone-cutting, repair engines, then there's the laundry, the leather goods workshop, the mail room, and the shoe and clothing shop."

"I don't have any experience with any of those." It wasn't a complete lie — my parents' store sold bulk fabric, but it was retail nonetheless and I didn't want to end up handing out clothes. "But I'd like to try carpentry if that's possible."

"This isn't a summer camp, kid," said Chief Keeper Flaherty.

"We may need him for the construction, Mr. Jagninski," said Deputy Warden Fowler, perusing his notebook the whole time. "I'll check over the work schedule and let you know."

Warden Craig then went into a long speech about reforming the convict and asked, did I want to be reformed, or did I want to end up a lifelong criminal?

"No, sir," I said, "I mean, yes, I want to be reformed." Was this the time they expected the defiant outburst? His question was hardly enough to make someone crack.

Warden Craig considered me then, squinted a little more through his monocle, and paused a few seconds as though to assess my sincerity. "Well, you have eleven years in here to work on that then," he said, cheerily, as though this might be something to which I would look forward.

Very slowly, Deputy Warden Fowler wrote one word in his notebook, paused to lift up his pen and cock his head, then wrote a second.

What did he write? I considered the possibilities:

Eleven years.

Stupid retard.

Dirty liar.

Watch him.

There were several more questions, including one about my faith. Father MacDonald asked if it were true that I was "of the Hebrew persuasion," and I confirmed that I was.

"You'll no doubt want to be observing the Sabbath with the other Hebrew inmates, then. I'll make sure you find out about that."

Warden Craig asked if I could read, and when I said I could, he handed me a mimeographed list of the prison rules and a separate list of punishments, said a few more words about discipline in these four walls, etcetera, etcetera, and the guard came back to escort me to my cell.

That evening, as we were lined up, waiting for the inspection before lockdown, I hummed a tune very quietly to calm a nervous stomach. I assumed I could barely be heard by the guy next to me, and besides, the guard, who had the droopy eyes of a basset hound, was standing twenty men down the line. He must've had a hound's hearing to match the droopy eyes because he jerked his head in my direction. He walked slowly, ominously towards me, stopping inches from my face and staring, close enough to smell his sour breath. Instinctively, I let my vision go out of focus.

"I'm assuming they gave you a list of the prison offences, new boy?" I felt his spittle.

I've never concentrated that hard, before or after, on calming myself in order to make my words come out clearly. Every inmate was waiting to hear what I was going to say and I'd found that if my speech impediment was too strong the first time people heard me, they didn't usually give a second chance.

"Yes, sir." It sounded clear, almost.

The guard smirked. Maybe he hadn't put his finger on

what was different. Maybe he'd assume I was French-Canadian, which probably wouldn't help much, but at least it wouldn't be as bad as if people thought I was stupid.

"And what do they say about singing?"

I closed my eyes and retrieved the image. "They say, 'A convict shall be guilty of an offence against Penitentiary Regulations if he sings, whistles or makes any unnecessary noise, or gives any unnecessary trouble,' sir."

"Yes, Offence Number Ten. No singing. And what did I just hear you doing?"

"I was humming, sir, not singing. And it's Offence Number Eleven, sir."

He cracked my left shin with his truncheon and I heard chuckles. I knew it wasn't wise to contradict him, but I couldn't help myself. It was worth it to be cheeky, to risk it just to show people I could be clever. I closed my eyes and waited for the pain to pass.

"Are you trying to be smart with me?"

"No, sir."

"Well then, why don't you tell me what Offence Number Four says about being smart with an officer?"

I knew it was Offence Number Three, but I didn't say so this time. "Treats with disrespect any officer of the penitentiary, or any visitor, or any person employed in connection with the penitentiary, sir."

He cracked my other shin. "Then don't contradict me, new boy."

"I'm sorry, sir." My legs felt wobbly.

He considered my apology, then said, "You think reciting the rules verbatim is gonna impress me?"

"No, sir."

He smiled, stepped back, and stood there, arms akimbo. His truncheon jutted out like a sword in a scabbard. "Okay, wise guy, what's Offence Number Twenty-Three?"

"Offering to an officer a bribe of any kind whatsoever."

"And Number Twenty-Six?"

"Neglecting to go to bed at the ringing of the retiring bell."

He pulled a small booklet out of his back pocket, opened it, and held it away from his face. "Hmph. What about Number Thirty, then?"

"There is no Offence Number Thirty, sir."

The guard laughed. "They couldn't have given you those rules more than five hours ago. You been sitting in your cell all this time memorizing them?"

"No, sir, I only read them once."

"Well, I'll be. He sounds like a gibbering idiot but has a few tricks up his sleeve." My throat tightened with disappointment. "I've heard about people like you." He put away the booklet, then gave a final crack, which sent me to my knees. "Watch out, new boy. I don't like smart alecs," he spat, then moved along, back to where he'd left off his inspection.

an open window

Ari and I took a walk in the neighbourhood around Baycrest while Bessie slept, Pearl watching over her at the bedside. My sister had not had a good week. Her cancer was progressing painfully, and painfully slowly. Unlike mine, it appeared not to bend to radiation or chemo. A month before, she'd sworn off treatment, opting for palliation, but they weren't doing a good job at pain management.

Chronic pain is a fire that can burn up hope, sizzle it to a crisp. The crack of a truncheon to the shins is a mere scalding, producing a temporary blister that will pop and heal, if anger or resentment aren't allowed to infect the wound. If the pain is severe or prolonged, it slow-cooks us until we're bereft, until hope is charred, desiccated, and not really hope at all, just its ashen remains, with longing for release rising up like a wisp of smoke.

Today, Bessie had shifted in her bed uncomfortably, and watching as she tried to hide her suffering from her grandson, watching her try to ignore the pain, was too much to bear, even more because she couldn't dissemble. I would certainly not end up like that. It confirmed my decision.

I could see how upset Ari was. I saw his face when we left Bessie's room; it was as if she'd let him down. He couldn't possibly blame her for it, and he'd get little comfort from me.

He didn't know the half of it.

"I need you to help me," I said, as we strolled along the

quiet residential street. The words sounded weak, frayed at the edges, betraying my nervousness. I couldn't delay any longer.

It was a bright, sunny spring day, one that gave people a sense of possibility after a harsh winter. Splashes of colour glinted in freshly turned flowerbeds. Trees protected red brick houses and newly sprouted leaves rustled from a light breeze. A beautiful cherry had sown a carpet of blossoms before us, making the air fragrant with the perfume of pollination.

Surrounded by all of this awakening life, I asked Ari to help me end mine.

After a few moments, he turned away, fighting back tears.

I put my hand on his shoulder. "Ari, I know I'm asking a lot. I'm sorry." When he didn't say anything, I hardened my voice. "Do you really want me to end up like Ellen did? You've seen that place." I pointed back at Baycrest. "Can you honestly say you'd want to live there, slowly waiting to die? Look at your grandma Bessie."

He pulled away from me and wiped his nose on his sleeve. "What *about* Grandma? Who will look in on her?" His tone was accusatory.

Since his aunt Lil died, Ari had become closer to Bessie than I gauged he'd be comfortable to admit. Closer than a twenty-something man should be to an old lady. I couldn't blame him; I'd been drawn in by the same qualities, many years before. With Bessie, you didn't talk about great ideas or concepts like you did with Lil, but she had qualities I'd needed much more than intellect, like loyalty and fairness and humanity. If you were beleaguered and confused, she had a way of slicing cleanly through the nonsense and flicking it to the side. She did this with wit and impatience and yet she didn't make you feel ashamed. Somehow, you felt she was agreeing with what you *would* have said, had you gotten it out first. She was more solicitous of Ari than any of us. His parents exacted excellence, pushing him higher and higher but in a hyper-critical manner. I usually followed Lil's example, trying to rein in his overconfidence. Bessie, while disapproving of the world around her, didn't care about excellence or worry about self-confidence in her loved ones. She was only concerned with goodness, good manners, and common sense. As a result, we felt no pressure from her, just the sweetness of her praise. When she offered congratulations, she somehow made success seem both expected and surprising all at once. Ari moved in an academic world that was competitive and harsh, and he cherished her support.

"Your grandma doesn't need me," I said. "She has her friend Pearl. And you and your parents."

He let my answer hang in the air a few seconds, then asked, "Why me? Why not Mom and Dad?"

"You told me last year you had a friend who was dying of AIDS and his friends helped him get the drugs he needed to end his life. You said you knew the nurse who got him what he needed."

"That friend wasn't close. And others helped him, not me."

"Your parents don't know who to ask. It would be too risky for them; they'd have to talk to too many people. You already know the right person."

"I'm just not sure," he said, and although he was apparently talking about the drugs, I knew it was more than that. This wasn't going well and I'd feared as much. "I need a few weeks," he added.

"I'm not necessarily planning to do anything right away. I just need a little insurance."

"It's not a question of when. You can't just ask me something like this and expect me to leap to it. I need time to think things through. I need to consider ... well ... things."

"Nobody will ever find out you helped me," I said.

He looked doubtful, and I couldn't blame him. If my life was a cautionary tale, its message was keep your nose clean. Why would *I* be asking him to break the law? "I'm not making this request lightly," I offered. "I wouldn't involve you unless I needed to. I'll take care of it; if the police get involved — not that they will — you won't be implicated in any way. I promise."

"Yeah? Well, you'll just have to cling to life a little longer," he said.

For the moment, I had to accept his answer, though I felt heavier to hear it. Besides, I shouldn't have expected him, quickly and easily, to make that kind of leap. I, of all people, should've known how difficult it was to sail out an open window, when the ground was far below and the night was dark, dark, dark.

the key to liberation

By 1933, when Emma Goldman moved to Toronto, my sister Lil was eighteen years old and in her first year of university. Lil had been encouraged in her schooling by a man named Irv Charney, who had begun to court Bessie the year before. Irv was going into his last year of pharmaceutical studies, and Bessie had taken a job at a local factory. Lil was working part-time in our parents' store because they were more flexible with her need to study. I still worked in the store too, and hated every moment. I could've worked the cash, but Ma had me sweeping, carrying boxes, and wrapping purchases, all the uninteresting jobs. Even though I had proved how useful I might be with the inventory, she put Lil in charge. Meanwhile, Lil also got to talk to customers and make sales.

When Irv started courting Bessie, she complained to him about Lil's radicalism, but her pride in her younger sister's academic accomplishments peeked through, and Irv was shrewd enough to ignore the sibling rivalry. Lil's success at school was an exciting curiosity in our family. Except for in arithmetic, Bessie's marks had been mediocre. As for my parents, they never had the chance to go past grade eight. Irv took Lil under his scientific wing and encouraged her academic pursuits, and his encouragement was just the push she needed. In her last year at Harbord Collegiate, she applied to and was accepted into biology at the University of Toronto. With the money Bessie had helped earn by working in the factory, our family scraped together enough to pay for Lil's tuition.

Irv Charney graduated as a pharmacist the next May, and in August he married Bessie, moving her out of our parents' place on St. Patrick Street and in with him in a rented flat above a dry goods shop on Spadina Avenue. Irv went to work for Mr. Rothbart, and being a good provider now, chipped in to help pay for Lil's tuition. The decision was clear: Bessie would quit her job at the factory. We didn't know then what a mistake that would be, how that decision was another switch on the tracks, diverting our lives to a course we couldn't reverse.

Lil took her studies seriously, but if there was a choice between school books and politics, activism took priority. All those years since we'd heard Emma speak, Lil had been learning about anarchism, going to meetings, making new friends who shared her political leanings. Furthermore, she'd devoured everything there was to know about Emma herself, read everything she could get her hands on.

In December of '33, Emma swept back into Toronto with almost fifty years of hardship and social struggle carved into the lines on her face, and I thought Lil would explode from excitement. Emma wasn't just visiting Toronto, she was moving here. Since Lil considered Toronto a dreary back-water town, she was amazed that someone with Emma's past, someone who'd travelled to all the major cities in North America and Europe, would choose to live here. Born in Lithuania in 1869, Emma immigrated as a teenager, with her family, to Rochester, New York. She married young but left her first husband because he was impotent, and moved to New York City, where she worked in a garment factory, became active politically with local anarchists, and quickly distinguished herself. After training as a nurse in Austria, she returned to New York and worked with the residents of the Lower East Side, even helping women to seek safe abortions. She was a masterful organizer, a keen thinker, and a clear and declarative writer, but she was best known, and most hated, for her public speaking.

When I learned about Emma's life, I felt an odd kinship with her that she would surely never have understood. I realized that she too had discovered how speech was a knife cutting both ways. It could draw people in, move their souls, but then, depending on what you said or how you spoke, fickly, it could provoke terrible retribution or crushing exclusion. Of course, Emma was more in control of when that happened than I ever was. She mastered the English language, which I believe was her sixth, after Lithuanian, Yiddish, Russian, German, and French, and she spoke it with barely any accent. The world knew Emma because she wove her words into unforgettable, sometimes shocking tapestries, and people were afraid of their powerful message.

She was ahead of her time and she paid for it. Hounded and imprisoned several times by the American government for her unorthodox views, she was eventually tried and deported to Russia in 1917, just after the October Revolution. There, she met with Lenin and other Bolshevik leaders, and quickly became disenchanted with the authoritarianism of the new Russian leadership. Before long, she denounced the Bolsheviks, left Russia, and took up residence in England and France, with numerous lengthy stays in other countries, including Canada.

Essentially, from 1926 to 1940, she moved back and forth several times between Toronto and the South of France, with a few years in London somewhere in the middle. After my family heard her speak in '26, she went to St-Tropez, then a sleepy village of artists and fishermen on the Mediterranean. It was cheaper to live there, and she rented a cottage found for her by patron of the arts and socialite Peggy Guggenheim. The next year, Guggenheim gave her the money to purchase it. Emma named her little sanctuary hopefully. She called it Bon Esprit — Good Spirits — and she installed herself to write her autobiography, *Living My Life*, which was published in 1931.

Lil read *Living My Life* cover to cover, all one thousand pages of it. Captivated by Emma when she'd heard her speak on Ibsen's *The Doll House*, Lil had set about to devour every idea that Emma had put to print. The most compelling to Lil was the call to critical thought. While the communists were busy talking about the bonds of capitalism, Emma was more concerned with the bonds of the human mind. She decried the shackles that convention and uncritical thinking can place on a person, communist, capitalist, anyone. Her experience with the Bolsheviks in Russia had confirmed to her that even communists could become tyrants and that even if the means of production had been changed, the proletariat could be duped if they didn't first free their minds.

EMMA HERALDED HER ARRIVAL in Toronto by launching a speaking tour at Hygeia Hall. I remember Lil's face brightening when she read the news — it meant not only that she might get to meet her idol but also that Rupert MacNabb's not-so-secret efforts to thwart the tour hadn't fully succeeded. MacNabb, a wealthy industrialist, had somehow discovered that Emma's comrades were scouting locations and was determined to erect as many roadblocks as he could. He called potential venues and raised the spectre of bad publicity from riots and police raids, urging them to turn Emma away. His connections and influence on the editorial board of both the *Mail and Empire* and the *Globe* ensured those newspapers ignored her visit, but he failed with the *Daily Star*, which wrote a favourable editorial a few days after the first lecture. And, though he couldn't get the tour cancelled, MacNabb caused just enough frustration that he inspired a lust for payback in many people. Most did nothing about it, but it drove Lil to actions we'd later regret.

MacNabb's opposition to Emma wasn't personal in nature. She'd never targeted him either publicly or privately; he merely detested her for what she espoused. Lil said that unlike the general public, MacNabb probably knew that anarchism wasn't about people setting off bombs, or mobs running wild and foaming at the mouth. That it didn't mean looting and fornicating in public. He knew that while anarchists criticized government, they didn't preach chaos. Lil suspected that MacNabb had actually read Emma's ideas and that what bothered him most was her belief that we should routinely question those with power and influence. Unlike the general public, MacNabb actually *had* power and influence.

Nonetheless, Emma wasn't as concerned with him as her supporters were. To her, MacNabb was a gadfly that she brushed away with a wave of the hand. Her mind was always on the bigger picture, overseas or south of the border, or on her own writing. She let others take care of the details while she prepared for her lecture.

On the opening night of the tour, my parents had another commitment, so Lil decided to go with friends. When she asked if I wanted to join, I agreed, but half-heartedly. I had a reputation to maintain as a surly seventeen-year-old, but I was secretly intrigued by Emma's notoriety and also simply looking for something to do on a Monday night in January. In the summer, I might've gone out to hang around in the park smoking, but in the winter, there weren't many places to congregate and do anything that I considered fun. My parents often suggested I have friends over, but that was out of the question. I didn't have friends, or not the kind you'd invite home, anyway. I couldn't imagine the guys I knew, who were this close to thugs, sitting on our living room couch while Ma served tea and Pop interrogated them. What an unmitigated disaster that would've been.

I went that night with Lil and her classmates. Emma's speech was "Germany's Tragedy and the Forces That Brought It About." For the rise of Hitler, she blamed the heavy industrialists and the landed gentry, the Social Democrats who didn't dare touch them, and the Communists who spent more time attacking the Social Democrats than the Hitlerites. When someone asked if the German Evangelical Church should be praised for its stand against tyranny, she lamented that they had stood by while the Jews were persecuted and only began to speak out when they were targeted themselves.

After the speech, a crowd gathered around the podium, and Lil announced that she wanted to go to the front to see if she could meet Emma. Her friends declared that she'd never get near her and that they didn't want to wait. I felt the same way but had to hang around because she was my sister. As Lil pushed her way forward, her copy of Emma's autobiography clutched in a sweaty palm, I followed a few steps behind. I stood on the outskirts of the gathering and craned my neck to see through. Lil hung back for a while, but then she saw an opening and shoved her way to the front.

I saw her stick out her hand. "I'm so pleased to meet you, Miss Goldman, I've been a very big fan of your writing for many years."

At first, Emma was warm and gracious, shaking Lil's hand and smiling generously. She looked her up and down and said, "Not that many years, by the look of you. You can't be more than twenty."

"I'm almost nineteen, but I heard you speak when I was eleven. I'd like to get more involved in the struggle and I wonder if you could tell me how I can help."

Emma held Lil's arm, up near the shoulder. "Read. Listen," she said, giving Lil's arm a shake with each word. "Then think for yourself. Question everything! The key to liberation is to first free one's mind," she said, tapping her own temple. Then she took Lil's copy of *Living My Life*, signed it without being asked, returned it, and turned her back to greet other admirers.

Lil searched for me in the crowd. She was annoyed, and I couldn't tell at whom. I moved towards her, but when she couldn't locate me, she turned back to Emma and tapped her on the shoulder.

"All right, Miss Goldman," she said. Her voice trembled, but she spoke loudly enough to interrupt others who had already started to talk. "I have a question: Is this how you treat someone who might just be a new ally? A sister in the struggle? By dismissing her with platitudes? With all due respect, I've been reading and thinking and questioning and trying to free my mind ever since I first heard you speak here in '26. I'm ready for more."

A hush came over the gathering. Emma did not turn around.

When there was no answer, Lil added, nervously, "And I'm not afraid of hard work."

Emma remained with her back to her for a few more seconds. Then, slowly, she turned around, fixed Lil in the eye, squinting through her round spectacles, and brushed aside a strand of grey hair. She was not smiling this time.

"What is your name, dear?" she asked. The people around them shifted about, glancing to the side, maybe checking out the nearest exit.

"Lillian Wolfman, Miss Goldman," Lil said, more feebly than her initial volley.

"Miss Wolfman, hard work is one thing, but courage is in short supply, and I can see you have that in spades. Or at the very least, you have chutzpah, and for now, that will do."

Lil's face flushed. "Yes, Miss Goldman. Thank you."

Emma took a pencil from behind her ear and wrote something down on a piece of paper she fished out of the pocket in her cardigan. "Come to this meeting. I am raising money for the anarchists being forced to flee repression in Germany, but shortly thereafter, I will be leaving Toronto for the United States. They have finally let me back in, if only for a few months. We need people to carry on the fundraising while I am gone."

"Yes, Miss Goldman, I'll be there. You can count on me."

"Call me Emma."

"In that case, you can call me Lil," she said, braver than she'd ever felt, I'm sure.

At that, Emma gave an explosive cackle, and said, "All right then, Lil. You and I are going to get along just fine."

Lil rushed back to find me and dragged me out of Hygeia Hall, talking incessantly all the way. You'd have thought she'd seen the Messiah; that was how elated she was. We went straight home, and Lil ran ahead. She burst through the door to tell our parents about her encounter, but shortly into her story realized that Ma's eyes were red and she was waiting for Lil to stop talking.

It was then that we noticed Bessie sitting in the living room, weeping in Pop's arms.

When you greet the morning like any other, rubbing sleep from yours eyes, it's hard to imagine that a day can flip over like that. Like a dog lying on its curved back, belly up, tongue out, paws slack, suddenly disturbed and leaping to its feet. One dog will flip over and be tail-wagging happy. The other, hackles raised. It was like that the day Lil met Emma and Bessie lost her new husband. Same day, two very different dogs leaping up at them.

Ma told us the awful news: Bessie's Irv had been killed in an accident. He was running to catch the trolley, crossing the street in front of it, and he slipped on a patch of ice. The trolley conductor tried to stop, but the wheels locked and slid, just enough to crush him under the front bumper.

The shiva lasted all week and was held at Irv's parents' house, a few blocks over on Bathurst Street. Bessie moved home. She spent most of the shiva with her face in Lil's shoulder. Lil held her close, patting her back, taking handkerchiefs from others and pressing them against Bessie's nose, warding off acquaintances who seemed only to want to gouge out a piece of Bessie's grief and take it home clutched to their chests. One girl made it through the protective wall. She was small and fair-skinned, with a pretty face and a kind smile. Instead of blocking her, Lil urged her forward. She sat down beside Bessie and put her arm over her shoulder, then drew a finger across her own bangs, uncovering a port wine stain on her forehead, just above her right eye. Its ruddy roughness mesmerized me for a moment, not to mention that it was sticking out there for all to see. Did she mean to uncover it, or was she so preoccupied with Bessie's grief that she'd forgotten she had it? I'd never seen a girl with a facial disfigurement before and wished I could've asked her about it, but that was impossible. A few minutes later, she made her apologies and left. I was too embarrassed to ask Lil her name.

Though Lil carried on protecting Bessie, by the third night of the shiva her face began to betray an uneasiness, a slight embarrassment. I thought it was because she was so unused to consoling anyone, especially her older sister. I'd never seen Lil be so tender before, so protective. When people tried to come to speak to Bessie, Lil continued to wave them away, and Ma, Pop, and Irv's father took them aside to receive their condolences.

That night, after the prayers had been said, Lil waited until our parents were in the other room, then dislodged Bessie from her shoulder, held her face in her palms, and said, "I have to go out for a little while, Bessie; I'll be back later."

"What? Where are you going?"

"There's a meeting I promised someone I'd go to." Her eyes flickered once in my direction. It was then that I understood. What I'd mistaken for uneasiness was really just impatience. Lil had promised Emma she'd attend that fundraising meeting.

"You're going to one of your political meetings? Lil, this is Irv's shiva!" She'd raised her voice a little and people turned to look.

"I have to, Bessie. I made a promise. I'll be back as soon as it's over." Then she turned and quickly left before Bessie could protest further and before our parents had a chance to stop her.

The comfort Lil provided that week apparently receded in Bessie's memory. As an older woman, she would tell people of how Lil chose politics over family. Everyone had come to expect such behaviour of Lil, she said. "Running out on me in my darkest hour to go to a meeting was only one instance of my sister's topsy-turvy priorities."

This one-sided version of those events lived on because it elicited no protest from Lil. She took her beating again and again. "That was only the first of many mistakes," she'd admit.

§

After I met with the prison classification board, I assumed I'd be transferred immediately to Collins Bay, given that its chief keeper was present at my interview, but instead I spent the first eight months in the main jail, Kingston Pen. Also, despite the talk of construction work and my request for the carpentry shop, I was sent to work on the farm. Every morning, a whole crew of us were marched through town escorted by guards. Townspeople would clear the roads to let us pass. Women stood on the sidewalks and held their children close, but the men largely walked on without stopping. Once we'd reached the outskirts of Kingston and arrived at the fields, which were, in actual fact, right by Collins Bay, we'd work from eight in the morning until five at night with a half-hour lunch break.

They operated the farm to provide produce for the two prisons — to reduce their operating costs. We cultivated hay, oats, buckwheat, potatoes, carrots, cabbage, onions, and tomatoes. The crops all ended up in prisoners' mess kits or in the bellies of the horses they kept for use by the guards and in the farm work itself. When Ma came to visit me in

August and found out they were teaching me to be a farmer, she wept, remembering her back-breaking labour as a girl in New Liskeard.

The field supervisor was Mr. Corey, an older man with a leathery face and a raspy voice. Overseer Jagninski had hired him from the Guelph Prison Farm, where Mr. Corey had worked for twenty years, ever since the bank had foreclosed on him and appropriated his family's land. They said his wife left him for a daguerreotype operator in Toronto, taking their son with her. Mr. Corey didn't speak much, but he was nice enough to those of us who worked hard.

I didn't know a thing about farming, but I learned fast. I'd missed planting season, but I was put to work with the others tending the fields or looking after the animals through the summer until the harvest. When it came time to pull in the crops, the most satisfying were the onions, potatoes, and cabbage, because they were weighty and it felt like you'd really grown something.

Even though the work was exhausting, I was glad to be outdoors. It would've been entirely bearable had there not been a couple of fellows who decided that I was an easy mark. They were the sort who had bitterness and cruelty sewn up inside of them, who were overstuffed with it. I knew, when occasionally they lapsed into periods of mercy, that nastiness would soon push out through the seams. The guards rarely did anything, and out there in the fields, Mr. Corey's attention was pulled in too many directions.

The worst offender was Red Humphries, a guy even uglier than me, only he didn't recognize it. He had no deformities, but his face was pocked and puffy and his ears stuck out farther than mine. He had a pear-shaped body on which the hard work in the fields had no effect whatsoever, but he was about six foot two and, because of his sheer bulk, I wasn't anxious to tangle with him. His red hair was shaved close (like all of us), revealing a lumpy skull, which I suspected came from being dropped on his head a few too many times.

His favourite method of torment was to cross his eyes and talk with his tongue between his teeth, pretending he was a retard. "Look at Wolfman, you guys. N-eye-thhh onionthhh, eh Wolfman?" he would slobber. "Look at the ppppwetty onionthhh!" I tried to ignore him, and his friends' laughter. For two months, I'd been doing my damnedest to stifle my rage and humiliation and just get on with the work. I found the best way to do this was to breathe out through my nose, as if opening my mouth would let loose an inadvertent scream or cause me to bare my teeth. I'd close my eyes and focus on a soothing memory: my mother stirring barley and carrot soup, or Nurse Grace stroking my cheek and saying "there, there," with her English accent.

One day in mid-September, we were harvesting the root crops. Rows of inmates crouched and waddled between furrows, hand-gathering potatoes that horse-drawn steel-wheeled diggers had turned up for us. We carried burlap sacks on ropes around our necks, and these were kept open by hooking one side of the sack onto a crossbar, which was itself attached to the rope. Just when you got used to the scratchy hemp digging a groove into your nape, the cross-bar would knock your chin. To keep a rhythm and not throw myself off balance, I jerked my head, shifting the rope into a temporarily more comfortable position. I tried to ignore the sweat that ran down my face and inevitably trickled into the notch in my lip.

"That's it, Wolfman. Good bending at the knees. Good pace," Mr. Corey rasped, as I straddled a mound of spuds and one hand after the other tossed them into my sack. "Humphries, you could pick it up a little."

Red Humphries and his friends were working two rows over. As Mr. Corey walked away to the other side of the field, Red flipped a finger in his direction. Beyond Mr. Corey, I could see that a digger had become stuck and men gathered around to pull potatoes out of it.

The bag slipped down my neck again. I jerked my head up.

"Hey guys, get a load of Wolfman and tell me who he reminds you of."

I was trying not to pay attention, but I saw one of them had a puzzled expression and shook his head, continuing to collect his potatoes.

"I'll give you a clue," said Red, and he started dancing about, crouched over, heaving one shoulder up and down. He twisted his face, crossed his eyes, and then covered his ears. "The bells! The bells!"

I breathed in and out through my nose and tried to picture Ma, but that day, all I could see was Red.

"Quasimodo!" one of them yelled, pointing at me. They all laughed.

I hadn't seen the movie, but I knew to whom he was referring.

"Take that back, Humphries," I said, straightening up.

His friends smirked. "Make me," Red snorted, and he puffed his chest out a bit, glancing briefly at his friends. Maybe he was a little surprised I'd responded.

The insult was no worse than a dozen he'd thrown my way. I didn't realize, until later when I'd cooled down, what set me off, what was different that day. Quasimodo had a deformed face. I was used to being teased about how I sounded, but I'd fooled myself into believing that my moustache covered the notch.

I was still breathing through my nose, as if it were doing a damned thing to calm me, and stepped across the furrow between us. I stood facing him. "I said, take it back!"

"Go back to your row, Quasimodo."

I went to push him, but he must've anticipated it because his hands caught mine on their way to hitting my chest. We shoved at the same time but he was stronger and I stumbled, destabilized by the potato sack around my neck. Stupid of me not to take it off. I fell into a furrow, on my back. The sack was upended and potatoes rained down on me.

Mr. Corey had finished with the digger and saw the fall on his way towards us.

"Humphries!" he barked. "Over to the far row with ya! I shoulda known to separate you two."

Having Mr. Corey send him away while I was lying there like a turtle on its back was even more humiliating than what Red had said about me. I'd been in scraps before back in Kensington, and I'd always come out the winner. Back in Toronto, people knew me as someone not to mess with. Ever since I'd pounded Bobby Fein in the schoolyard for calling me ugly as a chimp, there'd been respect accorded me, even though behind my back they'd probably still said things.

Here, there were different rules. I'd been told stories of knifings and people beaten to bloody pulps — not by Red, mind you, but he was big enough to set my imagination going. The law of the jail yard was the same as the schoolyard, only with bigger and more dangerous players, and in their pecking order, I was at the bottom of the heap, lying in a ditch.

§

The guard's grip on my arm was, as usual, much stronger than it needed to be. It was unnecessary when two burly men were posted by the visitors' door with guns ready to shoot us dead if we bolted past our relatives. He pushed me down into a chair behind a table, his fat fingers leaving divots in my skin, stood back a few feet, and motioned to the door that they could let my sisters in. I'd spent weeks waiting for Bessie and Lil's first visit and became even more excited when I'd learned they were coming without Ma and Pop — they had to visit in turns because it was too expensive to close down the store. I missed my parents, but Ma spent her visits weeping, and neither Pop nor I had any clue how to console her.

Bessie entered first, carrying a package. Immediately, a guard intercepted her. I couldn't hear them but she seemed to be explaining the contents of the package and was getting more and more agitated. Lil was becoming indignant but luckily Bessie had the sense to calm her down or they would've been thrown out. They looked over to me during the exchange, and I could read on Bessie's face her mounting disappointment as she realized her present would be confiscated.

They came over and we embraced. "I had such a nice spice cake for you!" said Bessie. "Do they think I'm bringing you a nail file? Damn guards." I'd never heard her swear before.

"She sobbed the whole time she was baking," said Lil.

"Did not."

"That cake?" She made a face. "Salty as a kosher chicken, from her tears. Trust me, those guards don't know what they're in for."

"It's okay." I smiled. "I'm just glad to see you."

"They're getting fat and you're wasting away," said Bessie. "Look at you, thin as a rail. They're not feeding you enough!"

"I'm fine. I'm just working in the fields, so I lost some weight."

"I'm going to write a letter," said Lil.

"Don't write a letter, Lil. You'll just get me in trouble. Write letters to *me*."

Bessie leaned in towards me. "You think *that* would be meddling? Ask her how she's been spending Thursday nights, Toshy."

Lil shot her a glance, but then, back stiffening, said, "I got involved with the Prisoners Support Guild, and you're not going to talk me out of it. I have to do *something* to help you while you're in here." I must've looked worried because she said, "It's mostly general prisoner supoort, about basic conditions and such. I promise we won't campaign to have them tuck you in at night."

Bessie'd been holding my hands, rubbing the skin over my knuckles, and generally pumping them as though if she squeezed often enough, it might kick-start my circulation. "Well, I couldn't do what Lil does, but she does have a point. Look at these hands. They're like cracked desert mud."

"I don't mind working on the farm, really."

"You see, Bessie? He needs something to do. That's why we met with the unions the other day. They've been protesting the work you do here in prison; they say you're doing union work and getting paid too little for it. Personally, I know it's exploitation, but you have to have something or you'll go out of your mind. All the unions care about is drumming up more work for themselves."

That was just like Lil. Jumping to a conclusion without asking. The fact that she happened to be right wasn't the point. "What else is this guild getting up to?" I asked, trying very little to hide the irritation in my voice.

"Well, the other issue is that the inmates they're transferring to the new Collins Bay Prison are mostly adults despite the fact they're supposed to be building it for youth. Do you know that Parliament is completely unaware that Kingston has quietly changed its policy?"

"They don't really give us political updates."

"Well, I'd much rather you be transferred to a facility with young people, as it was intended to be, rather than staying with all of these older, hardened men. I mean, look at them!" She twisted her face in horror and pointed to a man at the next table, who turned to glare at her. I lowered my head and so did Bessie.

"I don't mind being with the older guys."

Bessie said, "Lil, wouldn't it be good to *ask* Toshy what he thinks you should be fighting for?"

"Of course! I want to hear all about everything."

But from her tone, I could tell she didn't really want to know. Bessie leaned back in her chair and rolled her eyes heavenwards.

Even if it was futile, I started to tell them about what it had been like for me, how my cell was cramped, about our daily routine, how terrible the food was, all of the stuff I knew would be easiest to hear. I didn't mention Red Humphries.

A few minutes into my stories, Lil interrupted mid-sentence. "Oh my god! I almost forgot to tell you. Guess who's in the guild with me?"

Bessie put her face in her hands. "As if he'll ever guess."

She elbowed Bessie. "Stop picking. It's a figure of speech." She turned to me and resumed her smile. "Lady Grace Fister. I could hardly believe it."

"Nurse Grace?"

"One and the same. At first, I couldn't bring myself to tell her that you were in jail for stealing her hawked wedding gift. But eventually, after a few meetings, I screwed up my courage. Of course, she knew all along. She'd followed the trial in the papers and remembered caring for you when you had your operation."

I felt a rush of heat to my face. "She remembered me?"

"Said you were one of her most adorable patients."

"You're making that up."

"I swear to God."

"You don't even believe in God," said Bessie.

"Do I have to show you the dictionary definition for 'expression,' Bessie? Anyway, when I said how sorry I was about the diamond, she said, 'I'm not. I'm sorry for your brother, the poor dear.'" Lil did a terrible British accent, but it made me chuckle. "Then she said, 'But I was delighted that vile and wretched Oonagh MacNabb doesn't have my precious diamond anymore!' Can you believe it? What a hoot. Ever since, I've been trying to find ways to use the words 'vile' and 'wretched' in a sentence."

"What a lady," I said.

"I know. I felt sick listening to her, especially when she said, 'It's only a shame that diamond will never bring joy to anyone again.'"

Now I felt sick too, just to hear Lil repeat Nurse Grace's words. "How is she doing? I mean, what's she like?"

"You never met someone nicer. She's invited me over for tea a few times. Doesn't really understand my politics, but that's okay; her heart's in the right place, and we have our interest in health care in common. I think she trusts me too. She even told me the story of how she met her husband."

"Didn't we read that in the papers?" asked Bessie.

"Some of it — the stuff she'd be too modest to tell me herself, like how the British Army rewarded her for her excellent nursing with the Royal Red Cross and the Queen's South Africa Medal. But I don't remember it saying she was born a commoner, or how when the Boer War broke out, they sent her fresh out of school to work in a field hospital in the Cape of Good Hope. Also, I didn't know about her family. Apparently, her sister went into nursing first and worked at Wandsworth, a prison in London. Grace followed her into the profession but decided on paediatrics. Her sister's career was how she's come to have an interest in prisoners' health."

"She could teach the old battleaxe they have here a few things about bedside manner," I said. I already knew the story Lil was telling me. Nurse Grace had told it to me when I was five years old, in the hospital to have my palate sewn shut, but I liked to hear Lil tell it again, so I pretended it was new to me. "Did she tell you how come she came to Canada?"

"Well, it seems she met Lord Fister when he was visiting a wounded comrade-in-arms. She and Lord Fister were immediately lovestruck and he knew he wanted her for his bride. So, when the war ended and Grace went back to England, he set about to find a suitable wedding present. The Orange Sunset was for sale in its raw form in Port Elizabeth. Apparently, it was named for its colour — a light amber — and patriotically for its origins, because it was discovered in a mine in the middle of South Africa's Orange Free State. Its original Afrikaans name meant the Glory of the Orangemen, but Lord Fister renamed it the Orange Sunset because, after all, the British won the Boer War and the Orange Free State was no longer.

"On the way home, Lord Fister stopped off in Amsterdam to have the diamond cut and set into a brooch. Then he went on to London, where he presented it to his fiancée. Apparently, Lord Fister Senior was not impressed. When he heard of his son's engagement to a commoner, he reduced his supply of money to a trickle and virtually wrote his son out of his will. But he and Grace had predicted this. They got married anyway, took the money they had, and sailed for Canada!"

I smiled, reflecting Lil's expression because she was clearly looking for a reaction. In my heart, though, I was jealous. Nurse Grace was special to me. I was her most adorable patient, she'd said. It wasn't fair for Lil to move in and befriend her. I wanted to say, get your own sweet little old lady.

Through it all, I hadn't really noticed Bessie, but when I looked at her now, she was pale.

"Let's not talk about this anymore," she said.

"Oh c'mon, Bessie. What's done is done," said Lil. "What you've gotta take out of that story is that there's a lot of love in the Fister home, and a diamond brooch doesn't make a difference to them, so don't worry."

The sounds of other families talking at the tables next to us filled the gap in our conversation. I knew if the subject was going to change, I'd have to take matters into hand.

"Bessie, you haven't said a word about how you've been, and Lil you haven't mentioned medical school at all."

"Oh, I've been fine," said Bessie. "You shouldn't worry about me. Ma and Pop are glad to have me back in the store with them, and it's not so bad, I guess."

"And Abe?"

I got a smile out of Bessie when I mentioned her boyfriend's name. "Things are good. He's never suspected anything."

"And there's no reason for him to," said Lil.

"I'm happy for you, Bessie."

"And ... my classes are going well enough, though it's only been two weeks." Lil had apparently decided Bessie was finished talking, and Bessie actually seemed relieved to shift the spotlight away again, so I said nothing. "The course load is heavy, but honestly, the hardest part is being one of only a handful of women in the medical school, and the four others are Gentiles. On my third day, one of the professors told me that only two Jewish women have ever graduated and that I would be the third. 'If you make it through,' he added ominously!"

"Do you know the other girls?"

"The five of us met on the first morning, and every day we huddle together in the middle of the lecture hall like a hamlet under siege from an army of men. An army of *vile* and *wretched* men. Ha ha! Did you like how I did that?"

"Very cute," I said.

"Whenever one of us dares to speak up, which, frankly, isn't often—"

"*You* don't speak up very often?" Bessie cut in. She put her hand on Lil's forehead. "What have they done with my sister?"

"As I was *saying* ... when we *do* speak up, the men act as though they're waiting for the signal to advance. If we give a wrong answer, they snicker, they roll their eyes..."

Bessie said, "You can't have expected it to be easy. They're just threatened by you."

"I know. I know I'm being sensitive. And they're not *all* vile and wretched. A few of them are quite nice, particularly this one Montrealer named Gerry. He says the Jewish fellows are angry I've taken one of their precious spots. I told him they should realize who their real enemy is. I may be an easier target, but they should direct their anger with the quota system at the University of Toronto, not at me."

I tilted my chin in the direction of the guards who had confiscated Bessie's cake. "I guess we all have our challenges."

"I guess..."

I waited for Lil to continue, but for once, she was speechless. I only meant to make conversation, but instead I'd shamed Lil for comparing her medical school challenges to my prison life, which, really, she hadn't actually done. I started to say something, but Bessie squeezed my hand and shook her head, so I stopped. It didn't hurt Lil to be chastened every so often.

Ever so slightly, the corners of Bessie's mouth lifted.

§

Letter from Lil to Emma Goldman, from the Berkeley archives:

Toronto, September 14th, 1935

Mrs. E.G. Colton,
St. Tropez (Var)
France

Dearest Emma,

How did you survive your years on Blackwell Island? How did Sasha survive his endless years in jail? I am fearing for my brother's health. Two weeks ago, before I began my classes, Bessie and I visited him for the first time in the Kingston Penitentiary.

Yes, he was convicted after all, not that there was much doubt about the outcome of the trial. What came as a shock was that they sent him away for eleven years. Eleven years! For that charge, such a sentence is almost unheard of, but because Toshy didn't apologize for throwing the brooch out the window, the judge got mad. I suppose that, in the end, my brother's clashes with the local police have not helped him either. When the sentence came down, we all wept, even my father. Poor Toshy was not frightened, though. He didn't shed a single tear or resist in any way as they led him out of the courtroom.

Kingston Penitentiary is a huge and awful place smack in the middle of town, surrounded by turrets and menacing walls — just exactly the way you'd expect a prison to look, I suppose. The difference is that you never imagine someone you love would ever be inside.

It broke our hearts to see Toshy brought in by the guard, even though he had an enormous smile for us. He was smaller and thinner in his oversized prison clothing, but when I saw his face, sunburned, peeling, and his hands, cracked, dry, a few fingers wrapped in strips of cloth, I recalled my mother's lament that they had him working out in the fields every day. I don't know what kind of medical care they're giving them in there. Maybe I should investigate a career in prison medicine.

Don't worry, I heard loud and clear the admonition about working on his release and on improving his prison conditions. You'll be pleased to know I recently joined the Toronto Prisoners Support Guild. The characters I have met in the guild are the oddest assortment. They come from all social strata, and surprisingly, there are many wealthy people who see this work as Christian charity. Only a few of us go because of a family member behind bars.

You will never guess who is helping me lead the charge: Lady Grace Fister! Surely, you remember that this is the original owner of the Orange Sunset, the woman whose husband sold the diamond to pay down his business debts. She has been a member for twelve years, ever since she retired from nursing. Now, this dear woman has provided help and comfort to our family on not one, but two occasions.

Emma, dear, you too have provided me with comfort, even in your absence. I wish I had your guidance now, for I am feeling quite tested these days and do not know where to turn. I often wish they'd locked me up instead of him. You remember the Tim Buck case last year? I'm not suggesting they'll do that to our Toshy because he's not a political agitator. What worries me is that he's in a place where prisoners riot and guards can get away with firing at a defenceless man.

My sister tells me I have to try not to dwell on it all the time, that we have to get on with our lives, and me especially because of my medical studies. Easier said than done. Sometimes, I get furious at those awful MacNabbs and have to restrain myself lest I go over there and do something terrible. There is much more to this story than you know, but I dare not write it in a letter.

Enough, or my blood will boil. Let me tell that my studies are going well. Whenever I have my doubts, I conjure up your image, sitting in that bar on College Street, tilting your spectacles and wagging your finger, saying, "Lil, if a woman is to be free, she has to have a stable and independent income, a profession preferably not tied to the forces of the market, and one that will lift her above the grind of poverty!" You won't believe me, but I have written it out and pinned it above my desk.

On another subject, I suppose you have been reading in the papers about Hitler's effects on Germany. Things are frightening in Europe, are they not? Comrades passed on copies of a couple of articles clipped from the *New York Times* and from the *N.Y. Jewish Forward*. Among them, I was surprised to see an interview with John Haynes Holmes, apparently expressing sympathetic leanings to Hitlerism. Is he not a friend of yours, and a long-standing labour organizer? I suppose even progressives can be guilty of lapses. I am including the *Times* clipping for you to see for yourself.

Emma, dear, I am still dreaming of visiting France one day, but for now, I must turn to the digestive system, a less appetizing prospect, if you'll pardon the joke. I saw Dien and Tom before they left for France and gave them a small present for you — just a silly nothing I picked up but I do hope you like it. If I can't be there in person, at least something of mine can enjoy the French countryside. I hope you'll place it on a windowsill, where it can enjoy the view of those vineyards you describe.

Please write and tell me what you are doing these days in your lovely cottage. I long for news from afar.

You have, as always, my enduring affection and steadfast friendship.

Lil.

Letter from Emma Goldman to Lil, from the Berkeley archives:

St. Tropez, Var, October 12th 35

Miss Lillian Wolfman
Toronto (Ontario)
Canada

Dearest Lil,

I was delighted, this morning, to receive a reply to my letter. I knew of course that you would have your mind elsewhere, but I confess I began to fear that my letter might not have reached you. I have placed your lovely figurine on the window as you requested. She has a coveted spot next to a potted plant and can see not only the vineyards but also the Italian Alps, on a clear day.

You asked me about surviving in jail. My time in Blackwell Island was indeed difficult, but it allowed me to better understand the human condition and our ability to withstand hardship. I emerged a stronger person and so will your brother. I can't say Sasha emerged unchanged, but his spirit kept him sane through those long years. To be sure, letters and visits sustained us both — you and your family must be sure to visit your brother at every opportunity. As I wrote in one of my essays, "the hope of liberty and of opportunity is the only incentive to life, especially the prisoner's life. Society has sinned so long against him — it ought at least to leave him that." If your brother has even a fraction of your spirit and determination, he will weather the storm.

It does not surprise me that there is more to the story than you have written. There almost always is, in matters involving the police or the judiciary. I look forward to hearing about it one day. As for wishing you were in jail instead of him, banish that from your mind. I agree with your sister: it is pointless and foolish to dwell on what might have been. As I said in my previous letter, do not forget about your brother, but do not let your guilt about him paralyze you. You have done the right thing by joining the prison support group. You must do everything you can to give your brother hope. That human need I remember most of all from my days in Blackwell. Good for you, as well, for throwing yourself right into your studies. You will make a fine doctor, Lillian. You must have really had spectacular grades to earn your spot.

What of my activities these days, you asked. I have been urging anarchist writers and editors of the movement's press — Rocker, Nettlau, Albert de Jong, and so on, to publish articles to mark Sasha's sixty-fifth birthday in November. Also, this house has had a host of visitors since July: Dien and Tom, of course, then Mollie Steimer and Senya Fleshin came from Paris and Modeste Stein from New York.

Modeste jokes about coming to visit his wife, because I listed him on my land deed as my first husband. My real first husband, Jacob Kershner, is long dead, but his American citizenship was revoked at the same time as mine and Sasha's, so it was safer to put down Modeste. The French have odd practices when it comes to selling land to women. Notaries require that a woman list all of her current and past husbands, though strangely, they then register the land deed under the woman's maiden name.

Thank you for the clipping from the *N.Y. Times*. I recently received a reply to a letter I sent to Holmes himself, and as I suspected he is no Hitler sympathizer. He wrote to me that he "found the Nazi regime strongly rooted in the country and that the opposition to it was negligible" and that Hitler had infected the masses of the people with an insane nationalistic fever in his support. Even without my experience with newspapers over a period of forty-five years, I should have hesitated to believe in the reliability of the reports. Remember that, my dear Lillian, when you read what was no doubt written about your brother.

Yes, my dear, the European situation is terrifying. By this time, you may have realized that England has not succeeded in frightening Italy. With its usual hypocrisy, the British government is once more trying to play the role of humanity's savior, while it is rushing the world headlong into a new devastating war. If only the people at large were less inert, less obsessed by the spirit of authority and "leadership," the situation would be different. As it is, one might despair but for the fact that in spite of all dictatorship and suppression, the spirit of liberty still lives and will continue to assert itself, though it is unchecked temporarily by the forces of darkness and oppression.

I am going to Paris and then England to do my share against the impending calamity. I am not foolish enough to believe that my voice will be heard by many, especially in England where I am little known. Nonetheless, I find it impossible to concentrate on writing at this appalling time. If only to soothe my own conscience, I have to go where I can speak out. Therefore I am going, whatever the possible consequences.

I am always happy to hear from you. The American Express will find me in Paris and then once in England kindly address me:

c/o Mrs. L. Koldofsky,
20 Beechcroft Court,
Beechcroft Avenue,
LONDON, N.N.11

Now I must go down to the market at the Place des Lices to pick up provisions. Please extend my regards to our comrades.

With deepest love and affection,
    Emma

burdens of survival

My new assisted-living complex, The Terrace, was designed to be a stage between independent living and an old age home. It was a mere five-minute stroll across a parking lot to get to Baycrest, or a brief shuttle bus ride, for those with limited mobility. They said both facilities were models for senior care in Canada, and though I didn't doubt it, that wasn't much comfort, if what you were really longing for was simply to be left alone.

The Terrace's rules were to protect the more fragile ones from injury, to protect the administrators from lawsuits, and generally to keep the peace. I didn't care. I'd lived with my share of rules, and all these years later, I still remembered them well enough.

Offence No. 1: Assaults any Penitentiary officer, employee, or servant. (A lady upstairs bit her attendant the other day. A psychiatrist was brought in for an assessment, and they've now assigned her someone who looks like a prizefighter in a dress.)

Offence No. 8: Is indecent in language or gesture. (Apparently, Mr. Kirsch down at the end of the hall was rebuked by Mrs. Dyment, the social worker, for telling a dirty joke to Mrs. Appelbaum in the dining hall last week.)

Offence No. 16: Commits any nuisance. (Mr. Kirsch got angry at the rebuke and started shouting until people gathered around and Mrs. Dyment finally had to call her colleagues for assistance. Mr. Kirsch was asked to switch tables for the rest of the week.)

Offence No. 24: Neglects to shut the gate of his cell after entering. (They only cared about this one if it was committed while cooking or in conjunction with Offence No. 8. I was told that last year, several women complained that Mr. Kirsch was strutting in front of his open door in a state of semi-arousal dressed only in his briefs.)

Offence No. 25: Neglects to rise promptly on the ringing of the first bell in the morning. (Well, they left you to the mercy of your own alarm clock here, but if you didn't show your face by eleven, it was a safe bet someone would knock on your door to see if you'd expired during the night.)

There was always a period of adjustment, wherever you went. Knowing this, I tried to see the positives, but it wasn't easy. The staff was nice enough and that counted for something. To make sure we didn't rot or stink or attract roaches, there were cleaning women, and in addition to tidying our apartments, they did our laundry. Unlike Baycrest, here, we didn't have nurses on the floors making it feel like a hospital, just one in the office downstairs.

The social worker, on the other hand, was more intrusive. When Mrs. Dyment introduced herself, she told me she mostly dealt with "family issues," which as far as I could tell was really a nice way of saying problems with residents that a family couldn't resolve on their own. Unfortunately, it turned out that she fancied herself some kind of Club Med employee, always urging us to join activities and nudging us into social interaction. This might have been tolerable if I'd been on a beach in Tahiti, and if the people with whom I had to interact were young, nubile women wearing string bikinis.

Instead, my next-door neighbour was the easily disturbed Mrs. Appelbaum, whose late husband was some big-shot lawyer, and she believed this entitled her to have an opinion on everything and everyone. Last week we got into an argument because she knocked on my door while I was frying myself up a little lunch, some kosher sausage and an egg.

"Your sausages are stinking up my apartment, Mr. Wolfman. You know too much fat is bad for your heart? Shouldn't you be worried about that?"

"No," I told her, "I should not. What the hell am I saving my body for? And what are you so worried about? You're even older than I am. Dropping dead of a heart attack at this point would be a goddamned blessing."

Then she said, "Well, I never!" and I realized she'd misunderstood.

"Ach, don't get your nose out of joint; I was talking about myself."

It crossed my mind that her keeling over in front of me wouldn't be such a bad thing, either.

"Nevertheless," she sniffed, "you shouldn't talk about death in such a cavalier fashion or use such profane language."

"Mind your own business. I can talk however the goddamned hell I please," I answered, as profanely as I could think to when put on the spot like that.

"You, Mr. Wolfman, are a Philistine!" she shouted, and then left in a huff, slamming her door.

Now, whenever she saw me, she snootily turned away, making sure others saw her gesture. Compared to her, Pearl Feffer was downright pleasant.

My neighbour to the right was Mr. Stein, a nice enough fellow, but a Holocaust survivor, poor thing. There were lots of survivors here. On some days, I felt like the piece of fruit that got hidden at the centre of the grocery bag, protected while those on the outside were bashed around on their way home. True, I wasn't exactly unmarked myself. The scars where my lip was repaired might catch the eye even more than a forearm tattoo, or a face that in unguarded moments let horrors re-emerge. None of that compared to what those people had lived through. Sure, I'd been in jail, but it wasn't a concentration camp. Yes, I was locked up, but it meant I didn't get conscripted and possibly mowed down at Dieppe.

I could hear Mr. Stein through the walls at night, crying out in the middle of a nightmare, maybe for a lost relative, or in fear of a dreaded camp guard. It made me embarrassed to talk to him in the morning.

Consequently, I stuck to my apartment more than most. It was brightly enough lit, and they let you paint your own place, but I didn't really care to. The walls were beige, which was pretty much how I'd describe this place. Nothing too exciting, lest it provoke too dramatic an increase in a resident's heart rate. Once a day they served a kosher meal downstairs, if you liked, and sat residents at assigned tables, afflicting us with company that we might not care for. I went because the food in the dining hall was actually very good — that was another positive thing, to be fair. A big difference from prison gruel. With Mrs. Appelbaum's snubbing me, I realized I'd better not make too many enemies here, or they'd run out of tables to shift me to.

Next to the dining hall was a room where they showed movies or sometimes had exercise classes, where people sat in chairs and waved their hands in the air or shrugged a lot because they couldn't do much else. I wasn't that far gone yet and got in enough shrugging and waving of my arms just from the peculiarities or annoyances of daily life.

As for non-physical activities, they had several options, none of which interested me. They had carpentry, sewing (they called it "tailoring" for the men), and then there were groups of different kinds. No pottery. Did I say that Mrs. Dyment only dealt with family issues? That wasn't altogether true. She came around the other day with a flyer announcing a new group she was promoting: "The Recollections Group," she was calling it. It was especially for Holocaust survivors.

.Not that I'd have signed up if it were for the rest of us. It was going to be a group where someone came in and helped people write down their experiences and memories, as a sort of therapy, I guessed, or maybe also a history project.

I was thinking yesterday, after visiting with Bessie, that being a survivor shouldn't be an everlasting state, a prison condemning a person to hang on until the bitter end. Even most prisoners eventually go free. Warren and Susan, who said I needed to give it time, mustn't have any idea what it was like to live in a place where a person usually didn't leave except if he went bonkers, became lame and incontinent, or died.

The burden of survival went beyond the physical encumbrances of body and home. Every person should be freed from survival, allowed to walk away from his past. People weren't as much motivated to survive as they were compelled. We carried on because of what we couldn't put out of our minds. Forget all the clichés about hanging on to hope, clinging to pride, or the motivating force of fear; none of those would keep a wretched soul hanging on for even one instant, if he weren't forced to remember the meaning and promise life held before there was pain.

I still remembered, and that was the worst of it. My memories hung on, not willing or ready to liberate me, not yet.

"LOOK, MRS. ROSENBERG! It's a *feygele*!"

Ari stopped, an escapee caught in a searchlight.

He felt his head. "Is it the new hairstyle?"

I laughed. "It's the bird, ya nudnik."

"What?" He stared at the cage he was holding. The budgie inside warbled, as if to scold him.

"Did your parents give you no Jewish education at all? It means little bird," I said, "as well as gay."

"Isn't it cute?" the Baycrest volunteer continued, as we approached her. "You see that nice young man? He's bringing us a new *feygele*."

Ari had stopped on the way to buy a replacement budgie for the residents on Bessie's floor, when he heard that the previous bird had died mysteriously in the night. Probably strangled by a crazed resident.

When we got to Bessie's room, he left the cage outside and we tiptoed in, in case she was asleep. Her eyes were closed, but she wasn't alone. Naturally, Pearl was there, sitting beside her with book in hand.

I made my whisper as flat as possible and pointing to her said, "This is Pearl Feffer, a long-time friend of your grandma's. Pearl, this is Ari, Bessie's grandson." Then, to keep us from disturbing Bessie, I beckoned them to the entranceway.

"Well aren't you a handsome fellow! Very nice to meet you, finally." Whispering like that, Pearl's voice was deep, a little sultry, like Lauren Bacall's. She took Ari's hand and nearly crushed it; there was some force packed into that tiny frame.

"He *is* a handsome devil. Takes after me," I said, smiling, nudging Ari in the ribs. We heard Bessie stirring. I went to her and pulled her covers up slightly, adjusting them at her waist. She smelled of Chanel No. 5, mixed with antiseptic soap.

"So you're studying at McGill. Bessie's told me a lot about you. Oh, do I have a young lady for you! Are you single? My granddaughter is at McGill."

Before Ari could answer, I turned and whispered, "Obviously Bessie hasn't told you everything, Pearl. Ari's gay. However…" I paused for emphasis. "I believe he *is* single — if you've got any grandsons at McGill…"

"Uncle Toshy!"

Pearl's cheeks flushed and I smiled.

"Oh, for heaven's sake, don't worry. You see? She hasn't fallen over with a heart attack, though I will say she seems a bit flummoxed."

"I'm right in front of you, and I'll thank you not to talk about me in the third person." She glared.

"Well, you haven't answered me, Pearl. I asked if you had any grandsons for him."

"Leave poor Pearl alone," said Ari, shaking his head. "I wish to God I hadn't come out to you."

He hadn't; I'd wormed it out of him, on a drive to his parents' cottage two summers before. With just the two of us in the car, I started to speak candidly about Ellen, how lucky I'd been to find her, even if it was late in life, and I kept at him about why he didn't have someone, being so handsome, I said. "Unless you do, and I don't know it," I'd added. "If I'd been as good-looking as you, there wouldn't have been any shilly-shallying." His grip tightened on the steering wheel.

"I told you, I don't have a girlfriend, Uncle Toshy."

"Who said anything about a girl?" I said, raising an eyebrow.

He pulled the car over to the side of the road. "How did you know?"

"I had a gay friend once; I judged him and regretted it. I know better now."

"Please don't say anything to Grandma," he pleaded. "I'm not ready to tell her." He eventually did, with my coaxing, though it hadn't gone all that well at first. She became weepy and called Warren to ask if Ari'd been taken to a psychiatrist, to lament that he would die from AIDS, or lonely and outcast, or both. A family conference calmed her down, and over the months, she settled into the news. I hadn't expected Bessie to be judgemental, not after what she did in her youth, but she obviously still had the same ignorance we all did, left over from our upbringing.

Pearl had somewhat recovered her colour. "I think it's lovely that you're gay, dear. I think gay people are wonderful. So creative and interesting. People consider me to be a very progressive woman, you know. My friends are always telling me I'm ahead of my time." She was dodging the issue of the grandson. "I once had a neighbour who was a homosexual. He was maybe a little older than you," she rambled on. "His name was Frank Shore — you don't know him, do you? A lovely man. Moved back to Regina because his mother got sick. Poor thing."

I didn't know whom she meant, the man or his mother, or if it was the illness or moving to Regina that was the reason for Pearl's pity.

"I'm sorry, I don't know him."

"He doesn't know every single gay person there is, Pearl. Do you know every single Jew in Toronto?"

"No, of course not, don't be ridiculous. I know they don't all know each other." She slapped me on the arm. "No harm in asking. You never know."

"It's okay," said Ari. "I don't mind, but I'm afraid I'm not that connected to the community here in Toronto. Ask me about Montreal, and maybe."

Pearl smiled, and then turned towards me and the smile constricted. Her eyes narrowed slightly too, to better aim the daggers.

"I have a little something for my grandma," Ari said to her, when he realized the conversation had come to a halt. "A *feygele* from the *feygele*."

This confused Pearl.

"Lemme show you." He picked up the cage.

"Oh, will you look at that," she said. "A new budgie. My, my, he is a cute little thing." She stuck a frosted nail through the bars and the bird nibbled at it.

I took the cage and placed it on the night table.

"Well then. I should let you all have a visit together as a family. Your uncle is very possessive about his family time, Ari, and I suppose I can't blame him." She brushed off her skirt, tugged at the hem of her jacket, and then turned to the mirror to fix her hairdo. She pulled out a compact and applied a touch-up to her face. I noticed she dabbed a little extra on her forehead to cover the discolouration, then fiddled with her bangs so that they fell down over it again. I felt a slight tightening in my chest, thinking about the first time we met; it hadn't gone well. Who knew how things might have turned out if I'd acted differently?

"I have to get back to the apartment anyway. My daughter's coming to take me shopping at the Yorkdale Mall. A pleasure to meet you, darling," she said, crushed his hand again, and left without addressing me.

Bessie was still sleeping, so I took the opportunity to probe Ari about his personal life.

"Now, tell me. Since it seems we're not going to be setting you up with Pearl's grandson after all, what's a good-looking kid like you doing still single anyway?"

He sat down on the chair Pearl had occupied and said, "Why? Why oh why can't my family ostracize me like normal people would?"

"Because we're not bigots. Be grateful."

"Grateful. Yeah. Anyway, what about you? Have you gotten any action lately?"

I snorted. "Oh, sure. The ladies are lined up in their wheelchairs to get in my room."

"You know Aunt Ellen would be mad you haven't tried to find someone else."

"I know. She told me when she was sick that she expected me to go out and find a young trophy wife." A lump thickened in my throat, and I started fiddling with the zipper on my windbreaker. "The thing she never understood was that she was my trophy. She was my prize for waiting all those years."

Ari squeezed my forearm.

Bessie was stirring beside us. "You were her prize too, you silly man." Her voice was froggy. "Come over here, you two; I can't kiss you over there."

We hugged her in turn, and she planted wet sloppy ones on our cheeks. They left a ring of saliva.

Bessie got out of her bed, put on a housecoat, and the three of us went down to the common room at the end of the hall to sit together in the sunshine by the window. We visited for a half-hour, while she asked Ari first when he was going back to Montreal, then moved to questions about Quebec separatism — did he believe there would be another referendum, and why couldn't they understand that we wanted them to stay a part of Canada, for heaven's sake. "You tell your French-Canadian friends, the next time they go on about how we hate them, that they should come to Toronto; we'll eat a nice coffee cake together and they can see people won't spit at them on the street."

To hear Bessie get fired up like this, I knew we'd caught her on a good day.

"Yes. Coffee cake will solve English-French relations in Canada, Grandma."

"You know what I mean."

"I don't understand all of this nonsense either," I added. "I never had any trouble with them in prison. We all got along just fine."

"That's such a test?" said Bessie. "What choice did you have but to get along with people in there?" She'd obviously forgotten all about what had happened between me and Red Humphries. "Ari, I want to know if you're going to get a decent apartment next year. Your mother tells me you've been living in a hovel, and that there are beautiful apartments to be had in Montreal."

"What? This from Mom, who lived for a summer in a wildflower-growing commune near Bancroft. Grandma, it's not a hovel. There's some paint peeling in one spot in the entranceway."

"Okay, okay, I'm only asking."

"It's perfectly fine, and I'm keeping it."

"Tell me about how your thesis is coming along, then, you're so defensive about your hovel."

"I'm taking a short break from it because I'm writing a paper on Emma Goldman's years in France. It might end up being useful. I got a research grant. And ... my place is *not* a hovel!"

"Hmph."

"I'm going to France in a few weeks to do my research."

"How lovely!"

"Yeah, it'll be great. Uncle Toshy gave me a few letters that'll help. They're ones that Aunt Lil sent him in jail just before she went there."

I'd forgotten to tell him not to mention that.

"What are you talking about, before she went there?"

"He means before Goldman went to France," I said.

"Not those ones. The ones before Aunt Lil went."

"You must be mistaken, dear. Your aunt Lil never went to France while your uncle Toshy was in jail. Her first trip was on her tenth wedding anniversary, after the war. Your grandpa Abe and I went with them."

Ari looked to me for help. Keeping secrets from Bessie had become second nature; my mind naturally dug around and around, trying to turn up a plausible explanation. I took a breath and turned to face my sister. "I'm sorry, Bessie. Lil and I never told you. Emma funded Lil's trip so that she could help with her political work."

"When did this happen?"

"It was my second summer in jail, when you and Ma and Pop thought she was in Montreal on her internship. She thought you'd scold her for neglecting her studies."

I prepared myself for her reaction, but Bessie still had the ability to surprise. She laughed.

"Well for God's sake, Toshy. You didn't think after Lil graduated from medical school that I might not care anymore about her neglecting her studies?"

"We got worried you'd be hurt that we'd lied to you."

"You should've been more worried that I'd be mad. I was working my fingers to the bone to help put Lil through school and she goes gallivanting off to France? If she were alive, I'd ask her for the money back. With interest!" I knew that wasn't true. Lil had more than earned Bessie's help, and Bessie knew it.

She turned to Ari, and said, finger wagging, "This only

goes to prove what I've always said. That Goldman woman has always churned things up for this family. Didn't mean to, she just couldn't help it. She was too busy trying to save the world to realize the toll her actions were taking on those closest to her."

She could just as well have been describing Lil.

"C'mon, Grandma. You're exaggerating again."

"I don't think so. Your aunt Lillian got caught up with that woman and there was no reasoning with her. If Lil hadn't been brilliant, and if we hadn't been hounding her about her studies, she might have flunked out of medical school. She was always over at the woman's apartment, or going to some damn meeting or another, or distributing leaflets on a blustery street corner."

"Oh, Bessie, she was young," I said. "We all did crazy things when we were young, even you."

She looked away. "At least I know what I did wrong."

So it was that, again.

I asked Ari if he wouldn't mind excusing us. "I'd like to spend a moment alone with your grandma. Can you wait for me in the lobby?"

When he'd left the room, I sat back down beside Bessie. "I know what's gotten into you."

"Nothing's gotten into me."

"Yes, it has. And it has to do with this newspaper clipping, doesn't it?" I brought it out and unfolded it onto her lap. We looked at the picture, lit up by the sun from the window.

"There sure is a resemblance," she said.

"It's uncanny."

She fiddled with the waistband on her housecoat. "So what do you think?"

"I think it wasn't your fault, Bessie. And that we've been over this many times."

"I just can't stop thinking of Lady Fister, Toshy. About what I did..." Tears welled in her eyes.

"Bessie, you thought you were doing the right thing. You couldn't have known what would happen."

"I've been reading about the granddaughter. She has no money, she's forever fundraising, and she's doing so much good. She's *such* a good person, just like her grandmother. Maybe she'd have the resources if only I hadn't … you know."

"Or if only I hadn't been caught. Or if only the Orange Sunset hadn't been lost…"

"All of that was after the fact. The diamond didn't belong to the Fisters by then, so none of that matters. What I did matters."

"What makes you think her granddaughter would sell it off now, if she had it?"

"It was an awful gaudy thing. Nobody wears that kind of jewellery anymore, especially not someone like her." She tapped on the photo, then smoothed over the clipping. "In any case, she should have the choice." She rubbed her eyes dry and new tears flowed through her lashes, like the pools that form in footprints on a saturated lawn. Most of us learned to live with the weight of past mistakes, but in Bessie, the torment didn't ease with the years. Lately, it seemed to cripple her more than ever.

We embraced, and I took the elevator to the lobby. Ari was in his usual chair, grimacing at the terrible coffee they'd sold him. I walked over and sat down across from him.

He pushed a travel brochure across the table. There was a picture of a bikini-clad woman arching her back into the sun's rays, while reclining, ocean-side, on a chaise longue. "You've never been to St-Tropez, have you?" he asked.

"Nope, never have."

"Of course not. You've never even been to Europe. Well, how'd you like to come with me? You might even change your mind about you-know-what."

"You mean…" I made a scratching sound and drew my finger across my throat.

"Yes," he said. "That. Good to see you're taking it so seriously."

I could hardly believe it. After all these years, I might actually make it there. I'd been thinking of little else since he'd last mentioned his trip but hadn't mustered the courage to ask if I could join him.

He swallowed his coffee and looked at me quizzically. It was perfect, I thought. He spoke French and he was looking for Bon Esprit, where Lil had been all those years ago, where I'd almost gone myself.

"You're sure I won't be a burden?"

"No, you'll be my research assistant."

"Then I'd love to come!"

He seemed surprised I'd agreed so readily, and though I wondered suddenly if the offer had been genuine, I wasn't about to push the issue. I wouldn't get this chance again.

a blur in the corner of her eye

I might not have been the sharpest kid, but even when I was little, I was smart enough to grasp that justice should never be confused with the law. In *Oliver Twist*, which Ma read to me when I was eleven, Mr. Bumble is told that the law holds him responsible for his wife's action, and he responds, "If the law supposes that, the law is a ass — a idiot."

I loved that line. Ma had said the word *ass* out loud and then, realizing it, put her hand to her mouth, and we both giggled. Ma said that *Oliver Twist* was an important story, even though Dickens was an anti-Semite for referring to Fagin as "the Jew" and for making him a villain. I didn't understand. He *was* a Jew, like we were, and she had always told me to be proud of it. Besides, I romanticized the life of his boys, and unbeknownst to my parents, I'd started my own life of petty thievery. Small fruits, a handful of nuts, a trinket from the shelf of a store. I fancied myself the Artful Dodger, except that I never had the guts to pickpocket anyone. Lil didn't know it, but her Robin Hood gesture of stealing from my parents to give fabric to the poor gave me the idea. Except I was only stealing for myself.

At eleven, I'd not yet been caught, and though I knew that the law would've held me responsible for my actions, I agreed with Mr. Bumble: the blame really lay elsewhere. In this case, I decided that it lay with capitalism, and that the law was an ass for saying otherwise. I've said before that, as a child, I didn't give a damn about communism, but in this case, it served my interests. I successfully twisted Pop's teachings until our family, and I in particular, became the struggling, drowning victims of "the Bourgeois Sea," that terrible frothing expanse of evil rich people submerging the poor and wretched. Constructing my life as Dickensian was pure eleven-year-old melodrama: the truth was, I started nicking things because I was bored and angry. I was a cliché: misunderstood — boo hoo — the disfigured kid who everyone believed was a bit slow and would therefore amount to nothing more than a helper in his parents' store. What would become of him when they died?

Well, I could at least outsmart the shopkeepers. I'd show them: I was quick and clever enough to pinch stuff without getting caught. I didn't really want the things I stole. If they were edible, I'd scoff them down soon afterwards just to get rid of the evidence. Otherwise, I'd chuck them in a ditch or, if they were small enough, stuff them into the wall behind Rothbart's, telling Lil I'd found them on the street. If she doubted me, she never let on.

Getting banned from a store because a shopkeeper suspected me but couldn't prove it was to be my badge of honour. There was a delicate balance to strike, and at first, I was too good to get it right, and that was no fun. My age protected me, as did my tagging along with Ma; people considered me her poor handicapped child.

A few years later, when I started doing errands without her, eyes finally began to twitch suspiciously in my direction. I knew why. My parents' neighbour had said my mouth looked like a serpent's, and that it gave me an aura of deceitfulness. This angered me, but I would play with it. I cultivated that aura, slithering in and out of stores, but not always stealing things. Ensuring there was always doubt surrounding me. Then, I'd frustrate them by never letting them have the proof. Without hard evidence, nobody reported me to my father. We didn't live right in Kensington, where I focused my crime spree; our store was south and to the west. To visit our place would've taken a special trip, and maybe they were afraid Pop would be insulted and throw them out in a rage. I imagined him red-faced and shouting at the accuser, "My son? Never! My boy knows how hard it is to make a living in retail. How narrow the margin is."

I didn't know. Sure, my parents worked long hours, but I was a kid and didn't understand how tiring that could be to an adult. Furthermore, nobody shoplifted from my parents' store (except Lil). How would they have done it, tuck a three-foot roll of cotton down their trousers? Hey, mister, is that a fabric bolt, or are ya happy to see me? No, my parents remained ignorant of my criminal activity until the day they were hauled into the police station because I'd been arrested at the MacNabbs'. The police told them it was a natural escalation from previous crimes. I'd long been a suspect, but I'd finally gotten cocky.

The cops knew about me because, even if the shopkeepers didn't alert my parents, they did call on the law. The first time was when I was fifteen and had just taken a few walnuts from a store on Augusta. The owner's wife, a sour-faced, hunchbacked woman, squinted angrily as I casually strolled out the door. As I walked down the street, I felt her eyes on my back and turned around, briefly, only to see that Constable Richards had arrived just then, and she was telling him something, pointing at me. I quickly turned my head away and heard him yell, "Hey, kid! Wait right there!"

I shot around the corner, praying he hadn't seen me clearly, especially my distinctive mouth. I darted down Wales Avenue and then up someone's driveway, where I hid behind the garage for a few minutes before snaking through the maze of houses, over fences or through holes in them until I emerged swaggering, thumbs in pockets, onto Bathurst Street.

Constable Richards must not have seen me that time, because he definitely knew who I was and would have said something when next our paths crossed. Approximately once every two weeks, he or another cop who shared the beat broke up a mobile craps game the guys I knew took up in any free alleyway we could find. And, once, he almost caught me reading a girlie magazine. I was flipping through the pages, wide-eyed and lust-filled, and hadn't seen him until his late-afternoon shadow covered me like tar sliding down a roof. I said, "Shit," and quick as a hare, bounded to the end of the alley and over the fence into an old lady's backyard. On the run, I rolled the magazine and stuffed it down my shorts, where my woody had been moments before.

One Friday in May of 1934, I had my closest call yet. Lil was at school and Bessie and I were working in the store. Mid-afternoon, Ma asked me to get her a few items, most importantly a chicken, from Nesker's on Baldwin Avenue. I had to rush to get there before sundown or there would be two nights of canned dinner. The blue laws prevented shops from opening on Sundays, and though my parents' fabric store opened on Saturdays, the Neskers were orthodox and didn't open until the Sabbath was over after sundown. Ma never bought from anyone else because she said kosher chicken was better and Nesker had the freshest birds, better than Groskopf. It was true about the chicken. Kosher beef might as well have been left to dry in the Sahara Desert before being stomped on with a leather sole, but for some reason, the blood draining and the brining made chicken taste delicious.

I headed up to Baldwin Street, pulling on a cardigan because of a chill in the air, one with pockets in case I saw anything along the way worth grabbing. I hated taking the streets; instead I cut through laneways and darted across backyards. I was eighteen and agile. Mrs. Debardeleben had said I looked like an ape, and in Kensington, I felt like one. I enjoyed the exhilaration of vaulting over a low fence, swinging through an urban jungle. Ladies scolding from kitchen windows were my hunters, street poles boomeranging me around a corner, my vines. Better yet, I pretended I was

Tarzan. Where was my Jane, I wondered. When would I ever find her?

On one fence, my open cardigan caught from the inside on a splinter and I was tugging it free when a man came out of his house, shaking his fist. "Get the hell out of here, or I'll call the cops!"

No time to be delicate, I pulled at the cardigan and felt the wool give way. Oh well, it wasn't a good sweater, and the hole was hidden by the pocket sewn over top.

I arrived at Nesker's out of breath and found it bustling, women hurrying to do their last-minute weekend shopping. I perused the bins out front before going in, dragging my hand close to the nuts but not touching them, not yet. My instincts were good: I picked my head up and saw Mrs. Nesker eyeing me.

I went inside and hovered near the windows where there were crates of vegetables. I found the scallions my mother liked, the ones with a sizeable bulb and long green shoots. After Mrs. Nesker rang up my change, she retreated through a door to the stockroom. Seeing Mr. Nesker at the counter busy with another customer, I decided I'd try my luck pinching a few almonds. Outside of the store, I stood next to the bin and fumbled inside the bag I'd been given, rearranging the chicken wrapped up inside. I was bold that day and tried something new. I let the paper bag slip, as though I'd lost hold of it, and it fell on top of the mound of almonds. I put my hands under the bottom, scooped up a couple of nuts in my palm, and then heaved the bag into my right arm, letting the almonds slip into my cardigan pocket.

I turned to leave, but standing in front of me, I don't know why I hadn't seen him there before, was Sid, the Neskers' enormous son. He was a few years older and probably a hundred pounds heavier. "Hold it right there, bucko. Ma!" He blocked my way. "Ma! Come out here, will ya?"

"What's wrong?" I winced, because I'd slurred my *s*. "C'mon, buddy, I'm in a hurry." I tapped my foot into the sawdust on the ground.

Mrs. Nesker came out and stood beside Sid, arms crossed.

"I'm pretty sure he grabbed some nuts, Ma."

"I'm sure he didn't take anything, did you, young man?" Despite the question, she sounded like she believed him.

"No…" My breath quickened.

"Of course you didn't. But my son is very careful. So, just to be sure, you'll understand if, as a precaution, I check your sweater pockets, won't you?"

I didn't know what to do. If I protested, it would raise more suspicion.

"Please," she continued. "I'm sure this will satisfy my son that you're not a thief." And before I could say anything, she dipped her hand into my left pocket and felt around. That wasn't the one into which the almonds had fallen. "And the other?" she said, pointing to the grocery bag I hugged tight against it.

I looked her in the eye, but kept my poker face, even though I was sure it was all about to end. I lifted the bag and felt her hand go in. It searched around, prodded into every corner, and then her finger poked through the sweater and tickled my side.

She pulled the unbuttoned cardigan away from my body and wiggled her finger at her son. "Holes in the pocket. You must have been mistaken, Sid. A thief would be smarter than to steal merchandise and then hide it in a holey sweater pocket. I'm very sorry, Toshy. My son is vigilant, and we appreciate it. When people take things from us, it only forces us to raise our prices. I'm sure you can understand that, your parents being shopkeepers and all."

"It's okay, I understand," I said. My face burned, and I wasn't sure if it was from guilt or embarrassment that she'd essentially called me a stupid thief.

I walked away, resisting the urge to turn around to check if the almonds were still visible in the sawdust beside the bin, where they must have dropped. I was frankly incredulous at my pure, dumb luck. Once I was around the corner, I felt inside the pocket. Sure enough, the hole was gaping, but in the corner of the pocket, there was still one almond, lodged in the knitting. Could Mrs. Nesker's hand have passed by without touching it? Or had she felt it and decided to let me go with a warning?

As I made my way home, I became fixated on the possibility that she might not have missed the almond. I still couldn't be sure, but I contemplated why she might have let me go. She felt sorry for me; that was the only plausible reason. Not only had I almost been caught, but Mrs. Nesker most likely thought I was a dimwit to be pitied because of my condition.

Feeling lower than I had in months, I shuffled back into our store. I handed the groceries and change over to Ma and made my way to the back to begin sweeping up. Ma went to the kitchen to prepare dinner, leaving me and Bessie to mind the shop.

A few minutes later, Bessie made her way over. She chucked me under the chin. "Why so glum?"

I looked into her eyes and felt ashamed. Even if under normal circumstances I could've confided in her, how could I talk about my stupid problems now, with Bessie's stoicism such a positive example? She'd found herself a childless widow at twenty-two and had adapted to her circumstances quickly, with little self-pity. After Irv Charney's shiva was over and she was settled in with our parents, she tried to get her job back at the factory, but it was the Depression. Jobs were precious and her spot had immediately been taken by another girl. To keep an eye on how Bessie was doing, my parents encouraged her to work in the store. Privately, Ma told us kids that Pop had been slowing down and experiencing occasional heartburn and shortness of breath for which he refused to see a doctor. She wanted Bessie to help her, she said. We didn't actually believe Ma at the time, because Pop appeared to be just fine, and we assumed that she was inventing the excuse to make Bessie feel needed.

In the evenings, Ma would try to get Bessie to come with her to meetings of a group she was involved in — the *Yiddisher Arbeiter Froyen Fareyn*, the Jewish Women's Labour League — but Bessie had no interest in that sort of group. The only time I ever saw her get excited about politics was when Pierre Trudeau ran for office.

It wasn't a lie that Ma wanted Bessie's help in the store. Of the three kids, my eldest sister had always been the best with customers. People had trouble understanding me, or so said my parents. As for Lil, she was often excused because of classes and studying. When she was available, she was impatient and curt. She found the concerns of retail shoppers to be petty and annoying and wasn't good at dissembling. Ma tried to get her to improve her manner, to no avail. She asked Lil to consider that working in the store might be practice for when she was a physician.

"Do you think all of your patients are going to be sensible and courteous? No. You'll have crazy people like your father, who refuses to recognize how grave his health is, and you'll have the malingerers. Taking a snooty attitude with them will not help you build your practice. It's going to be difficult enough convincing people to go to a lady doctor."

"Don't worry, Ma; I'll have a good bedside manner. I just can't pretend that choosing between light purple or pink, or between damask and duvetyn, is all that important a problem. People's health is different."

Ma and Bessie shook their heads.

"You've got to learn to pretend, Lil darling. Trust me, there will be moments in your life when those skills will come in handy. Look at your sister Bessie and how brave she's being."

It was true, and Lil fell silent when it was pointed out, just as I had there in the back of our store, when Bessie had asked me what was wrong. To watch her with a customer only weeks after Irv was killed, you would never have known she'd just suffered a great tragedy. In a private moment, you could catch her far away, but if she saw you watching, she'd quickly reanimate her smile and busy herself with chores.

"It's nothing," I said to Bessie. "I'm just fed up." I waved at the dust on the floor. "Same as all of us."

We heard the tinny jangle of the door chime and saw Lil swooping in, her book bag over one shoulder. "Look who I found." She pointed to the door.

A girl tentatively stepped inside, and I saw that it was the girl from the shiva, the one who'd consoled Bessie. My eyes went immediately to her forehead, in spite of trying not to stare. Her bangs covered the stain, but I could see it peek through. The wine colour bled slightly into her eyebrow.

"Pearl!" said Bessie. "It's *so* nice to see you." They embraced.

"Lil and I passed on the street. I was out doing some errands on my way home from work, and so thought I'd pop in and see how you're doing."

"Hanging in there, I guess." Then she caught sight of me looking on. "Oh, Pearl, I should introduce you to my kid brother, Toshy. Toshy, this is Pearl."

"Right!" said Lil. A look passed between my sisters that was unmistakably one of collusion. "Pearl, Toshy's the one I told you about."

Pearl approached me and extended her hand. I gave it two quick shakes, but avoided her eyes. Still, I could see she was blushing. "Hello," I said.

"Nice to meet you. Your sisters have told me a lot about you."

"Really? They never mentioned you before."

"We worked together in the factory, before Bessie quit. You know, before…"

"Before her husband was killed?"

She looked to Bessie apologetically. "I was going to say before she got married."

"Yeah, we don't like to talk about Irv in front of her."

She furrowed her brow. The stained skin above her eye crumpled like soft leather. "I didn't *mean* to talk about him … you were the one who…"

"How long have you had that thing on your forehead?"

She stared at me, mouth agape, then sputtered, "How long have you had that … that lip?"

"My sisters think I can't get a regular girl."

"What?" Her eyes widened even more.

"That's why they're introducing us. They think people like us aren't good-looking enough to—"

"Toshy!" Bessie said.

"It's okay, Bessie. I've gotta get going."

"And I've gotta get back to work," I said, turning away. I was furious.

"Yeah," I heard her say. "See you around."

I went into the stockroom, as I heard Bessie and Lil making apologies on my behalf, and stayed there until I heard the door chime. Stepping back into the storefront, I saw Bessie waiting for me, arms crossed. Lil was in the background, shaking her head.

"How could you be so rude?"

"Just because of my lip you two think all I can get is some homely girl like that?"

"Pearl's not homely," said Lil. "And neither are you. She's pretty, she's your age, and we just thought … you know…"

It was true Pearl was pretty, I had to admit it, in spite of the stain. But that was beside the point. "She has that huge … *thing* on her forehead, and so you thought, 'Let's get the two ugly people together. They'll never find anyone else anyway. They'll be perfect for one another!'"

"Don't be mean," said Bessie. "And that wasn't the reason."

"I can find a girl for myself, so you two can just butt out."
Bessie raised her palms to me and shrugged, backing away. Lil, still shaking her head, went to fix a display table. For what seemed an eternity, we went about doing our chores in silence. My sisters had no idea what it was like to be eighteen with no prospects of companionship. They both had had fellows calling on them. Bessie had even been married. Now, I learned that they saw me as a charity case, to be fobbed off on to the first disfigured girl they could find. While I fumed, I swept up by the cash, and my sisters kept to themselves, on the other side of the store. I moved dust from one spot to the next, back and forth, making little piles and then flattening them, like hopes that are raised and then get dashed.

A half-hour or so later, Lil broke the silence, perking up suddenly. "Hey, you guys. I just remembered. There's a party tonight I found out about. Wanna come with?"

I considered it for a moment, my anger beginning to drain away at the idea of something to do.

"Not me," said Bessie. "I'm exhausted. It's been a long week. Some of us work for a living."

"Oh c'mon, Bessie. It'll do you a world of good to get out again. We've all been itching for a bit of excitement. Ever since Irv died, you've been moping around here with Ma and Pop and I've been cooped up with exams. Now, with exams done, all I've been doing is writing a stupid paper I got an extension on, and looking for an apartment for Emma for when she gets back from her tour. I'm ready to have *fun*, you guys!"

"I guess I'll come," I said.

We looked to Bessie. "I don't know…"

"We can just go for a while," said Lil. "C'mon, Bessie, come with us."

She hesitated just a moment, but it was enough.

"It's settled then. We'll leave at nine."

The party was in a large apartment above a restaurant on

College Street, near the Rose Café, a popular local hangout. Lil said she hadn't personally been invited, but that people were encouraged to bring friends. She told our parents who was hosting it and they were surprisingly agreeable that we should go. They were probably happy Bessie was getting out of the house.

Ma made us promise to be home by midnight and gave us change to run out and get flowers to bring for the host. We arrived, a sad bouquet of carnations in hand because it was all we could afford, and a bottle of wine procured by one of Lil's university friends.

Bessie clung to us, more nervous to talk to people than I was. "Do you think it's right that I should be at a party," she said, "this soon after my husband's death?"

"We've been over this a thousand times," said Lil. "This isn't the nineteenth century. People don't expect you to stay inside draped in black for years on end. You're twenty-two and beautiful, and you're not dead, Irv is."

I slapped Lil on the arm.

"What? It's true."

"You have a real way with words," said Bessie.

"Oh piffle, you know what I mean. I'm going to talk to those people over there," she said. "There are drinks and snacks on that table. Why don't you go get some and then you two can be wallflowers if you want."

I left Bessie and sidled my way through the crowd, over to a table where vegetables, coffee cake, and punch were on offer. I filled a small plate, and as I was pouring drinks, I looked up and was surprised to see Pearl standing there. She seemed equally flustered. Lil hadn't mentioned she'd be at the party; perhaps she didn't know.

"Oh, hi, I…"

But as soon as I'd opened my mouth, Pearl glared, turned her back, and walked away. I stood in stunned silence as she disappeared into another room. A girl beside me started giggling, then brought a hand up to cover her mouth. I felt winded, and although I deserved her snub, I could hardly believe what had just happened. Gingerly, I picked up the punch glasses and plate, and carrying them slowly, wended my way back to Bessie. I didn't mention the encounter with Pearl.

As Lil predicted, Bessie and I huddled in the corner for the next twenty minutes or so. It seemed since I'd stepped away from Bessie, the apartment had become even more packed and it now smelled of smoke and oil from a kerosene lamp someone had lighted for the mood even though there was electricity. I scanned the crowd and recognized a few people, but nobody I knew well enough to say hello to. Pearl, fortunately, was in another room.

Then, leaning against a doorframe at the far wall, was the most beautiful girl I'd ever seen. She was surrounded by people, but the light settled on her like icing sugar, making her sparkle. Her lips were full and perfectly shaped and she had rosy, flawless skin. Her eyes conveyed such confidence and such mischief, and her body … she was a knockout. Her dress was elegantly simple, as though she was trying to dress down, but those curves wouldn't let her. I prayed she'd turn my way, but when she did, it was only to smile at someone between us.

Bessie engaged me in small talk, pointing out people at the party and commenting on what they were wearing, and I answered in monosyllables, trying hard to pretend I was interested, but as often as I dared, I stole glances at the girl. This was the sort of girl I wished my sisters would introduce me to, not someone like Pearl. There were two guys next to her leaning in close, and occasionally she laughed at their jokes, pressing her hand against her chest and throwing her head back. The laugh looked fake, but once or twice she squeezed their forearms and, by doing so, put the men into trances.

"I'm going to find the washroom," I said, cutting Bessie off mid-sentence. I handed her my drink.

"Don't you dare leave me alone here!"

"Be back in a sec."

I moved off and made my way across the room, the struggle to squeeze through the bodies becoming more difficult the closer I got to that girl. It was as though the whole party was her private security force. Eventually, I reached the doorframe where she stood. Now there was only one person between us — one of the fellows she was talking with. I was close enough that I could have touched her. I breathed her perfume in through my nostrils and it intoxicated me, filling me with lust I'd never before felt, a vacuum that sucked at the back of my throat and across my back, that pulled my diaphragm up, pushed out my chest, and caused my lips to part. I must have been staring because she turned and met my eyes. I quickly looked away. My heart pounded. I wished I'd had the nerve to say something, but I was sure Bessie was watching; how could she not be watching? My face was so warm it felt like I'd broken out in a throbbing rash that the whole room could see.

Suddenly, I really did have to use the washroom.

Behind the closed door, I splashed water on my face and tried to muster the courage to say hello. Then I looked in the mirror, and the air I'd been holding in escaped in a hiss through the gaps in my teeth. My fever was broken, replaced by the sobriety of my reflection. I'd never seen a girl before who'd made me forget I was homely.

When I made my way back through the room, it came as a slight relief that she wasn't standing in the doorway anymore.

"Bessie, did you see the girl that was just over there?"

She craned her neck to see where I was pointing, but before she could answer, staccato laughter came from the group Lil had joined. Then she made a beeline for us, face pinched, teeth gritted.

A man in the group called out, "We knew you'd come over to our side, Lillian Wolfman. It's okay to admit you were wrong."

"You wish!" she shouted back. Then, to us, "C'mon. We're leaving."

"What? We just got here!" I looked back again to find the girl, but that side of the room was blocked from my view. "What happened, Lil?"

"You guys didn't notice? No, of course not, why would you? Can't you see? This isn't just *any* party."

We looked at her, stupidly, not getting her meaning.

"It's a *Party* party!"

Since Lil had begun associating with Emma, she'd become known as a staunch anarchist, much to our parents' chagrin. The communists and anarchists were enemies or, at best, rivals. Their favourite sport was lobbing public denunciations at one another.

Bessie chuckled. "Didn't you know that before coming here? It was your friend who mentioned it."

"Sure, I knew. It's important to have dialogue with your enemy. To build bridges."

Bessie and I looked at each other, then back at Lil.

"I did *too* know! But these … *people* … don't want dialogue. There's no reason for us to stay."

I was going to leave it, but Bessie couldn't resist. "You're incredible, Lil. You can't even admit that you made a mistake. You're not interested in building bridges. In fact, if there *was* one, you'd let your enemies drown in the moat, eaten by crocodiles, while you pulled the bridge up."

"Think what you will."

"Ma and Pop knew what kind of party this was," I said, realizing it only an instant before the words came out. "Why else would they be happy we were coming here?"

The man who'd taunted Lil came over and handed her a leaflet. "Here, Miss Wolfman. It has the date and time of our next meeting. I'm sure you'll want to mark it in your calendar."

Lil threw the paper on the floor and stomped on it, then ground it under her heel. She stuck out her tongue, but the man laughed and turned away.

"Very mature," said Bessie.

"I know! Like children."

"I was talking about you."

"Oh, shut up. C'mon — we're leaving."

"But there was a really pretty girl over there!" I pointed back at the doorframe where she'd been. "I think she noticed me."

"Really?" Bessie looked across the room.

"Yeah, she's been making eyes at me."

"No kidding." If she knew I'd lied, she was kind enough to pretend. Lil, on the other hand, didn't even react.

"Yeah. She's not there anymore. But I told you I could find someone by myself."

Lil said, "Are you guys coming or not?"

"C'mon, Toshy. We can't just stay here and let them make fun of Lil, even though she deserves it *soooo* much."

Lil wasn't going to just slink out of there. She called back to her tormenter, "Who are you kidding anyway, Bill Diamond? Your meetings aren't about politics. All you ever do is throw parties, and they're not even good ones!"

She grabbed Bessie's hand and pulled her along. Bessie caught my arm and we let Lil drag us from that party, barely scooping up our coats from the table beside the door. I left the room walking backwards, still scanning the crowd.

§

They were watching me those first months in Kingston Pen, to assess whether or not I was fit for transfer to Collins Bay. As Lil had informed me, the new prison, located just outside of Kingston, was originally intended to be a facility for youth, but the warden had ignored this and filled it with inmates working on the farm or on the ongoing construction of the prison itself. Only about 10 percent of the inmates at Collins Bay were under eighteen, identifiable, apart from visibly being just kids, by the letter *y* sewn on the shoulder of our uniforms.

The Parliament of Canada didn't know any of this until the report of the Royal Commission came out in '38, and even then, they did nothing. If Lil hadn't told me about the Royal Commission, we wouldn't have found out about it until Agnes McPhail herself came to visit us once from Ottawa and asked people a whole bunch of questions. They made a big fuss about it — a member of Parliament nosing about in their business, and a woman at that.

While in Kingston Pen, I'd survived the planting season and a winter spent in the stables, with only two more incidents with Red Humphries. It took every ounce of self-restraint to ignore him, but being taunted and not fighting back was to suffer slightly less indignity than getting whooped again.

I didn't know it, but it was lucky for me that I held myself back; in February of '36, Warden Craig decided I didn't meet any of the exclusion criteria for Collins Bay. I was not a murderer, scheduled to be deported upon release, an agitator, an incorrigible, physically unfit for hard labour, or a "homosexual pervert." Despite now being closer to the farm, Overseer Jagninski put me on prison construction duty, something else I knew nothing about. It wasn't very difficult to learn, given that my tasks mostly involved brute strength — carrying or stacking bricks, mixing cement, and so forth.

A month later, as soon as it got warm enough, we were pulled off construction and taken to work on the wharfs. I hated that — the St. Lawrence is always cold, even in summer. In early March, the lingering snow reminded us that the whole river would still be frozen solid were it not for the currents. During the first few months, we worked on dry ground, finishing work started by the autumn crew. Later, in July and August, we'd take turns going into the water to install the barriers in order to pump out an area and then dig and set the wharf posts. After an hour, we'd emerge, even on the hottest day, with our jaws clacking and lips blue. Even on the dock, there was a risk of being chilled. On blustery days,

waves broke against the posts and surged up, slapping us fro
underneath, through the planks we were nailing or fastening
with ropes of hemp. Then the wind lashed from the side in a
one-two punch.

I did love the smell of the water, though — fresh and
tangy with the slightest hint of fishiness, what I imagined
must be from algae waving at us offshore, just below the
winking surface. I'd never been to the seaside and wondered
what ocean spray might smell like. Because the sea was salty,
I figured it might be odourless, like the bowl of salt water at
Passover, which reminds us of the tears of Hebrew slaves.

That Passover I spent alone in my cell, staring at the
walls and reading over a letter I'd just received. Lil had written me of Pop's sudden death from a heart attack. He was
lifting boxes in the back of the store, a job I used to do. Ma
found him there. Pop and I weren't close, but we weren't
distant either. He was a gentle man and I never doubted he
was in my corner. His disappointment never edged towards
disdain or dislike; he simply wanted the best for me, and I
hadn't aimed for the best, not even close to it. We'd had a
relationship that many fathers and sons had, one of mutual
love, but muted by a general machismo that gave us the
same magnetic polarity: both positive, so we could never get
close enough to express how we really felt. I experienced
Pop's death as an ache that had to remain dull so I wouldn't
fall apart in front of my prison mates.

It helped to focus on Ma. With Pop gone, I worried how
she'd make ends meet now, how they'd put Lil through
school. All of this work on the wharf, this hard work that
could've been spent helping at home, felt like pennies into a
well. Wasted.

However, being on a different work crew in Collins
Bay meant, for a brief blessed month, I didn't have to con-
tend with Red Humphries. Sadly, that reprieve was short-
lived; in April he too was shifted over. I didn't hear the
news, and he ended up with a cell far from mine, making

his appearance at the wharfs the day after his transfer a complete surprise. I was nailing in a plank midway down the dock when I saw the foreman directing him towards the very end.

"Aw, shit," I said, under my breath. He must've been at the back of the procession. I looked around for his friends, but they weren't with him.

"Well, look who it is," he said, spotting me. "The guys are still in Kingston, in case you're wondering, but it looks like you and me are together again." He crouched down beside me, leaned in, and whispered in my ear, "Think you can take me now that I'm all alone?"

I slammed down my hammer near his toe, causing him to jump.

"Hey! Watch it!"

I stood up. "No, you watch it, Humphries. I don't want any trouble."

"Yeah, well, then steer clear of me," he said, giving me a slight shove.

"Gladly," I said and shoved him back.

He shoved again, harder, and I stumbled backwards to where we hadn't yet nailed any boards into the dock. It had happened again. I fell into the hole, catching myself with my arms, leaving my legs dangling below, a few feet above the water.

There was laughter from the other prisoners.

"Same wimpy Wolfman," he said, then sauntered down to join his crew.

His transfer meant I was back to my existence of nervous vigilance and periodic humiliation. Every day, I avoided catching Red's eye so that I could avert another altercation. This was a mostly successful strategy, but as any abused person will tell you, it's never possible to anticipate all of the excuses a bully will find to launch an attack. The curious thing about my life was that every time I was knocked over, something or someone came along to pull me up.

Bernie Koffler was just such a deliverance.

I remember the day we met, because it came the morning after I'd received an extremely tearful visit from Ma, the first I'd had since Pop died. I'd gone to sleep exhausted, yes from work, but more from consoling Ma and from the strain of bottling up my own grief, which I was terrified if amplified by hers would become uncontained. Had I lost control, I feared she'd leave at my most vulnerable moment, and I'd be alone and exposed like that, utterly raw.

The next morning I lay in my cell, which I had to myself; that was the way things were organized at Collins Bay. It consisted of a metal-framed bunk, a thin grey blanket, a small toilet with no seat, and a small desk with a narrow shelf. There was a rickety chair on the verge of imminent collapse tucked under the desk and a small lamp perched atop.

A wireless set was nestled into one corner of the shelf, with a set of headphones plugged in. These had been installed the year before, paid for by deducting an amount from the inmates' peculium, a monthly stipend we received to buy cigarettes and such. In the first year that I spent in Collins Bay, that radio was a godsend; I'd not yet discovered the pleasures a library could bring. I listened to the news broadcasts and sports scores from the newly established Canadian Broadcasting Corporation, and sometimes on a clear day we even picked up a station in Prescott. Often, in the early evening before we had to turn off our sets, I lay in my bunk and jerked off under the blanket to the sound of low music. I wondered how many of the guys were doing this, and if so, when and how often. I'd close my eyes, or keep them open and let my eyes melt into the off-white walls, which still had a faint smell of paint. Only a few scribbles. When I was spent, I drew circles and lines in the semen on my stomach until it dried into a brittle crust, then scrubbed it away with my blanket.

From the outside wall of my cell, they'd cut an ungenerous window with bars on it, about six feet up. At my

height, I had to stand on the chair to see the courtyard —
barren except for wooden benches and a few tables for card-
playing at the perimeter. If the window was open and I
pressed my face between the bars, I could see a line of weeds
sprouting through a crack in the cement that split the yard
in half. Our yard had a cleft of its own and it started right
under the window, making me wish that the earth might one
day open up, dividing my cell and the yard neatly in two and
sending me tumbling into an abyss.

Every day, we walked around that yard during a half-hour
"open air parade." A thick white line painted on the ground
directed us round and round. This practice of idiotically
trudging in circles was more appropriate for those who spent
their days working indoors, but when prison or wharf
construction involved hard labour in the blazing sun or pouring rain, the parade felt at best redundant and at worst a
bloody nuisance.

Beside the toilet, against the far wall, was a small mirror.
Sometimes, before bed, I stared in it and contemplated how
Lil and Bessie had been right. Manual labour and prison
food had made my face ropy, my arms sinewy. I traced my
jawline with an index finger, down to my chin, and then up
to my bottom lip. Then I hesitated, but eventually made
that short, painful leap. I closed my eyes and rubbed my
rough, callused fingertip over the notch. Then, I made a
moustache out of the finger, a better one than the scraggly
mess that was growing there, and opened my eyes. I tried to
imagine what I might've looked like if I'd been born normal.

The fourth wall consisted mostly of a door made up of
bars leading onto the corridor. If someone walked by while I
was doing this, they would've seen me, but my back would've
been to them and they might've assumed I was brushing my
teeth. In the mornings, I really did brush them, but I dreaded
it. They provided us with toothpaste made of camphorated
chalk and salt to mix in. Most of the prisoners complained
about the unpleasant grittiness and terrible taste, but what I

hated most was the feeling of numbness it gave my lips and gums. I had enough trouble talking without worrying I might be drooling on top of it all. What we didn't know then was that camphor is absorbed through the skin, acts as a slight local anaesthetic, and is mildly poisonous. They say that in high doses it can cause seizures, mental confusion, irritability, and neuromuscular hyperactivity; no wonder so many of us were jumpy.

After we used the toilet and brushed our teeth in the morning, a burly guard opened our cell doors by shoving a huge lever at the end of the row, up and then down, in one grand arc of 180 degrees.

These were the sounds I heard shortly after the morning bell: the squeaking of the poorly greased lever, the grunting of the guard, and the grinding of the long metal bar to which the lever was attached and which ran along the top of each cell, connected to the doors. Then, there was a clunk, as dozens of metal bolts were set free of their latches. Finally, you heard the doors creak as they swung open, letting us stagger forth onto the balcony for inspection.

That morning, while I was waiting for the guard to call out my name, I observed there was a new man standing opposite me on the balcony across the inner courtyard. Why did I always miss the news of a transfer? After inspection, we marched single file to the cafeteria area, walking by the open door to the galley. I caught a glimpse of the kitchen floor, slick with a thin film of dirty water in which were sitting various open bags and piles of produce, and on the counter, uncovered jars and meat parts. All of these were attended to busily by a hoard of flies, unbothered by the kitchen staff, who were listlessly chopping vegetables for lunch.

I picked up a tray, poured myself a cup of tea, and followed the line until I reached Mrs. Duckworth, a bony, jaundiced woman who smoked too much and was missing her front teeth. A cigarette dangled from the corner of her mouth as she slopped porridge into a bowl and thrust it at me, growling

"Mor-ning!" in as pleasant a manner as I'm sure she knew how. The cigarette bobbed up and down on each syllable.

"Morning," I replied with a smile, knowing how important it was to keep on the good side of the kitchen staff. You might get an extra portion if there was ever anything good, which was rare, granted. Most everything was boiled to within an inch of its life, ending up a mushy paste of grey and green and brown. Best to take advantage of fresh produce; I grabbed a bright red McIntosh and moved on to the self-service table.

Standing there pouring himself a glass of milk was the new man I'd seen across the range. He was ten to fifteen years older and slightly taller, with a sturdy build, apple cheeks, and already thinning brown hair.

Seeing me approach, he thrust forward a meaty hand. "Hey there, kid. Name's Bernie Koffler. We're neighbours across the way. I just transferred last night from Kingston." A few hairs stuck out of his ears and vibrated when he spoke.

I took his hand and shook it. "Herman Wolfman. My friends call me Toshy." I paid attention to my words to form them properly.

"Well then, I hope you'll let me call you Toshy." He smiled.

I scooped sugar onto the glutinous blob in the centre of my bowl and poured a bit of milk around it, forming a moat between the edge of the bowl and the gruel castle with its brown turret.

Bernie asked, "Going to the Sabbath study group this morning?"

"I usually don't, if the truth be known."

"Why not go this time? There's no rabbi; Father MacDonald said he'd give us permission to use one of the rooms. I'm organizing a little discussion you might find interesting." He winked when he said that. "We'll speak in Yiddish — the guards can't understand. You speak Yiddish, don't you?"

"Not very well."

"You'll do fine."

"I'll think about it," I said, curious about what the discussion might be but not wanting to ask because it might only get his hopes up. The last thing I needed was some religious fanatic preaching to me. On Saturday mornings after breakfast and on Sunday afternoons, we were given time for so-called free activities. Usually during this period, I went outside if it was a nice day and sat in the sun, smoked, played a game of cards, or kicked a ball around.

Bernie shrugged. "Suit yourself."

Just then, a guard came up and nudged us on, herding us into a single file back to our cells to eat alone. A half-hour later, I was on my way outside with a deck of cards when I ran into Bernie again.

"C'mon — give it a chance," he said.

"Naw," I answered, turning the card deck over and over in my hand.

"We're not meeting in the chapel. They let us meet in another room, a bigger one with windows that open up. C'mon, it's a hot day, it'll be good to be in the shade in a place where there's a bit of fresh air."

So much for not being a fanatic; he'd only been regrouping for a fresh assault.

"I don't really feel like religious discussion."

"Who said it was religious?" He cocked an eyebrow.

Intrigued, I followed him. As we made our way over to a guard, a few other guys fell into line. The guard led us into a long room that I'd never seen before. It had a few folding tables and chairs to sit on, many more than we needed, and it did indeed have five tall windows they'd opened wide. I could feel a breeze tickle my face.

We set up a table, and the guys sat around it, on the edges of their chairs, knees open and leaning forward, forearms on the table and hands clasped. We were all looking at Bernie, as though a great secret were about to be told.

Bernie cleared his throat and said in Yiddish, "We should begin with a prayer. Someone remind us every now and then, to make sure we look like we're talking religion. Everybody bow your heads."

We did, and from the corner of my eye, I caught the guard scrutinizing us. Then I heard Bernie say, first in Hebrew, then continuing on in Yiddish, "*Baruch ata adonai*, grant us the strength, that we should tolerate this cursed hell hole, eat this dreadful food that tastes like shit and might be poisoning us, and smile at these stinking *tuchus*-heads day in and day out until we get the hell out of here, Amen."

I started to laugh, but someone kicked me under the table and I clamped my mouth shut.

Then we lifted our heads. Bernie told us that he was friends with Tim Buck and Sam Carr, two of the leaders of the Canadian Communist Party, both of whom had spent four years in Kingston Pen. Buck and Carr had been convicted in '31, along with six others, of preaching to overthrow the government through violence. They were sentenced to ten years, but a lengthy campaign was waged to secure their early release, charging that they were political prisoners. In '34, the "group of eight," as they'd become known, were granted clemency by the Governor General.

The newly free Sam Carr had told Bernie that when he was in Kingston, he used to get together with the other Jewish inmates and hold political discussions during their supposed Sabbath prayer meetings. Two years after that conversation, Bernie was charged and convicted of embezzling funds from a dry goods store he owned with his brother-in-law. He claimed the brother-in-law had framed him, that they'd had a falling out over another business venture.

I never did know the truth surrounding Bernie's conviction, but who was I to question, given the strange events that had sent me to jail? Whatever the real story, his apolitical charges explained why Warden Craig considered him a common thief and not an agitator, and how he had therefore been permitted to transfer to Collins Bay after a year, as I had. In his year at Kingston, he'd met with a couple of fellows who were part of Sam Carr's group: Fred Rosenberg and Coleman Green. Together they'd carried on the meetings, and now that he was in Collins Bay, Bernie had decided he'd begin a new group.

And that's how, during Saturday morning prayer meetings in prison, I became a communist. A Stalinist, as a matter of fact, but those were the days when Stalin was still in power and hadn't been exposed for the anti-Semite and the murderer that he was. My father, I hate to admit, was more or less right in the end. I considered with sadness what he might've felt had he heard I was learning about Stalinism in jail. Probably, he would've been angry that I was leaning towards being a party member, that I hadn't embraced Menchevism or remained unaffiliated, as he and Ma had. Most of all, he would've been angry that someone else was penetrating my consciousness when in all of those years he hadn't.

What Pop couldn't know is that he'd chipped through a fair distance. I wouldn't have been open to what Bernie and his friends had to say had I not grown up absorbing my parents' lessons. Now, with Pop dead, I could form opinions freely, feeling untethered to his beliefs. Also, Bernie offered me politics with a side of social interaction. I'd spent months and months a prisoner of my own thoughts, surviving on radio broadcasts, letters from home, and the occasional visit. When I felt laughter escape my throat, and after so long, I thought, I can't survive eleven years like this. Not without stimulation. Not without laughter. And not without friends.

the best defence

My cereal bowl clanged as it hit the sink in the kitchen of my apartment in The Terrace. I wiped my mouth with a napkin and saw my reflection in the metal. A mad scientist stared back. Years of slow balding had depleted my hair, once full and thick and shiny, and the lustre had not returned after my last radiation treatment. I considered it now, dry, thin — defeated and yet somehow unruly. No matter. I ran the comb under the tap, went to the mirror in the hall, and made a side part. I dragged what fell to the sides away from my face and behind my ears, and was satisfied that I looked less frightening.

I was going to the lobby to meet with Ari, to discuss our trip. Out in the hallway, Mrs. Dyment had posted a new schedule of activities. There was another recollections group, this time for people who weren't survivors of the camps. I considered what it would be like to join it; probably a room full of old farts kvetching or sobbing about things they couldn't change anyway. I thought of Bernie Koffler and felt an aching, clawing hollow deep within my chest. If Bernie'd been there, he'd probably have tried to convince me to attend, but there were no Bernies in this place. Anyone old enough to be wiser than me was too addled to share his wisdom.

As I perused the rest of the schedule, Pearl Feffer emerged with another woman from the common room at the end of the hall. They were laughing and they walked arm in arm. Her companion was much older than Pearl and obviously needed assistance. I turned back to the schedule to pretend I hadn't seen them, but I was spotted.

"Hello there, Herman!"

I was taken off guard. Nobody had called me by that name since my father died. What the hell made her think she was special? Still, I didn't want to correct her in front of her friend.

"Hello, Pearl, how are you today?"

"I'm fine, thanks. That's a nice shirt you have on."

"You must need your eyes checked. It's the same ugly thing I always wear."

She was wearing a blue sleeveless dress and had a purple scarf twisted about her head, tied off on the side. The colour matched the flowers on her dress. I considered the woman's figure; not bad for seventy-seven, I had to admit. Especially in comparison to the woman beside her.

"And you, my dear, must learn to take a compliment. Gert, this is Herman Wolfman. Everybody calls him Toshy, but I like Herman; it's a good solid name. You'll soon find out Herman's a bit of a pill, but he has a nice sister who's been a good friend since forever. Bessie is the one I visit every day over at the home. She's the one I lost touch with when I lived out west, but we've picked up where we left off. I'm forced to be civil towards the brother. By the way" — she came up to me, stood toe to toe, and woodpeckered my chest with her finger — "you should do things with her every now and then. Take her out a bit more."

"You should butt out." I poked her back, once, with my index finger, but hit a slightly soft part too close to her bosom, and so I didn't repeat the gesture. My face felt hot. "What I do with my sister is none of your business. I'm her family, not you."

"Oh, for heaven's sake, don't give me that nonsense. I know I'm not family; that's why I'm telling *you* that you should be spending more time with her."

"And just who the hell are you, to be telling me how to behave with my own sister?"

My blood pressure was rising, but maybe I wasn't the only one. The colour in Pearl's cheeks and the flash in her eye gave me hope that I'd finally succeeded in annoying her. She puffed her chest out and her cotton print dress pulled taut. Her friend Gert looked away in discomfort.

"Bessie was a good friend. We've been through illnesses and the deaths of our husbands and I owe it to her to be looking in on her now."

"I thought you lived out west when Abe died." I knew she was talking about Irv, but it felt good to get in a dig.

"What is your problem? Bessie needs stimulation. Besides, there's no ownership over treating someone well, Herman. What is the big deal, anyway? It wouldn't hurt you to take her out to a show sometime, or to the museum. It's not like you're all that busy here. You never participate in anything..." She waved her hand up and down, as though slathering paint on the activity board. "All you do is skulk about the hallways and the lobby."

"Do you know what a production it would be to take Bessie out? I'm not exactly twenty-five anymore."

"Well, getting out and doing things makes you feel younger. I swim thirty laps in the pool every day, to keep in shape."

"Congratulations. I have cancer and you don't."

"Oh, piffle. It's in remission," she said, no pause, no surprise whatsoever.

"How do you know?"

"Bessie told me. She said you've been clear for over eight months. You can stop feeling sorry for yourself."

"Don't tell me how I'm feeling! I am *not* feeling sorry for myself!"

There was silence, and then Pearl said, "I apologize. Listen, I'll help you if you'd like. We can take her out together."

I thought about it for a minute, and then said, "Fine," just to shut her up.

"Good. Then it's settled. We can take her tomorrow to see the new exhibit at the Royal Ontario Museum."

"Okay, but I'm not saying I'll make a habit of it."

"My goodness, you're a stubborn man."

"Yeah? Well, you're no pushover yourself." I turned to her friend. "Gert, I'm sorry you had to witness that. You should take Pearl with a grain of salt. She says things to hear herself talk."

"Ach, such nonsense. C'mon." They walked a little and then Pearl turned around and said, "You want to know what your problem is, Herman?"

"No," I said, "but I'm sure you'll tell me anyway." How dare she use my formal name without asking my permission?

"Your problem is that you put up too many defences," she said. "You don't need to guard yourself like a fortress."

"Hmph."

They continued towards the elevator. Then with her back to me, Pearl called out, "You're trying to keep people out, but you're the one who will end up feeling trapped." She pressed the down button and glanced back.

I waved her away, and she returned the gesture, and then — I couldn't believe it — she actually turned around and stuck her tongue out at me. The last time I'd seen a grown woman stick out her tongue was when Lil did it at that party, years ago. I turned to the board and pretended to read the schedule again, waiting until the elevator came and took them down to the lobby. Until I'd had time to stew. Defences, she said. Nonsense; I'd been launching pre-emptive strikes.

I composed myself, took the next elevator down, and met with Ari, trying to banish Pearl Feffer from my thoughts.

My great-nephew had been a busy fellow. He'd set about to do as much research as he could, good little academic that he was. He had contacted the Emma Goldman Archives in Berkeley, and the director, Dr. Falk, had promised to send him copies of Emma's letters that I'd forwarded to her, as well as the letters to her from Lil, which I was anxious to read because I'd never seen them before.

He'd asked Dr. Falk for any information she might have regarding the location of Bon Esprit, the cottage in which Emma had stayed. She confirmed what we feared: nobody knew its exact location. She had a few old photographs, but none had a clear enough image of the house or any surrounding landmarks to be of much use. Of all the academic research done on Emma, apparently nobody had considered this piece of real estate to be of much interest.

Ari also made calls to France. With help from the St-Tropez Tourism Board, he reached a pleasant transplanted Brit who after a quick conference with his colleagues told him to try François Provencher, a volunteer with the local heritage society. Monsieur Provencher was working as a curator at the town's citadel and told Ari he also didn't know anything, but that there was a very elderly gentleman, Monsieur Sanschagrin, a man in his nineties with an exceptional memory, who was somewhat of a local history buff. Monsieur Provencher had his mother call the old man — they'd been neighbours when they were children — and the mother reported back that we were in luck: the old man did remember something about a woman named Goldman. Ari thanked Monsieur Provencher profusely, saying we'd like to meet with them both and that we'd call when we arrived.

In the next few days, Ari tried several times to reach Monsieur Sanschagrin by phone, finally reaching his granddaughter, who was reticent to give out much information. Ari decided at that point that the best he could do was check with her that her grandfather would be in St-Tropez during the period when we planned to visit. He would be, she said, and so Ari asked her to pass on the message that we would be contacting him in a few weeks.

As Ari told me all of this, as well as other details he picked up in the university library, we walked over to Bathurst Street for a bite. By the time he got to the part about the old man, we were at a table sipping coffee. I could see Bessie's window from where we were sitting. I considered this old man in St-Tropez. Did he have the same problem as me, that he couldn't forget a damned thing, try though he might? God help me, I would *not* live 'til my nineties, people pestering me for quaint remembrances or to help them with their research.

On that note, I said, "Ari, what have you decided?"

"About?"

"About ... you know."

"Aw, c'mon. We were talking about our trip to France, for God's sake."

We'd spoken a couple of times since I'd asked him to help me end my life, but I'd not probed him again for an answer. He'd asked me to give him time, and though I was trying to be patient, the question felt lashed to my throat, desperate to wriggle itself free. If he was going to keep me waiting forever for an answer, time might just do the dirty work for him, and that was what I was trying to avoid. I stared at him until he spoke.

"When you agreed to come to France with me, I hoped you might give up on the other idea."

"I haven't."

"All of this talk about our trip and all you can think about is death?"

"No, not all. Anyway, when would be a good time to bring up something like this?"

"Never, and so I wish you wouldn't."

I glared at him, waiting until he continued.

"I still need some time. You've been watching TV too much. This Rodriguez case is making you obsess."

"I can form ideas on my own, believe it or not, without the influence of the media."

"Of course you can. I'm just saying ... with all that's happening in the news ... maybe, if you tuned it out, you'd—"

"My situation is different."

"It sure as hell is. She has an irreversible, debilitating disease. She's trapped in her own body and soon she won't even be able to tell people what she's thinking, what she's feeling. Look at you. You're going to the French Riviera."

"I thought you agreed with assisted suicide."

"I don't agree or disagree with it. There are times when…"

"It should be a person's choice."

"I was going to say, times when there are no other humane options."

"Are you afraid of the law? Because you shouldn't be."

"No…"

"Nobody will know. They won't trace it back to you."

"It's not that. I'm just … I have to be sure."

"I'm surprised. You've always given the impression that you had this all figured out. Politically, I mean."

"Yeah, well, I've realized lately that politics can kind of fall apart when you're faced with a personal choice. When it's about one person, someone you love, who's staring you in the face. If there's one thing I know from studying Emma Goldman, it's that she knew how important each individual was. And Aunt Lil taught me that too. Know what I mean?"

"Your aunt Lil taught you *that*? Well, if she figured that out, she learned it late in life. She didn't always think of the consequences her actions might have on the people right next to her. Remember, I knew her much better than you."

He reached into his knapsack and handed me a manila envelope. "Well, I'm getting to know her better through these. They arrived yesterday from Berkeley."

I wouldn't get an answer from him today, that was clear. In any case, something important had to be taken care of before I did anything drastic, something all the way across the ocean, in St-Tropez.

prisons

was my life worth living?

If anyone had the courage to ask, "Was my life worth living?" it was Emma. Personally, I'd never have asked such a question. Unless I'd been damn sure the answer was "yes," that is, and then why would I have bothered, unless I'd had something to prove?

Emma had something to prove.

In September of 1934, when Lil and I helped her type the famous essay she was to have printed in *Harper's Magazine*, I was only eighteen and without much existential angst. Bitterness, yes; angst, no. Nonetheless, even then I sensed the question was perilous. I would've asked something safer, less black and white. How about: How much have I accomplished?; or What influence have I had?; or How many shmoes have I outwitted this month?

Lil said, "Forget it; she never does anything in half measures," as we hurried up Spadina Avenue towards Emma's apartment. "I asked if she was sure about it and all she said was, 'I must!'"

The night before, Lil had lied to our parents to get us out of work at the store. She'd just started the second-last semester of her biology degree at University College, and she said she needed my help quizzing her for an upcoming test. On the way to Emma's, she told the truth: Lil was typing up Emma's notes and she need me to read them out to her.

"She hasn't been in the best spirits. Her lover just left town and Rupert MacNabb got another one of her lectures cancelled. I swear, Toshy, if I had the chance, I'd strangle that man. Here's Emma, who's only exercising free speech, just asking people to think for themselves, and never sure where her next dollar will come from…"

"Didn't she write a book?"

"Yeah, I guess it's hard to earn a living that way. Now, she's under attack — left, right, and centre — from critics who say anarchism is dead, passé. Imagine having to prove your life was worthwhile, after nearly forty years of struggle and sacrifice. Being asked over and over again if everything she's done has had any effect."

"Who keeps asking?"

"Journalists, mostly. And lately they've been asking so often that you can't help wondering if there's some truth to the accusation. I tell ya, that alone would make me want to end it all."

We arrived at Emma's, a one-bedroom stacked on top of a busy store, and I was nervous as we climbed the stairs. I'd never met her before, but I was intimidated by Lil's stories, and by what I'd witnessed the first time Lil had introduced herself. I didn't have the kind of gumption Lil did, not when it came to direct confrontation.

I shouldn't have worried; when the door opened, Emma smiled warmly.

"You must be Herman, Lil's brother! Lil talks about you all the time."

I doubted she did, and Lil's response proved me right: "Call him Toshy, everyone does." Emma reached past Lil and engulfed my hand in hers. She gave Lil a kiss on the cheek and ushered us in. "Sit yourselves down at the table. I've made tea and fresh-baked coffee cake."

I was surprised that the great Emma Goldman baked coffee cake. I figured that she should have protegés or admirers doing that for her, that maybe we should have baked her one ourselves.

"The place is a mess, as always, but no matter, I'll have

to clean it up in a few days when I move out of here and in with the Langbords."

"I forgot you're moving so soon."

"Yes, and it'll save me a lot of money."

I scanned the apartment. It was relatively dark, despite a window that looked onto the street, with exposed wires running along the walls and peeling brown paint that might at one time have been beige. On a desk by the window, the typewriter was barely visible for the papers and leaflets stacked around it. There was a small kitchen table on which she'd placed the cake, a teapot, and three cups, and between the table and the desk, a loveseat.

Emma sat and poured us tea. There was a book beside the pot that she brushed her hand over and sighed.

Lil said, "Good reading?"

"I haven't started it. Frank left it for me." Then she did something even more surprising than baking coffee cake: she began crying. She grabbed a serviette and turned away to honk loudly into it. "This is very awkward. His absence shouldn't be affecting me so much. We've only just become lovers, after all."

"Don't be embarrassed," said Lil. "You're only human."

"I'm not afraid to show my feelings among friends." She pulled herself together, sat upright, and gulped down some tea. "It's just that I've never met your poor brother before and here he is watching an old lady cry over a man she's just met. You must promise never to tell anyone, Toshy, or my reputation as an independent woman will be shot. People will say that deep down I have longings like every other woman — to be a wife."

"I promise," I said, staring at my teacup.

"People don't understand that I get lonely like everyone else. Why must they conclude that just because I long for the touch of a man against my skin, for companionship, that it means I want to be subservient to him?"

"People are small-minded, you know that," said Lil. "You *taught* me that. We live in a moralistic society that says a woman can't have sexual relations without getting married. Women like us are considered a threat. Anyway, it's sweet that you miss him."

"I don't really miss Frank, that's the thing. He just left. It's just ... it has dawned on me that every man I've cared about lives somewhere else. Time with them is scarce and precious. We lie in bed, pressing against each other, clutching at each other, as if starved for the intimacy we have. We grasp at each other's skin as if we were wild, ravenous animals who haven't eaten for months. And we haven't, of course."

Speaking of skin, I wished I could crawl out of mine. The last thing I'd expected was to hear my sister talk about sex with someone who, now that I saw her sipping tea, looked uncannily like our dead grandmother. Still, a part of me wondered what Lil had meant when she said "women like us." Did she have sex, too, and with men she'd just met and wasn't married to?

"Careful, Toshy," said Emma, reaching out to steady my cup. It was listing and I hadn't noticed. Emma chuckled. "I'm afraid I really have scandalized your brother. The last time I saw someone so red-faced was when a policeman in Chicago was forced to release me from jail against his wishes."

"Don't worry about him — he's fine, aren't you?"

"Oh, yeah," I said, though I was sure I was blushing now more than ever.

"Tell me: how's the article coming along?" Lil asked, changing the subject in a rare and blessed moment of mercy.

"Ach, it's coming. You're just in time: the beginning is done and waiting for you by the typewriter, but I'm distracted by what happened with MacNabb. That little pustulous toad: how dare he suggest I'm irrelevant? I have to remind myself that outside of Canada, he's nobody. He thinks I'm afraid to look the truth in the eye? I know things aren't what they were thirty years ago. Wait until he reads my article. I'm going to take the wind out of that man's sails."

"He's just afraid of you, Emma."

"He's afraid of my ideas, not me."

We settled down at the desk, me in a chair beside it, and Lil's fingers poised above the keyboard. I read in a low voice so as not to disturb Emma: "It is strange what time does to political causes. A generation ago it seemed to many American conservatives as if the opinions which Emma Goldman was expressing might sweep the world. Now she fights almost alone for what seems to be a lost cause."

Lil stopped typing. "Alone? What am I, chopped liver?"

"My dear," Emma called out from the other side of the room. "I don't mean that I am *literally* alone, but on the world scene, what other voices are there but mine? Beside, wait a few pages, it's not all doom and gloom. Who do you think you're dealing with?"

Lil got on with the typing, but it was slow going. First, Lil was not a trained secretary. She hunted and pecked, stopping frequently to express editorial comments. Emma's voice would cut through as well, with statements that broke up the flow as we decided whether or not they were rhetorical.

"Maybe I should dramatize *Living My Life* for film," she said. "It could top up my royalties, although with the new Hays Code coming into effect in Hollywood, there would be nothing left of my life that the censors would find moral enough for the screen."

A few minutes later, she said, "Perhaps I should write another book on all the famous people I've known. Maybe that would bring me a bit more security."

"Emma, it was only one lecture cancelled. There will be others. And money always comes your way."

"I know, dear. You know, maybe I'll go back to France to write my book. Toronto is really turning out to be stifling for me."

"I wouldn't mind going to France," I whispered. Lil continued typing, making me embarrassed to have said it. "I know, that was stupid."

"No, no. It's never stupid to want to travel. It's just ... I was thinking it might not be safe."

"Why not?"

"For someone like you, I mean. You never know how people might react. They might see your lip and assume you're dangerous, like you got it in a fight or something."

I hadn't considered until then that I might look dangerous. Cute as a bunny, devious as a serpent, thick as an ape: yes, all those things. Not dangerous; I *liked* dangerous.

"Plus, they probably wouldn't be able to understand you, even if they did speak English."

I'd never thought of this either. "Well, what about England, then?"

"Same problem, unfortunately. They might speak English, but they have a completely different accent, and *they* already think *we* speak funny. I'm just worried you'd be made fun of."

"Nurse Grace was English and she didn't make fun of me."

"Of course not. She's a nurse. She's supposed to be nice."

"What if I went with you, then?"

"Sure. That might be a plan," she conceded.

"It would be a *lovely* plan," said Emma, from the kitchen. "If I ever go back there, you'll both have to come and visit me. Perhaps I can raise some money to pay your way. But you'll have to earn your keep by being as helpful there as you're being here today."

"That would be terrific!" I said.

"It sure would be," echoed Lil, but by the look on her face, I knew she wouldn't want me tagging along with her if she ever got the opportunity to go to Europe.

Emma jumped up from the table. "I just heard the mail being delivered." In a minute, she came in with a thick stack of letters, far more than our family ever received, and there were five of us. She shuffled rapidly through them and came upon one that she tore open.

"Aha!" Her monocle popped out. "Well, isn't this fantastic. Forester's Hall has accepted to host eight lectures, and Rupert MacNabb be damned."

"Terrific!" Lil got up to read over her shoulder.

"I knew something would come unstuck."

They hugged there in the middle of the apartment, while I sat in my chair and muddled over what Lil had said to me. I'd spent a long time developing an arsenal against cruelty in my own backyard. I never considered my defences would be ineffective against foreign invaders. I didn't question how Lil might know anything at all about France or England, having never been farther than Camp Naivelt, a secular Jewish cottage community near Toronto. Despite this, she projected an aura of sophistication and worldliness, so I trusted she knew what was best.

After Lil and I finished typing up Emma's article and had put it in an envelope addressed to *Harper's*, we went home for supper. Our parents discussed store business while I attacked a brisket hungrily, my knife tearing at the delicious, stringy meat soaked in tomato sauce.

"The numbers aren't great this month, Manya."

"They'll pick up when people start planning for spring and summer weddings."

"Still, it's going to be a difficult winter. No new boots, kids."

"That's okay, mine are fine," said Lil.

"Good. Anything extra, we'll need to put aside for your schooling. I'm glad to see you're working hard, because getting you through school will nearly kill this family, and we're going to need your medical skills to revive us when you graduate."

"I know, Pop. I appreciate it, I really do."

I hoped Lil would change the subject. I couldn't bear that he was talking about sacrifices made for her studies and we'd just wiggled out of working in the store. This was Lil's last year of her bachelor of science degree and she was our family's only hope for a university graduate. Certainly there was no hope for me, and Bessie simply didn't have the inclination, though she probably could've gone to university had she wanted to. Lil was applying to medical school and that was something to be proud of. We considered her degree a family venture.

"I've made a decision that will help," Bessie said, but she almost whispered it and didn't look up from her plate. That she was speaking at all was a surprise; she'd been so quiet lately. Quieter than me. "I've found a job. It starts next week."

Pop said, "Bessie, we need you in the store, sweetheart."

"We need the money more; you just said so. Toshy can help out front, if you let him. You'd see he's good with customers if you only gave him a chance."

"What's the job?" asked Ma, avoiding the subject of my dubious competency.

"Working as a maid."

My parents exchanged glances.

"I don't like it," said Pop. "Domestic servants are among the most exploited class in society."

"More than seamstresses?"

"Don't start with me. At least a seamstress can organize. Where's your union going to be if you go work for those people?"

"He has a point, Bessie." I couldn't remember Lil ever agreeing with Pop on a point of politics. Bessie was stung.

"This has nothing to do with unions, Lil; Ma and Pop are embarrassed because they don't know any Jewish families with daughters working as maids. Some communists."

"It's not that," said Ma. "You've been through a lot. Wouldn't it be better if you stayed here?"

"I've accepted the position. I'm going to be an old maid anyway; why not *literally* be one?"

Nobody laughed.

"I'm kidding. I want to do this."

"You're not an old maid, you're a widow," said Ma, but it didn't sound very comforting.

"How did you hear about it?" asked Lil.

"A friend of a friend. The couple doesn't have kids, so I won't live in, but they do need me from eight in the morning until nine at night; a little later for parties and the holidays. Cleaning, laundry, preparing and serving supper…"

"We'll never see you!"

"I'll be *living* here, Ma. C'mon; their help just quit and the lady has been worried about what to do for the holidays. It's decent pay."

"Sabbath off?" asked Pop.

"What do you care? We're not religious."

"You could help in the store."

Ma gave Pop a withering stare. "We are *not* going to make her work on her only day off."

"The *Christian* Sabbath, Pop. But Mrs. MacNabb will let me have the evening and the day for Passover, Rosh Hashanah, and Yom Kippur."

Lil straightened her back. "Did you say MacNabb? As in *the* MacNabbs?"

"Yes, *the* MacNabbs, and don't you dare start with your politics. I'm doing this for you."

"I wasn't going to; I'm grateful, believe me. Plus now you can spy for me and Emma."

Pop said, "There won't be any spying," as if Bessie would ever have entertained it. His frown showed his displeasure, but from his admonition, we knew he'd agreed to the job.

In the end, Lil's interests always came first.

§

Letter from Lil to me, from my collection:

Toronto, April 22nd 36

Herman Wolfman
c/o Collins Bay Penitentiary
Bath Road, Collins Bay, Ontario

My Dearest Toshy,

I have wonderful news to report: I'm going to Europe. Can you believe it? Remember Emma talked about bringing us there one day if she ever went back to France? Well, she did go back, and now she's sent me a fully paid return passage from Montreal to Le Havre. I know she would've done the same for you if only you'd not been in jail. I've dreamed about this for so long that I can't believe it is actually happening.

I should be ashamed of expressing such joy, with Pop so recently buried, and you stuck in prison, not even able to travel to the end of the road, but I can't help it. I had to tell someone, and you and I have always shared secrets, haven't we? You see, Bessie and Ma don't know. They would never approve of my trip when it means giving up an internship in order to be "a secretary," but since you and I talked about going there together, I knew you'd understand. Frankly, it irks me that I should have to hide my trip from Ma. For a person who professes to be a communist, Ma sure does make you feel ashamed to have a proletarian job. As soon as you tell a person you're to become a doctor, it is as if they undergo a brain transplant. Suddenly, they assume we must spend all of our waking hours thinking of medicine. There is life for medical students beyond the study of blood and cells and organs.

In any case, I have another job waiting when I get back — working with Dr. Frank in Toronto. That will give me some of the experience I need. Who says you can't dance at all the weddings?

Here's what I've told Ma and Bessie (you must remember this when they come in turn to visit you in June): I'm going to Montreal for the month to do an internship with a Dr. Bellow who runs a clinic out of the Jewish General, and I'll be far too busy to call or write because he's a veritable slave-driver with his interns. Dr. Bellow is actually a friend of Gerry Dunkelman, a fellow student who is sweet on me, and Gerry assured me he would keep up the ruse if ever Ma contacted him. That is unlikely, in any case.

Here's what I'm actually doing: On May 4th, I'll board the morning train but I'll stop in Kingston and visit you on the way. Then it's a ten-day crossing from Montreal. Ten days! I have no idea if I'll be seasick or if I'll enjoy the journey, because when have I ever stepped foot in a boat, except to catch the ferry to the Toronto Islands? I take the train from Le Havre to Nice, with only one and a half days in Paris on the way.

My trip is not a holiday, though you can't blame me if I'm thinking of it as an adventure. Emma's lifelong friend and comrade Sasha Berkman has taken ill. I wrote to Emma in January in London. She replied, saying that Sasha had undergone an operation and was scheduled for another, that she would be going to stay with him in Nice, and would I come to help with secretarial duties while she played nurse-maid. For Emma, politics are never forgotten, even during a personal crisis. Now that there is a newly elected anti-fascist government in Spain, she is anxious to continue her support of the Spanish anarchists and trusts me enough to help her.

She said she had mentioned this idea to her good friend Peggy Guggenheim, the famous one who has more money than God, and Miss Guggenheim offered to pay my way to Europe, as well as a small stipend once I arrive in France. I replied immediately that of course I'd love to come, and Emma wired a few weeks later with the details. My return voyage is June 15th and that means I'll visit you on the 26th, on the way back to Toronto. Since I've only been able to

visit once a month, you won't even miss me. Is there anything special you want me to bring you back from France?
Make sure the guards will let you keep it; I will not spend
money to have them enjoy your gift.

There you have it, my dear brother. Your older sister will
most likely become a European fashion plate, dressed in
fancy French clothing, wearing a large, silly hat. When you
see me in June, you won't recognize me, so glamorous I'll be.

On another subject, I am very anxious to be done with my
last exam, which is tomorrow. I can hear you scolding me all
the way from Kingston: "Why aren't you studying? Why
don't you write me tomorrow night?" Don't worry, little
brother. The subject is anatomy and I have a very good
memory. Not as good as yours, but with subjects like this,
things stick. I am simplifying it to say that it's mostly memorizing body parts, but if you can remember them all, it's a
strong foundation. I have been at the books for the last week
and felt the need for a break. To add to my restlessness, I
received the news about France today and absolutely had to
tell someone or I would scream. Rest assured, after I put
down my pen, I'll study into the late night.

Bessie is happy to take on extra duties in the store during
my exam period, but I'm sure she would not be happy if she
knew I was using that time to write you, and she'd like it even
less if she knew about France. Normally, she doesn't complain about the work, even though it is partly through her
labour that I am able to go to medical school. I don't know if
she feels it is a kind of penance she is doing for what happened at the MacNabbs', but if there's a debt to be paid, it's
to you she owes it, not to me.

Did she tell you things are very serious between her and
Abe Kagan? He is very kind to her and is over for dinner
almost every Friday night. It wouldn't surprise me if he
asked for her hand soon. Just remember that, when you're
feeling low. We did a good thing for our sister, and she's
going to have a happy life for it.

I worry about Ma, though. She is already run off her feet. If Bessie gets married and starts working in Abe's store, it will just be me and Ma, and then when I graduate, who will Ma have? She'll have to hire someone, I suppose. Wouldn't that be a hoot? Communist Ma, the evil boss-lady. Perhaps if Abe's business goes well, he'll offer to help her out.

Last time I visited, you asked me to write to you with any news or funny stories from the neighbourhood. There's not much to report, but here goes: Someone threw a rock through a window of Halpern's seltzer factory last week. I thought it might be anti-Semites, but there was no evidence of it. Maybe it was just kids getting up to no good. Poor Mr. Halpern was standing outside, or so I'm told, pulling at the few tufts of hair he has left on his head.

Oh, I almost forgot! I'm sure it will give you a chuckle to hear that there was a daring escape attempt from Groskopf Poultry last Tuesday. Some prankster left the pen door open and all of the chickens, ducks, and geese got loose in two seconds flat. They waddled and flapped their way down the alley to the front of the store and out onto Baldwin Street. Mr. Groskopf and his son ran out to scoop the birds up in their arms, while Mrs. Groskopf and the old lady who plucks chickens just stood there yelling, "Git zat one!" I heard some ended up a few streets over on Fitzroy Terrace, you know that lane that sounds fancy but looks like a Polish village. I didn't witness any of this, of course, because I've had my face in the books. But I have my spies.

Well, my dear brother, speaking of those books, I should get back to them if you ever want to see me wearing a white lab coat. I will see you in a few weeks, and I am very much looking forward to it. Remember, not a word about my trip to France if you write to Ma or Bessie.

Love,
   Lil

§

During the weeks after I joined Bernie's secret communist prison meetings, for the first time I felt my life might be worth living, just maybe.

Belonging to a group was a completely foreign and exhilarating experience. Now, I was stretching my mind, and Bernie and the others treated me like one of them. We debated ideas, shared news from the outside, and discussed events happening out there in the world as though we were part of it. Never mind that we were in jail. We weren't outsiders, not really. We were part of an international movement, doing what we could, in preparation, maybe, for the more useful role we'd play once we got out. Bernie and I even got together, just the two of us, outside in the yard or in his room, and talked more one-on-one.

I'd have been embarrassed to admit it then, but for the first time ever, I felt superior, and that buoyed my spirits. I was part of a small clique who saw the world unveiled, while everyone else, poor clods, stumbled around with ignorance clouding their vision. For the first time, I really understood Lil. This new feeling of superiority made me more aloof, made me want to get to know others even less. It was my first insight into how people had always felt about me.

And yet, worry irritated and scratched at my smugness. If I felt superiority, belonging, and purpose, I couldn't forget that I'd screwed my life up and it might never be salvaged. The other fellows in the group had done things prior to being convicted that might prepare them for when they got out. They'd gone to school, learned a trade, had jobs. What had I done? I hadn't gotten my diploma, I'd acquired barely any useful skills in my parents' store, and I'd garnered a reputation for dishonesty even before my arrest. I'd done nothing constructive to overcome the prejudice strangers felt when they looked at me or heard me speak. When the prison system finally spat me onto the streets, nobody would care that I'd developed a political consciousness. My family would take me in out of obligation, and while Ma would be thrilled I'd improved my Yiddish, she'd wonder how, and when I told her, she wouldn't be pleased. Ma and Lil would both argue with me, but from opposite sides of the political spectrum. Bessie would roll her eyes, and Pop would turn over in his grave.

Bernie must've sensed this was on my mind. I was his pet project, as well as his friend, and he put on his agenda convincing me to further my education. I'd almost flunked out of school in Toronto, despite being put in a class with the slow students. The subject matter was dull, and they treated us like imbeciles. To be fair to the teachers, I pretty much acted like one too, and eventually failed my grade twelve year. I wanted to drop out, but Ma and Pop wouldn't let me. They may have considered me stupid, but they placed faith in the ability of the educational system to give me whatever leg up it could. I was held back to repeat the year and may have eventually received my high school diploma had I not landed in jail.

They offered high school classes right there in the prison and Bernie encouraged me to go. I was intrigued, but I was finally with a group of people kind enough not to treat me like I was dumb. I didn't want to be back in a classroom, with all of the risks that entailed. I offered up excuses: I had another ten years ahead of me; there was lots of time. The discussion group was teaching me more than school ever could. Eventually, Bernie backed off.

IN MAY, LIL CAME TO VISIT ME on the way to France. She sat across the table while the guards watched us closely, lest she pass me a bobby pin to pick a lock, and her heavy suitcase was propped up beside her. She took off a long wool coat, which she said was for the boat because she intended to go out on the deck and watch the ocean.

"Can you believe it, Toshy? Me, going to France?"

"You're so lucky."

She took my hand and said, "I know. I'm so sorry you can't come with me." Her forced earnestness immediately made me regret saying anything. I was probably not supposed to be too obvious about longing for freedom; it made the non-incarcerated uncomfortable. Better to pretend you were hanging in there, chin up, making the best of it. Besides, that was partly true now, thanks to Bernie and his group.

"It's okay. You'll write me, tell me all about it. Anyway, I made a friend here. He's a good guy." I decided not to mention the discussion group; I didn't want to waste our visit on a political argument.

"That's wonderful!" she said, sounding even more fake than when she'd said she was sorry I couldn't come to France. "Who is he?"

She didn't really care. She wanted to talk more about herself and her trip, and she was only being polite. "Just some guy named Bernie who was transferred from Kingston a while back. We get together and talk about stuff. Play cards sometimes."

"Well, thank God you have someone in here. Now that Emma's in France, I rely on the Prisoners Support Guild. It's hard to talk to most people about all this. The guild members have been wonderful, especially Grace."

"You call her Grace now?"

"Oh sure, she's very down-to-earth. In fact, she rode on the train with me to Kingston, in the second-class compartment. She's over at the main prison now, meeting with the warden and the prison doctor."

"How come?"

"She's concerned about the shoddy medical facilities, and also, because I raised the issue with her, she's talking to them about how they've mixed older adults in with the youth in this prison. Someone like me would never be granted a meeting, but being a Lady gets you in anywhere."

"I already told you, Lil, I don't mind the older guys being here. Bernie's older. If he hadn't been able to transfer, I wouldn't have any friends at all. Don't you even listen to what I say?"

"I do listen, but this issue has bigger implications than just you, Toshy. They just went ahead and changed the policy without even telling Parliament! Think about it: if they can do that, what else can they get away with? In the long run, we're only looking out for your best interests. You have to trust us and consider the big picture."

Lil didn't get it. For me, there was no big picture; I knew then that my discussion group hadn't changed a thing. If circumstances pushed me down, I saw the floor. If they pulled me up, I saw prison walls or supposed do-gooders like Lil who didn't hear a word I said. Either way, the picture was small, and so close that I had to let my eyes go out of focus, just so that I could stand to look at it.

IN JUNE, KINGSTON EXPERIENCED an early heat wave that knocked us flat on our backs, practically naked on our bunks, lungs barely able to rise and fall from the weight of the air accumulating in the small cells. Each wave of heavy, humid air squeezed through the bars or windows only to be compressed by the next wave that lost its way inside and stacked itself under the last, until the stifling air was even pressed flush against the floor.

Feeling nearly crazy from the constant sweating and several sticky, sleepless nights, I was awakened by the morning bell, followed by the low grumbling and muttering of my neighbours. Because I'd only just a half-hour before achieved a state of fitful dozing, the ringing reached into my chest and felt like despair.

I got up and stumbled to the small toilet to relieve myself. The air reeked of sewage water fermented by the heat, despite the fact that I'd covered the bowl with my blanket the night before. The stench might also have been coming from my neighbours' cells or mixed in with my own body odour. I longed for a shower, one of the three we got every week. Bernie and I were in the Saturday-Tuesday-Thursday rotation and usually we went after coming back from work detail. On Saturdays, though, we went just after our group met and before he went to a pottery class run by a local Christian woman who came in to the prison to teach crafts.

There'd been a breeze coming through the windows of the room where we held our group, so by the time we'd finished, I was in much better spirits. Bernie and I went to have our showers and stood in line, waiting our turn. I chuckled to myself, remembering the blessing he'd given at the start of our fake prayer meeting. Every week, he found new Yiddish curses or insults for the guards. One week it was, "He should have Pharaoh's plagues sprinkled with Job's scabies," and another, it was, "All his teeth should fall out except one to make him suffer." Today, in a sing-song as if he were a cantor in a synagogue, he said, "*Baruch ata adonai*, let it be that the dried old farts who run this cursed hell-hole shit and then fall all over it, and let us have strength not to laugh too much at their stupidity, Amen."

Two showers came free and Bernie and I took them. I rubbed the coarse soap bar over my body and enjoyed the cooling spray, even if it came chugging out of the showerhead in spurts and the water was sulphurous and discoloured. Before I was in jail, I'd never showered with other men before, and it was hard not to stare. At the beginning, it would've been nearly impossible to ignore what was in front of me, like keeping your eyes ahead when you walked by an accident. I snuck peeks to see whose penis was bigger than mine, or smaller, or to look at the ones with foreskins, because I'd certainly never seen one of those before. Frankly, it was a novelty just to see the different shapes people's bodies could come in: which ones had rolls of fat around their waist, who had muscles, or who had strange wrinkles or pockmarks in the skin of their bottoms.

The problem was that people sometimes looked back, and you had to quickly avert your eyes or they'd get the wrong idea. It would take me a while before the novelty had worn off and I could keep my eyes down, or closed, or forward and unfocused.

What made me more nervous than worrying if I'd be caught staring was when I saw someone staring back. It happened if I wasn't paying attention, or when I opened my eyes after soaping up my face or washing my hair. The first few times, I assumed they were checking me out, just like I was, and maybe a couple of them were, but I couldn't be sure. Then, Bernie warned me not to shower next to a few of the fellows who were known to have wandering hands.

I didn't know much about the gays then, and I didn't really know any nice word for them either. The rules said they didn't transfer people from Kingston Pen if they were deemed a "homosexual pervert"; I'd assumed nobody at Collins Bay would be that way. Of course, then I remembered that they weren't supposed to transfer political agitators either, and there was Bernie holding clandestine meetings on Stalinism. Why shouldn't there be people with secret homosexual desires, too?

Sometimes I caught Bernie looking, which was confusing, given his warning. It was also awkward, since usually he showered facing away from me and staring meant craning his neck around and I didn't know what to make of that. Was he looking back to see if I was almost finished? That morning, when I opened my eyes after washing my hair, I caught him looking again. His eyes had been unmistakably looking down there, too, I was sure of it. Then, more unnerving than that, they flickered quickly up to my face and he smiled. Until that day, I'd pretended not to notice, and he'd always glance down at the tiles, just as I would've, if I'd been sneaking a look. The smile caught me off guard. I smiled back, but in a clipped sort of way, as though I might've just been wincing from soap in my eyes.

I rinsed off quickly and went to get my towel. Bernie lingered a few minutes more, his back to me, facing the showerhead. If he was a homosexual pervert, I didn't really want to know about it. I didn't actually care if he was or he wasn't, as long as he didn't direct his perversion at me.

We dried off and got dressed. Neither of us spoke until we'd pulled on our clothes. While Bernie was combing his hair in the mirror, he said, "Hey, Toshy, wanna come to pottery class?"

"I dunno. I don't really know how to make anything."

"Well, that's the whole point, isn't it? They'll teach you. C'mon, it's fun. You get to squish clay between your fingers. You can imagine it's a guard's head." He said the last part in Yiddish.

"I guess."

I followed him to the arts and crafts room, where a middle-aged woman wearing a smock was rolling a huge mound of clay on the countertop.

"Oh good, a new student!" she said, barely looking at me. "Take a seat over there. Bernie, get him a lump of clay and show him how to knead it. We'll start him with a pinch-pot."

"Everybody starts with a pinch-pot, then never makes one again," said Bernie, winking. "It's like once you've learned cursive writing, nobody bothers to print anymore."

He grabbed a hunk of clay from a mound next to the teacher and tore it in two, throwing one part on the table in front of me. He threw it on an angle but it stuck there, frozen to the surface, like a dinosaur caught in the tar pits. Then he grabbed a smock and showed me how to put it on. Facing me but looking to the side, he took the straps and reached behind me. I put my arms up and sucked in my stomach. He crossed the straps behind my back and then pulled them forward and tied them off.

We sat side by side and Bernie took his mound of clay. "You have to knead it to get the air bubbles out or it'll explode when you fire it. Also, it makes it easier to work with. Pretend you're making dough."

"I thought we were pretending it was the guard's head that we—"

"Shh!"

I kneaded the clay until my hands cramped, but it was nice and cool between my fingers.

The teacher shouted from the front, "Start your pinch-pot by hollowing out the clay in your palm, making it into the shape of a small sugar bowl." Then she turned her attention to another fellow who'd come in late.

I made a passable pinch-pot, which Bernie helped me even out. "Here, take your fingers, like this." He drew his thumbs to his index fingers and pinched the edges of the pot to make them more or less flat. I followed his example, and when we were done, he said I was ready for a coil-pot. He fetched a bowl of mushy, watery clay and plopped it down.

"This is slurry. You roll coils into circles and then stack them. The slurry, you use to hold them together like glue."

I couldn't get the coils even. They looked like earth-worms who'd swallowed large pebbles. Bernie said, "Not like that. Evenly, with your palms flat."

I tried, but the worms still had hernias.

He pulled his stool over and said, "Even pressure." He brought his hands down on top of mine.

I jerked my hands away. "I can do it myself."

"I know you can. You just have to—"

"I'm not stupid, Bernie!" I snapped. "Just let me work on my own pot, will ya?"

He moved his stool back and I saw that his face had dried and hardened. I felt slightly ill and wasn't sure if it was because of Bernie's touching me or because I felt bad for shouting at him. For the next half-hour, he worked beside me as if I wasn't even there. I worked on perfecting my coil-pot, but despondently. Meanwhile, he was painstaking in his creation. Frequently he got up to add more clay to it, then fiddled and fussed with its shape. I didn't know what the hell he was making, and I didn't ask — some sort of animal, that was sure — but which one, I couldn't tell.

Finally, he added the trunk, looked over, and raised his eyebrows at me. Subtlety was not Bernie's strong suit. He'd fashioned his clay into the elephant, huge and unspoken, that we both knew was standing in the room.

bench of lies

I still had about an hour before Ari arrived with the airport limo and we'd be off to France. Rather than wait in my room, I decided to go down and sit on a bench in the lobby. Two ladies by the window whispered to each other, glancing my way. People didn't travel very often once they moved into The Terrace, with the exception of one or two who still went to Florida in the winter. A summer trip was rare, and mid-week with all that luggage? It wasn't likely I was visiting a cottage.

"Where are ya going?" a man hollered from another bench. The ladies turned to hear the answer.

"To St-Tropez!" I called back. The man squinted skeptically. I might as well have said I was going alligator wrestling in the Amazon; in that lobby, declaring that I was off to the French Riviera sounded preposterous. They probably assumed I was escaping, or more likely, that I was being kicked out.

About fifteen minutes later, Pearl appeared out of an elevator. She approached me, arms crossed. What did she want from me now? My heart raced.

"And just what's this all about, Mr. Wolfman?" She brushed the air in front of my suitcase then put her hands on her hips. The rough, red skin on her forehead wrinkled under the fine, grey hair of her bangs.

"I'm off for ten days," I said, trying to make it sound like no big deal.

"You're off to *France*, and you weren't even going to tell me."

"Seems you knew, anyway. Were you testing me to see if I'd lie? Besides, I don't see what concern it is to you."

"I had to find out from your sister. And it's not a *concern*, you silly man." She smiled and shooed me over so she could sit down. I was uncomfortably close to an enormous mutant leaf growing on a plant next to the bench, causing me to lean slightly in her direction.

"You are the most peculiar man I've ever met. All of that time we spent together the last few Saturdays taking Bessie on outings and you didn't think this might be news worth mentioning? Something exciting in our lives, for goodness' sake. Travel! And to France, at that."

"I guess I didn't think you'd care," I lied. Why should I have to tell her everything about my life, just because we were spending time together now? Already, she knew too much for my liking.

"Of course I'd care. It's a nice trip for you. And we'll miss you, Bessie and I. Besides, the only place anybody here ever goes to is Boca Raton, Miami, or St. Pete's Beach."

"Or out of here in a coffin."

"Right." She laughed. "I suppose you're going on one of those package tours. I went on those for years after my husband died. India, Indonesia, Kenya, Bulgaria, Colombia, you name it."

"It's not a tour — I'm going with Ari. A little holiday," I said. Part of that was true.

"How exciting!" She squeezed my forearm. "And isn't it lovely that you get to spend all that time with your nephew."

Goddamn it — here I was again, telling her things about my life that I'd later regret mentioning. I'd begun to notice that Pearl had an unsettling ability to get me to open up against my better judgement. We'd be talking about a current event, or she'd mention something from her past, and then she'd make an apparently benign inquiry that tricked me into a revelation I never intended to make.

For instance, when we were at the museum admiring a display case of European porcelain, she said, "My mother had a set similar to this." She was pointing to a small figurine of a girl, ornately decorated with red and gold flowers. "But my daughter dropped a box when we were moving and it shattered. Oh, I was heartbroken! Maybe it's a female thing — you probably wouldn't understand what it's like to lose something like that, with such sentimental value."

I found myself telling her about Lil's plates and how Ari broke one of them a few weeks before while we were packing, and before I knew it, Pearl had me telling her all about Lil's illness, and her death.

I couldn't figure out why she wanted to gather this information, but I didn't trust it. I considered she might genuinely be interested and it made me nervous. Life had made me wary of that kind of attention. I dismissed the notion as preposterous. Besides, we still bickered a lot; what if she threw something back in my face?

Bessie wasn't helping; she was offering information up wholesale. Like last weekend, when, in the middle of a gallery of contemporary ceramic sculpture, she said, "Toshy's pottery is better than some of these pieces. Did you know my brother was a potter?"

Pearl replied, "No, I did not! Well, well, he is full of surprises," and then she stared at me with such astonishment that I had to turn away. "You've never mentioned it before, Herman — you should teach a class in the creative arts program."

Sheer chutzpah, using my real name, and right in front of my sister. Maybe Bessie'd told her to call me that. No, she'd never do that; this was Pearl's idea. How could I tell her to call me Toshy? It would only make it sound like I wanted her to be more familiar, instead of less.

"You'll have to show me your work," she said, and

because I wasn't sure I wanted to, I grumbled something I hoped was either ambiguous or inaudible and moved on into the next gallery.

As Pearl sat next to me then, on that bench in the lobby of The Terrace, I could feel her eyes bore deeply, searching for even more secrets, and I worried she could see too much. A man had a right to his private feelings, after all, especially if he wasn't sure what they were yet. Especially if he knew he wouldn't have the guts to act on them anyway, even if he ever did figure them out.

"Well, good thing you at least told your sister you're going away." She ran a finger across my Samsonite suitcase. Her nails were painted a frosted white and her hand was brown with liver spots, but the skin was smooth and smelled of lotion.

"Of course I told her." I thought of Bessie's reaction. She was glad for me but worried about my making such a long trip. "I'd be grateful, Pearl, if you could keep her company while I'm gone. Reassure her that I'll be back soon." I was sorry to be missing these days with my sister. There'd be so little time left when I got back.

"I will, don't you worry. You just go and have fun. And don't waste your time sending postcards; you'll be back before they arrive anyway. We'll miss you for the next couple of weeks on our outings, though."

My face felt hot. That was the second time she said she'd miss me. "Nonsense. I've just been slowing you down."

We both sat there a moment. I wasn't sure what to add now that we weren't jousting and parrying.

"Pearl, there's something that's been weighing on my mind. Something I need to get off my chest." She smiled at me, as if she'd been waiting for it, which made me want to say it even less than I had before. "All those years ago, I was an ass…"

"Forget it. We were both young and filled with insecurity."

I looked at my shoes, scuffing the tiled floor. I was still insecure, but I could see now that she'd grown strong and confident. Maybe my callousness had affected her much less than I'd thought it had. I sat silently, intensely uncomfortable, wondering what next to say, but fortunately, Pearl asked me more details about my trip. This time, I happily answered. Besides, it would also pass the time.

THE PLANE TOOK OFF TWO HOURS LATE, but I didn't mind — I was giddy as a child on his first flight. I'd flown a few times, but it had only been to Chicago, to visit Ellen's family. Ellen never wanted to go back to Jamaica — I had the misfortune to be married to maybe the only Jamaican person ever who didn't like the heat and whose immediate family were all in America anyway. Besides, she had a terrible fear of flying. I was embarrassed to tell Pearl that I'd never even been to Boca Raton, and as for Europe — it had felt too far away to go on my own, and there was the problem of the language. Lil's caution had dug itself into my gut and festered there long after I realized it was nonsense.

The Air France stewardesses doted on me and I basked in the attention — they were fetching and their perfume made me think of gilded Parisian salons and fine linen. Of luxury. One of them, a brunette with a name tag that said Christine, brought me extra wine and snacks, and another, a blonde named Océane, gave me a special package from first class that included a pair of slippers, a razor, shaving cream, a facecloth, and a blinder you strapped on to help you sleep. Ari was envious — he was seated across the aisle getting bubkes.

The trip to St-Tropez soon went downhill. To say it was a schlep getting there would be an understatement. Arriving in Paris, we learned that a wildcat strike of air traffic controllers the previous day meant the morning's flights were clogged and we were bumped until the afternoon. When we finally got to

Nice, the airport was crawling with nervous police officers armed with assault rifles and funny pillbox caps with large visors. They blew up a piece of unattended luggage while we were herded to a safe distance.

Because of the delays, we were told we wouldn't be able to get to our final destination that night. We had to change buses in St-Raphael anyway, a larger town also on the coast, but we wouldn't make it in time for the last connecting bus to St-Tropez, which left at 7:30 p.m. The driver explained to us that the Tropéziens had fought improvements in access to their town because it was already overrun with visitors and they were worried that if it became easier to get to, the town would lose its charm. A taxi would take us there, but it would cost an outrageous sum that we refused on principle to pay.

It had been a long day. We decided to stay overnight in St-Raphael and catch the first morning bus. Ari informed me that in Peggy Guggenheim's autobiography, he'd read a description of her encountering similar problems nearly seventy years earlier. He meant that it should comfort me, but it didn't, not one bit: what kind of country didn't improve its transportation system in over seventy years?

I spent the bus ride watching the scenery. The sun was setting and fatigue was catching up. Gentle hills dotted with pastel-coloured houses lulled me. Palms, giant ferns, and pine trees rustled in the breeze, the densely forested country-side broken up now and then by vineyards. When fields whirred by, I saw short, gnarly stalks supporting pruned, grape-laden branches that split the earth in perfect rows. In my exhaustion, I imagined the branches to be claws of escaped monsters, tunnelling through the earth and finally breaking free, piercing the soil. Why I was conjuring up monsters in such a beautiful place, I didn't know. This was just life reawakening, a more hopeful image to sit with, as sleep swept over me for the remainder of the journey.

We arrived in St-Raphael after sundown and found space in the Hotel Europe, a small, grimy place that I hoped wasn't as representative of continental accommodation as its name suggested. I slept for about eight hours, but finally the morning tugged at me impatiently. I acquiesced and threw back my sheets in the damp, sticky room. That I should be up so early didn't make sense to me, since we were six hours ahead, not behind, and when I planted my feet on the floor at five, it was actually just eleven at night back in Toronto, about the time I'd normally be feeling sleepy. This was the first time I'd crossed more than one time zone and it made my mind wander as I showered and brushed my teeth.

What would Bessie be doing? Was she wondering how I was making out? Feeling guilty about the risks I was taking? I hoped not. This time I took sole responsibility, even if she'd encouraged me to make the trip. She was probably long since asleep anyway. Maybe the attendants were checking in on her. Then I thought of Pearl. Would she just be slipping into her bed? I pictured her in a silk nightgown, sitting up and propped against a pillow, her legs covered by a thin, smooth blanket, the sheet underneath folded just so, once over top of it. She'd be watching the evening news, or would she be reading one of her books? Did Pearl wear her hair in curlers or sleep with a night cap? Or maybe she'd put on one of those kerchiefs that I'd seen her wear.

I stopped myself, shifted back to Bessie, because why the hell should I be thinking of Pearl now, when I was in Europe for the first time, with everything new and old ahead of me to discover? When it occurred to me that physically, we were at a different point on the earth's curvature, I reformulated Pearl's and Bessie's images, perpendicular to me. It was difficult to conceive of people and beds and cars and buildings existing in a different orientation to what was obviously up and down, and yet not falling off the earth. I found myself whistling and then stopped so Ari could sleep a while longer.

The road to St-Tropez curved south to head along the shoreline of Var province. I saw on my map in the Lonely Planet guide that the coast appeared to have dripped down when the earth was being formed and then congealed into barbed and curly peninsulas, St-Tropez clinging to one of them, near the tip, facing east.

Ari read from my guidebook. "It says artists discovered its location near the turn of the century and chose it over other small towns we're passing through because of the light."

As we rounded the bay through Ste-Maxime, we spotted St-Tropez on the far side and I could see what they meant about the light. It was just a cluster of glowing houses from that distance, but they were finely cut amber diamonds glinting their welcome. The final stretch of road into town was thin, winding, and blocked with cars: serpents with rabbits caught in their throats. The bus fought its way, stop and go, finally pulling into the station by ten o'clock.

The apartment Ari had found us was on the Chemin des Amoureux — Lover's Lane, he translated. It had everything we needed, a kitchenette, a bedroom, a living room with a Murphy bed, and a bathroom with a contraption Ari explained was a bidet — he said it was for washing your privates, but he might've been pulling my leg. The bidet really just looked like an uncovered toilet, and it reminded me of the one in my prison cell, only glistening and white instead of a putrid brown. A small balcony looked over the parking lot, but we could see the entranceway was planted with brightly coloured annuals and several bougainvilleas. I inhaled the sweetness of pink flowers from a tree I couldn't identify. Lil's letter had described how much she'd enjoyed the fragrances here. We didn't linger long; we'd made an appointment at eleven to see Monsieur Provencher, the curator of the St-Tropez Citadel, with whom Ari had spoken.

The citadel, built in the sixteenth century to protect St-Tropez from foreign invaders, stood at the top of a hill, as any self-respecting fortress might. What surprised us was that, after all these years, it pretty much demarcated the edge of town. Observing the cobbled streets and patchwork of houses as we made our way up the hill, it was easy to understand why people would covet this place. The midday sun scattered its rays liberally on the uneven topography of the town's roofs, and though it tried hard to outshine their colours, the soft pink and rust of the clay tiles fought back.

Monsieur Provencher met us at the gate and shook our hands vigorously. With a broad smile, he said, "Welcome. You must call me François."

He couldn't have been more than thirty-five and had a face round and smooth enough to suggest it probably hadn't changed much since the age of four. He wore a light cotton short-sleeved shirt and brown corduroys, and once he'd shaken our hands, he planted his palms firmly against his thighs, inside his pant pockets, removing them only when he started walking.

"*Suivez-moi!*" he said, and led us through the citadel's outer gates, carrying on in French with Ari. His introduction was the extent of his English. He beckoned us over a bridge that spanned a dried-out moat and led to the inner wall of the fortress. There were small windows not far up the wall, making me question whether the moat had ever been filled or if it was only a place to let invaders collect while you tossed boiling oil on them.

François's tiny cramped office had one of the small windows I'd just seen, looking into the moat. I stiffened — the room had the same dimensions and dank smell as my old cell, only there was even less room because of the stacks of paper, desk, shelves, and boxes.

François pointed me to the one chair in front of his desk and I sat while Ari explained that we were trying to locate a house once occupied by Emma Goldman. He explained to François that the location of Bon Esprit had been lost over time, that much mention had been made of it in historical documents, but that no address was ever given. François said that back then there was no need. You simply gave the street name — sometimes even that was unnecessary — and the letter carrier knew where he should deliver it.

Ari translated the conversation.

"What clues do you have?" François asked.

"We know the street name, Chemin St-Antoine, and one letter is addressed to the Maison Mussier. Other than that, she makes reference to seeing the Italian Alps and mentions that there were vineyards nearby."

"Well, at least that is something," he said.

Ari asked about Monsieur Sanschagrin, the old man he'd tried to contact from Toronto, the one with the long memory.

François said he was waiting at the head offices of La Bravade, the town's annual celebration of military independence. François had taken the liberty of arranging an appointment, but now that he realized I didn't speak French, he suggested something else, picking up the phone and dialling as he explained. He had another local contact who spoke English.

He explained, somewhat cryptically, that she was "*assez spéciale*" — "rather special." I didn't know this expression, but Ari said it was a euphemism for saying she was eccentric. In my experience, when people said eccentric, they meant crazy as a loon but were being polite. François spent no more than thirty seconds on the phone and then I heard him say "*D'accord*," and he put down the receiver, amused. The woman with whom he'd spoken had insisted she meet us right away.

Véronique Borduas, a local history buff, François explained, took only ten minutes to arrive, and we were waiting for her on the other side of the moat. She was a sturdy woman — edging towards hefty — and though it was quite hot, she wore a woollen jacket over a shirt splattered with flecks of white and blue paint. The jacket was brightly embroidered at the wrists, open, and hanging down below her hips. A long blue tie-dyed skirt rustled with each stride. Under the skirt, she wore some sort of beige Indian or Pakistani silk pants that fit snugly and crumpled near her feet, making her ankles appear to be wrapped with Tensor bandages.

She extended a limp hand. "Do not press too firmly; I have a strain from painting," she said. The other hand patted the side of her head. She had wiry, greying hair tied in a tight bun, like Aunt Bea from the *Andy Griffith Show*.

After greeting us warmly, she turned to François and her expression abruptly changed. She glared at him through round glasses, whipped a brochure out of a satchel, and waved it about in the air. She proceeded to rant on about something, while François, like a chastened schoolchild, nodded or shook his head obediently each time her voice rose in a question. Ari whispered that she was threatening to resign from the heritage society over the offending brochure. It misquoted a poem by Verlaine, and when she complained to the people who produced it, they weren't sufficiently concerned.

She turned to us as though we'd both understood what she said, and in English puffed, "I have a certain reputation to maintain!" François listened patiently to the outburst and then gently directed her back to the purpose of her visit.

Apparently, she only needed to vent, because hostility changed to friendliness and she began to question us excitedly. Occasionally as an afterthought, she translated for François. As Ari explained things, she nodded vigorously, leaned on one leg, and clasped her hands behind her back. Gnarled toes wiggled out of canvas espadrilles, maybe to relieve the pain of corns or arthritis, I don't know.

After hearing us out, she said, "I do not know of this Goldman woman, but there was a woman from the same period known to people as May la révolutionnaire — could they be one and the same?"

Ari's voice raised half an octave, he was that excited. "Maybe Goldman was known to the townsfolk by another name!" His enthusiasm was short-lived. This "May" had been married to a local fisherman and was a communist from Paris. Goldman was Russian-American, he explained, and was an anarchist. Not only were they different people, but likely they wouldn't even have been friends. Nonetheless, Madame B — that was how I thought of her since I couldn't get my lips around her name — felt she needed to explain to us in detail who May was, and how the town had been somewhat scandalized by her fiery nature and radical politics.

I asked Madame B, "Do you know if it was illegal to be a communist back then?"

"I'm not certain."

"In Canada it was — for quite some time. I knew many people who went to jail for their beliefs."

"How fascinating!"

We showed her Ari's copy of *Living My Life*, which used to be Lil's, so that she could see the pictures. In one of them, Goldman was standing with Modeste Stein and Alexander Berkman. It was taken right in St-Tropez but was so tightly cropped that they might've been anywhere. It impressed Madame B to see that books had been written about Goldman and that St-Tropez was mentioned in them. She considered the photographs and then flipped through the pages as though by feeling the breeze from their fluttering, she might divine a helpful clue.

"Might Goldman have been a friend of Colette's?" She turned to me for the answer. She appeared to have decided that May the Revolutionary was a dead end and also that I was the expert.

"They were only acquaintances," I said. "My sister knew Mrs. Goldman and they met Colette at a party once."

"Your sister met Colette? How marvellous!" she cooed. "You must tell me all about the encounter." Over our ten days there, I was to discover how obsessed the people of St-Tropez were with Colette. Few had ever heard of Goldman, but they prattled on incessantly about Colette this, and Colette that, and did you know Colette wrote *La treille muscate* right here in her house by the same name, and by the way have you been to see her house yet? Though both women lived in St-Tropez during almost exactly the same period, and Colette wasn't even as famous as Goldman in their day, Colette was French and Goldman was a foreigner.

Madame B said, forgetting Colette for a moment, "Will you be speaking to Lucien?" She translated for François.

François said, "She means Monsieur Sanschagrin."

Ari answered, "I'm meeting with him shortly, but my uncle doesn't speak French."

"Yes, yes, your uncle can come with me, of course," she said, and put a finger to her lips, then turned to me. "I know who you must speak to — we must go now to see Pascaline. My own memories will be useless to you; I am only sixty-five and anyway I grew up in northern France. Pascaline, on the other hand, is a woman in her eighties and has lived here her whole life."

"Sounds fine to me," I said, and with that, François and Ari left me to Madame B's mercy and I followed her down the hill and back to town.

We hunted all over town for Pascaline. The woman was elusive but Madame B was dogged. And also chatty. During one of a series of monologues over the course of the few hours we spent walking, she told me she was a retired poetry professor, which explained her outrage at the misquoting of Verlaine, and a history lover — a member of the St-Tropez Heritage Society. "Perhaps for not very much longer!" she added. Her academic area of expertise was an obscure French poet, but she'd taken a particular interest in the life of Colette when she moved to the region in the 1960s.

"Have you ever been to Canada?" I asked.

"No, I won't go to North America," she answered, flatly.

"Why not?"

"I was invited to a conference in Washington once but then I heard that an airplane crashed into the Potomac River from too much ice on its wings. I cancelled my trip. It is too dangerous to travel to such a place."

I didn't understand. "Didn't you say you were from northern France? Aren't the winters just as cold there?"

"Frightfully cold."

"Well ... you could make a trip during the summer," I offered.

"No, I could not. I ask you, what does it say about a civilization where one lives in a place where ice on the wings of an airplane is a known hazard, almost a certainty, given the climate, but one doesn't take reasonable measures to prevent it? What other terrible things might happen to me if I went there?"

She had a point, and besides, had I not just judged St-Tropez for its antiquated transportation infrastructure?

Pascaline proved to be quite mobile for a woman in her eighties. We covered every inch of St-Tropez that afternoon, and everywhere we went, people either told us we must've just missed her (though none had actually seen the woman) or we were pointed to another location where she was likely to be.

As we walked, Madame B stopped any person with grey hair. With my basic French and her occasional translations, I understood that she would start by asking them if they'd heard of Emma. She was likely a friend of Colette's, she said to them, extrapolating from the one time they'd met. Nobody had heard of her. "*Non, vous êtes trop jeune* — she is too young, of course," she'd say, turning to me.

Then she'd ask them if they'd heard of May la révolutionnaire, apparently changing her mind about May's importance and deciding that she should now be a part of our investigation, though Madame B was the one who'd raised her in the first place, and we'd only expressed the slightest interest. None of them had heard of May until she prodded them: "You remember May, she was married to Niel, the fisherman — not his second wife, the one who had the child, but the first one?" Then they all remembered her, but only vaguely, and that line of questioning would peter out. Finally, she asked if they'd seen Pascaline, and though nobody had, they were full of suggestions about where she might be found. Try the Place des Lices. Try her nephew's travel agency. Try the harbour. There had been a funeral that morning at the cathedral and she might be attending.

"Oh, we will go there — it will be letting out now," Madame B said.

"Do you think we should be pestering Pascaline when she's mourning the death of a friend?"

"When you are her age, your friends are dying all the time. It is not a worry."

Did she not realize I wasn't all that much younger than Pascaline myself?

Madame B led us to the cathedral, a majestic building nestled into the oldest part of St-Tropez, amidst a maze of narrow streets that cars squeezed through, causing us to flatten ourselves against building walls, sucking in our guts.

At the cathedral, the funeral had already ended and a few mourners remained to sign the condolence book. Out of embarrassment, I shrank into the shadows while Madame B accosted people, ignoring the fact that some were wiping tears from their eyes. She asked the same three questions. "Emma Goldman?" "May la révolutionnaire — the one married to Niel the fisherman; not the second wife, the one who had the child, but the first?" "Pascaline?" The answers were, no, oh yes — vaguely, and Pascaline? She might be on her way to the cemetery, with the procession we'd just missed.

Surely, she wouldn't...

"Come!" she urged.

The cemetery was sitting on probably the most envied piece of real estate in the whole town. Lying below the sloping face of the citadel, it was a lip of land pouting over the water's edge. Gravestones and crypts were grouped four deep into three aisles, from a white brick wall that fell into the ocean to where the cemetery met the road leading up the side of the hill. The graves were almost all grey or white, and they were planted in white gravel, not grass. On several plots, mourners had deposited five, six, seven pots of brightly coloured flowers.

It was a clear day and by now the early afternoon sun shone from behind us, over the top of the fortress. The sky was an unbroken blue screen stretched over the bay, a colour I'd never before seen and without a single cloud to provide contrast. I craned my neck and the colour deepened the higher I looked, until the sky became the reflection and the ocean the light source.

I realized we were virtually the only ones in the cemetery, that, thank God, we'd missed the funeral procession entirely. For a minute or two, that place — the exquisiteness of it — made me forget the reason we were there. Then, when the nature of our location reminded me of my plans back in Toronto, I wished I could've wrapped that feeling in my arms and held it tight. I'd seen precious few moments of such beauty and tranquility, and when I went home, I'd be giving them up again, for sure. The difference was that this time there'd be no parole, no release.

I sat down on a bench to rest my feet — we'd been walking for two hours now — while Madame B went up to an old man in a small hut, probably the groundskeeper. She came back to say he'd seen Pascaline — the first actual sighting — and that she most likely was on her way to the Banc des mensonges, where she spent the afternoons.

"Banc des mensonges?"

"The Bench of Lies," said Madame B, as if this explained everything.

Off we went to the old harbour. We emerged from one of the side streets on the south end near the Senequier Restaurant, a busy local landmark next to the tourist office. Madame B promised we'd stop for a drink and a bite to eat very soon, but first we shouldn't let Pascaline slip away. Buildings lined the harbour on two adjacent sides, sheltering it from the town like a peaked hat, like the French accent that sometimes covers their vowels. Breathtaking, old, multi-coloured, four- and five-storey structures extended burgundy awnings out onto the boardwalk at street level — they made me think of tongues hanging out in the heat. Peeking through a dense forest of sailboat masts, I watched a motorized yacht come into view and manoeuvre itself to find a place to throw anchor.

The smell of fries and something syrupy reached my nostrils and a steady hum of conversation also wafted from the patios as tourists lounged around tables, facing out to watch the parade of lethargic afternoon wanderers. At the edge of the water, yacht owners hosed down already sparkling decks.

The Bench of Lies was actually two benches, both of them pressed against the wall of a tall stone breakwater that ran parallel to the shore and protected the inner harbour from the eastern sea. Next to the two benches was a staircase leading to the top of the breakwater, where tourists could climb to take pictures of the bay. On one of the benches sat a row of old men, and on the bench next to them, old women. The benches had earned their nickname because old fishermen and their wives sat there weaving tall tales, inflating long-ago catches to the size of legend, or exaggerating the accomplishments of grandchildren.

In the middle of the row of women sat a hunched figure wearing a kerchief, a flowery sundress, and flip-flops. The woman was telling a story, and somehow I knew immediately this was Pascaline. Had her husband been a fisherman? Or maybe she herself had commandeered a boat in her day? Madame B caught the woman's eye, and she stopped speaking to clasp Madame B's hands in hers and kissed her on each cheek. When we were introduced, she gave a gap-toothed smile.

Pascaline urged a few women down to the other end of the bench so that we could sit beside her. The men on the other bench stared disapprovingly. Madame B explained our situation in French, and then there was gesticulation on the part of Pascaline, and pointing towards the ancient tower at the end of the jetty and at the adjacent restaurant. At one point, she waved the back of her hand in the direction of a gap between the restaurant and the tower, as if to sweep invisible dirt through it. Through the gap, we could see a small patch of sandy beach. I heard Pascaline say the word *merde* — shit — and she made a face.

Then Pascaline started talking to me, and I fumbled the phrase, "*Je m'excuse, mais je ne parle pas le français.*" Not very well, in any case, and my accent was appalling. She cackled hysterically and squeezed my arm.

Madame B translated: "When Pascaline was a young woman in the '20s and '30s, she worked as a waitress over there next to the tower." She pointed to a seafood place with a red roof. "It was of course a different restaurant then and it had a sort of — how do you say — trellis that extended over to the tower."

"That must be where my sister and Emma Goldman met Colette."

"How marvellous. You see, we are getting somewhere."

Really, we were getting nowhere. None of this information helped us find Bon Esprit.

"Ask her if she knew Emma Goldman." I hoped I didn't sound too impatient.

"She didn't. Not really. She was telling me of a weekly gathering with a very rude name. People were very disgusting then, with poor sanitation habits. The point of the story was that Pascaline served Madame Goldman drinks at this gathering, but that is all. They exchanged pleasantries. But at least people knew who she was."

"Can you ask if she remembers a Mr. Mussier, and if she knows which house was his? Tell her this was the house that Mrs. Goldman bought when she moved here. It was on the address line of one of Lil's letters."

There was a brief exchange, and then Madame B said,

"She does remember Mr. Mussier. He was a mechanic and she went to grammar school with his wife. They are both dead now and their children have moved away."

"And the house?"

"She doesn't remember exactly which house was theirs, but she says an old neighbour sold the house on behalf of Mrs. Goldman when she left St-Tropez. The neighbour's grand-daughter lives on the Lot des Carles. Perhaps we should go and speak with her. Pascaline says we should also speak to Lucien, but then, your nephew is there with him now, is he not?"

"Yes, that's right," I said, and I had half a mind to go find this neighbour's granddaughter right away, if I could, while Ari was occupied. If I could find Bon Esprit without Ari, in some ways, it would make things a lot simpler, except for how I would explain to him that I'd gone there first, without him.

Madame B squeezed Pascaline's forearm and got up to leave without saying either thank you or goodbye. She rushed on ahead, pointing to restaurants. "We will find your little house eventually, but first, some lunch."

§

Letter from Lil to me, from my collection:

St-Tropez, June 10th, 36

Herman Wolfman
Collins Bay Penitentiary
Collins Bay, Ontario
Canada

Dearest Toshy,

This is the letter I have owed you since arriving in this beautiful country. You deserve much more than the post-cards I've been sending, though you may not even receive any of them before I return home. It's been almost two weeks since I arrived in France, and I never stop marvelling at how glorious it is. Every building, every neatly tended field, and every cobbled street has been tastefully crafted or planted or set in just the right place and then loved, adored, and fawned over by generations of devoted Frenchmen.

We have striking beauty in Canada, but it is of a different kind. A rough and wild vastness, with jagged granite jutting out from between scratchy blueberry bushes, sharp mountains looming over messy pine needle expanses. France just has a certain gentleness to it.

One of the things I like the most is the market, with its pleasing, orderly loveliness. The presentation of the vegetables is something else. The merchants back home could learn a thing or two about how to make them appealing by placing them in precise formations and pyramids, instead of dumping produce carelessly into bins so that fat-fingered women have to drag their knuckles through them to find the one head of lettuce that hasn't had half of its leaves torn off. Of course, the merchants here won't let you touch the produce. That's how it stays nice. Let them serve you, I say. If everything is perfect, why would you care to choose it yourself?

And the fragrances! Peculiar how one's perspective changes when one is overseas. When I think of Canada from far away, the first thing that jumps to mind is Kensington, with its salty fish and sharp cheeses and tangy pickles. I think of Mrs. Eisen's spicy kosher sausages and the sweet scent of Ma's tomato brisket. Here, the aromas are different. Flowers first tickle the nostrils. Flowers I don't know the names of, red and blue and pink ones that grow on vines clinging to the sides of houses or blossoming on trees lining the narrow cobbled streets. And at the market, flavours waft under the canvas awnings, up and down each aisle. Freshly baked berry pies, various loaves and baguettes, and delicate soft cheeses made from the milk of goats! I've spent hours walking through this town just breathing deeply and feeling my heart sing.

You may be asking yourself why I am writing you from St-Tropez when I was supposed to be in Nice. I did go there at first, and spent a week with Emma, helping her type up propaganda material. We stayed in Sasha's apartment, a small place he shares with his companion, Emmy Eckstein. Emmy is the complete opposite of Emma. To think he's been lovers with both women is laughable. Emmy is fearful and unable to cope with his illness in any way, while Emma swoops in and takes charge.

While I typed like a madwoman, Emma spent most of her days at the hospital caring for Sasha. You remember when we helped her type her essay reviewing her life? Well, Sasha's illness has caused her to examine it, yet again. She puts on a brave face, but her oldest friend is terribly ill and could die. I know it is affecting her.

After a week, the apartment was feeling very cramped. Emma asked if I would like to go and visit Bon Esprit, to have a little holiday. I was hurt and embarrassed at first, but Emma assured me I had been a lifesaver but that I'd been too efficient; she'd calculated that the work would take a month and I'd done it in a week. Furthermore, Sasha would soon be well enough to return home and it would be too much with four of us. So, without guilt, I took her keys and set off on the bus to this beautiful little town down the coast.

Sasha did get discharged from the hospital last week, and after I'd been here on my own for a week, Emma returned on Saturday morning. She arrived in the mood for celebration and immediately dragged me to send a wire to a nearby town inviting her friend Peggy Guggenheim and Miss Guggenheim's husband, Arthur, to join us that evening for dinner. (Apparently, when you are as wealthy as she is, you get to keep your maiden name and everyone still calls you "Miss.") Unfortunately, Arthur was in bed with a summer cold, so Miss Guggenheim arrived in her motorcar, husbandless.

It was a spectacular evening. Emma prepared a sumptuous feast, and after two bottles of wine, we tumbled out of the house and walked down to the port. Lanterns were hung everywhere and beer flowed from large barrels. People were laughing and talking and dancing to tinny gramophone recordings out in the open air.

The only thing was the odour. If I have gone on about the pleasant fragrances, I might as well retract everything. I won't go into it except to say that for all of their aesthetic aptitudes, the French can be quite crude. Many people still chuck their "waste" into the nearby ocean and some do this upon arrival at the party. Everyone prays the wind is heading out to sea, but it often isn't. For this reason, they call it "Le Bal de la Merde." I won't translate it. You can ask one of the French Canadian inmates to tell you what it means if you can't figure it out for yourself.

Despite this rather vulgar practice, the pier was so busy you'd have believed the beer were free. After an hour or so, we spotted a woman with the most eccentric attire hanging on the arm of a man twenty years her junior. She had feathers arranged in her hair, Toshy, can you imagine? And jewels everywhere and a pink and green low-cut silk chiffon dress that made her look like an aging harem girl. She turned out to be Colette, the famous French author, who lives right outside of town. Miss Guggenheim was shocked to find out that Emma and Colette had never met, despite having lived for many years in the same small place, and she chastised Emma for being too focused on her international community to see the treasures in her own backyard. Both Madame Colette and Emma have achieved international notoriety for their views on the liberation of female sexuality, though later Emma told me that she found Colette's stand more about hedonism and attention-seeking than a coherent philosophy of sexual freedom for women.

Before you could spit, Miss Guggenheim had marched over and dragged Colette away from her friends to meet Emma and me. Of course, she only included me in the introductions to be polite, and when she mentioned I was studying to be a doctor, I couldn't help but feel it was to prove somehow that I was worth meeting. I'm sure Madame Colette didn't care about me one whit but she was pleased to meet Emma and carried on for a time in halting English, with Emma occasionally switching to halting French to help her out. Finally, Madame Colette said she was leaving town for a few weeks but would we come for dinner upon her return. I had to decline, silently regretting the schedule imposed on me by my medical studies. Emma and Miss Guggenheim accepted her invitation, though, which is for the better, I suppose. What would I have contributed to the conversation? Later, Emma said that she should really meet and talk with the woman before judging her so harshly, but I confess I would love to be a fly on the wall at that dinner. If Emma's judgement turns out to be confirmed, that is to say if she concludes that Colette is an apolitical narcissist, then the polite dinner might turn out to be anything but.

Emma, Miss Guggenheim, and I left the harbour well past midnight, and what was very nice was that for an entire evening, Emma had forgotten sick Sasha and morose Emmy back in Nice.

Before I finish this letter, I should tell you that I have finally been able to talk to Emma about our little concern, and I was relieved that she agreed to help. While she was still in Nice, I had lots of time to find just the right spot (I will tell you all about it when I see you) and now all we have to do is wait for Emma to make her contacts.

My dear Toshy, please keep yourself out of harm's way in that horrible place, and be assured that I will be back there for a return visit sooner than you think.

With all my love,
Your big sister Lil, a.k.a. Woman of the World.

cupid's warped bow

When I was young, very young, I lived with one eye closed, the other squinting, trying to gauge my destiny. I'll admit to a few blushes of optimism along the way, but mostly I was skeptical, apprehensive, as if the day were a land-mine waiting to blow me up if I stepped in the wrong spot. Later, I learned to live in the present, but not in gleeful abandon, the way people suggest when they use that expression. It was more like a minute-by-minute, second-by-second crawl, with my head down and eyes averted, afraid that if I peeked ahead, what I'd see would just be worse.

This was the truth of it: I was never a good-looking man. When I say that, it isn't false modesty, just the mirror's painful honesty slapping me in the face. Even after my lip operation, there was never a perfect Cupid's bow. The scarring was thick, prominent. And before it? That little notch stood out plainly for all to see.

When I was in my teens, my physique wasn't bad, but it was as much a curse as the lip. I played baseball and street hockey, and running was a speciality, even if it was only from the cops. The five-hundred-yard dash down an alleyway and the high vault over a fence were events that kept me in good shape. My muscles would draw a girl in, especially in the summer if I was in short sleeves or wearing an undershirt. Then it never failed: I'd watch her smile flicker as her eyes settled on my mouth. I grew a sparse moustache as soon as hair sprouted up there, but it was just tufts of grass in cracked cement.

Then one of two things would happen: either her smile would deepen, broadening and losing its flirtatiousness so that it became one of generosity or pity, or else her eyes would move to a distant point beyond me, or beside me, or at my feet, and the girl would begin to fumble in her purse as if she'd just remembered to search for something. Something. Anything but me.

One day in October — the October of the year before I went to jail — I was hanging around Baldwin Street in front of Nesker's, killing time in the late afternoon. As I've mentioned, I knew Kensington best from the backside, the yards behind stores, the alleys and secret laneways, which ones gave onto escape routes or holes under fences and which ones ended in brick walls or had clothesline spider-webs to tangle you on the run. Baldwin Street I knew from the front too. That was where I nicked produce most often, because it was one of the busiest places, easiest to tuck something away while women haggled with the shop-keep.

That day in October, I stood leaning against a rickety staircase that led to the apartments above Nesker's. My hands were in my pockets but my coat was unbuttoned even though it was cold out, because when it was done up I looked square, and I already had enough working against me in that area. The air was crisp but it had been a sunny day, and long shadows raced ahead as people walked briskly down the street.

When I was sure the Neskers and their enormous son were occupied with customers, I slipped a few dried figs into my pocket. Because the produce the Neskers displayed out-side was meagre, they didn't often come out of their shop. Childlike paintings of a chicken on one window and a duck on the other tipped people off to the fact that they sold poultry inside, but they didn't really need to advertise. As I've mentioned, their produce was the best.

I surveyed the local activity. Across the street, between two electricity poles, a few vegetable stands were set up in front of another shop and several women were milling about inspecting tomatoes and beets. A fishy scent filled the air; it was coming from the store beside the vegetables.

That's when I saw her — the girl I'd spotted at the *Party* party, the one Lil had brought us to and then dragged us away from shortly thereafter. I couldn't believe my luck. She paused in front of the fish store, and as the owner was wrapping her selection in newspaper, the girl glanced my way. I quickly averted my eyes, not wanting to suffer the usual embarrassment, but five months had passed; I knew I should take another look, just to be sure.

She was staring right at me, smiling. A large, stylish hat covered one eye, but the other held its regard and was clearly directed at me. There was no mistaking it because my back was to a wall and nobody else was near me. I found myself smiling too, until from sheer awkwardness I looked away again, this time down at my shabby shoes. I assumed she couldn't see me very well.

When I looked back, the girl was crossing the street. She stopped at Nesker's, a few feet away, and I felt my heart race. She picked at the fingers of a lambskin glove and then with a fingernail casually made furrows in the dried beans. Up close, her figure was even more terrific than I'd remembered. A winter coat cinched her waist, highlighting breathtaking curves. Her brown hair was pinned up, under the hat. The fish she'd bought was tucked under her arm, wrapped in the latest issue of the *Vochenblatt*. She began looking at the produce.

"They have more inside," I said, then immediately wanted to kick myself. The *s* had come out slurred, and I was sure I'd grimaced, my cheeks apelike.

She smiled at me and said, "Thanks. I'm just browsing." Even that close, the smile didn't change. No pity whatsoever, only sparkle. Such full, perfect lips.

Just then, Nesker came out of his shop. He had his eye on me and at first didn't see the girl. Nesker was a short man with a brown, neatly trimmed beard, and that day he was wearing a long dark coat smeared with chicken guts, and under it a shirt and tie.

"G'won — get lost, kid. You can't hang around here."

"It's a free world," I protested, and I didn't move. "I'm not in front of your store; I can be here if I want."

"Go and be free over there," he said, pointing to the curb. "You hang around here and I'll call the cops on you, Toshy. Don't think I don't know what you're up to. Don't make me pay a visit to your father." Then he saw the girl. "If this young lady weren't here, I'd ask you to empty your pockets right now, but I won't embarrass you in front of her."

What a joke that was; I was already humiliated.

The girl said, "Actually, he's with me," and held her arm out. "Come; let's get going now, Toshy. I don't believe I want to shop here after all."

Astonished, but trying not to show it, I took her arm and we crossed the street, leaving Mr. Nesker shaking his head. When he'd gone inside and we were a block away, she unlaced her arm.

"I'm Gussie Kander."

I wiped my palms and shook her hand. "Toshy Wolfman," I said. "I remember you from that party." She was still smiling. Could she actually be flirting with me? "Thanks for ... you know, back there."

"My pleasure."

"You know, I didn't take anything."

"Of course not." She winked. My neck felt as if a steaming cloth had been laid upon it, and suddenly I was warm enough that I could've thrown my coat off altogether. I remembered that Lil had said my lip projected danger; maybe this girl was attracted to danger.

We went and had a soda that afternoon, and the next, and the next, and the next. I could hardly believe what was happening. It was as though I'd suddenly inhabited someone else's life — someone more popular, someone normal. Gussie Kander was from a different world, one where shopping for fish was a diversion, indulged in when servants had their day off or to get out of the house. I learned her father was a big-shot milliner with several factories and her mother's parents had been rich importers-exporters back in Chemnitz. The Kanders had a huge home on Highland Avenue with a coach house for the help. She'd travelled to Germany and Holland in the summer. I was embarrassed to tell her my parents were shopkeepers and that my sister had been working as a maid. I didn't mention Lil's political work. I didn't know what Gussie would've said about that. If she'd been at the *Party* party because she had communist leanings, mentioning the anarchists might have turned things sour.

I was so smitten that it took me five weeks to realize she hadn't introduced me to a single person. When I suggested we meet some of her friends, she made excuses. After that, I became aware of little things. Like we'd be walking down Spadina and suddenly she'd pull me into a shop. I'd turn back to see a couple of rich ladies standing across the street. Once, she suggested that she buy me a nicer pair of pants or a new shirt. I refused, saying I couldn't take presents from her, even though I was secretly wishing she'd buy them anyway. She didn't. Gussie didn't go to College Street. Too noisy, she said, and yet we'd spend time on Spadina, where the ruckus sometimes made College seem like a monastery.

Also, we'd only ever been out together once on the week-end, to go dancing. There were several dance halls nearby, and I'd only been to one of them, the Embassy, at Bloor and Belair, the year before when my sisters took me to hear the Ferde Mowry Orchestra. I suggested we go to the Palais Royale because I'd never been there. It was just at the foot of Bathurst Street, and Bert Niosi had been making a name for himself there for several years already. Gussie didn't want to go there. She said she'd never been to the Balmy Beach Club.

"Doesn't that anti-Semitic gang hang around there?"

"Are you thinking of wearing a *kipa*?"

"No, it's just…"

"Well, then don't worry about it. They exaggerate all that stuff. Besides, we won't be advertising."

I gave in. One Saturday in November, Bessie and Lil lent me money and I took Gussie on the Queen Street car all the way over to Woodbine.

It turned out it was a taxi-dance, which meant you paid as you went, and I could see lots of guys and girls had gone with their friends instead of on dates. The boys milled about the edges behind barriers leading to the dance floor. Were these the gang members? They'd lean against any wall or post, trying to act nonchalant, but eventually I saw they were only getting up the nerve to ask a girl to dance. The brave ones bought a ticket at a booth and the ticket-takers let them on the dance floor at the next set. It smelled of beer and freshly baked pretzels.

I was proud to be there with Gussie, relieved I wasn't with my sisters, or worse, alone. I was also proud to be with someone as fancy as her. My parents had tried to drum working-class pride into me, but that would only really come with age and maturity, and back then I had neither. I must've behaved like a damned fool that night, strutting about with Gussie on my arm, faking my way through the foxtrot and the waltz. It was only later that I admitted the truth: Gussie had been looking at everyone except me, hardly ever meeting my eyes.

One Thursday evening, just over a month after our first date, we arranged to meet at a small ice cream parlour in Kensington. We sat at a table at the back, away from the window. She took the chair facing the door, as she always did, and in the middle of describing her family's plans to go skiing in Quebec, I saw her blanch. I turned to see two young women had walked in. Noticing us, they came over to give Gussie a kiss.

Silence followed, and then Gussie finally said, "Um, this is Toshy Wolfman. Toshy, my friends Shirley and Bernice."

"Gussie and I have been going together," I added, enunciating each syllable.

Gussie looked like she'd just swallowed a caterpillar. Was it the way my words had sounded? I'd been so careful; nonetheless, I immediately wished I'd kept my mouth shut, my big gaping maw. Maybe it was obvious we were going together and drawing attention to it was crass. Maybe Gussie wasn't ready to tell anyone. Maybe she wanted it to be our little secret for a while and I'd ruined the romance. Those were my thoughts then, naïve as I was.

Until that moment, her friends didn't really have a good view of me. Now, their smiles, huge and open when I'd started to speak, shifted ever so slightly. Another person might not have seen it, but I was used to this. I hunted for it, in the corners of a girl's mouth, in the lines beside her eyes, in the tightening of her cheek muscles. They'd seen my lip, or maybe in this case, my clothes too. Not only were they drab and ordinary, but the kind of shirt I wore that day was billowy, shapeless, and didn't even show my muscles. I might as well have been a little boy being introduced to wealthy relatives.

They said, "Pleased to meet you," and then quickly explained how they were looking for someone but must've gotten the wrong place. How nice it was that they'd met me. There were quick goodbyes, and when they left it was as though they swept all the air out with them.

That was the last time Gussie and I saw one another. That evening, we finished our ice cream without saying much, and though we made plans — for Monday, of course — Monday came and I waited by Nesker's for an hour before admitting to myself that she wasn't going to show. Finally Mrs. Nesker came out to close shop and tsk-tsked.

Gussie never came by my parents' store or called with an explanation. I would've called her — by that point I was way beyond pride — but she'd never given me her number. Each time we'd had a date, the arrangements had been made at the end of the previous one. A week later, I considered going to her house, but I was afraid to run into her father.

When two weeks had come and gone without word I ventured out on Saturday night for a walk. I ended up over on College Street, and as I walked past the Rose Café, I looked in the window. There was Gussie, sitting with friends, sharing a laugh.

She did go out on College, after all.

Her eyes flickered my way, and her smile wilted. Then, as quickly as it had happened, she glanced away and continued talking with her friends.

A block later, a wave of nausea surged up until I felt it in my chest, then at the back of my throat, and, though I tried to hold it back by closing my mouth, it was as though I was still a baby and my palate had never been repaired. The sick came up and out my nostrils. It seeped through my teeth and oozed through the notch. Finally, I gave up, choking and spewing, open-jawed, into the gutter.

Later that night, when Bessie came back from the MacNabbs, she found me sulking on my bed. She parked herself beside me and tilted my chin up.

"Hey, hey. What's wrong?"

"Aw, Bessie, how could I have been so stupid?" I pulled my face away.

"Gussie?"

"*Gussie.*" I said it as if it were a disease. "How could I have thought she'd really *like* me?"

She put her arm around me. "One day, you'll meet someone who sees how beautiful you are." I looked at her and frowned, but then she clarified: "You're a good person, not like that stuck-up snob."

"No, I won't, because I'm never letting anyone make a fool of me like that. Never again."

"You shouldn't be so hard on yourself. We all do silly things when we're lonely. People like that make us feel better for a short time, even if we know that in the long run, they might make us feel worse."

Bessie was giving me more credit than I deserved. I'd

had no idea things with Gussie might sour, that I could feel that bad.

I turned to her and saw she was miles away. Was she thinking about Irv? That didn't make sense; how could she have known he'd be struck by a streetcar and leave her a widow? Plus, Irv really *was* a good person, and besides, if Bessie ever did get into a situation like mine, and I couldn't imagine she would, it'd be different. She was wise to the ways of the world, I was beginning to see that for the first time. Not prone to brazen impulses, like Lil. Not silly and blind, like me.

BESSIE TRIED VALIANTLY to lift my spirits, as did the rest of the family, but there was no being around me for the next five months. When I was arrested and convicted that spring, I'm sure nobody imagined what I really felt. It was a relief. I wasn't going to have to worry anymore whether or not I'd run into Gussie, and the possibility of female rejection would be delayed for more than a decade.

§

After that first pottery lesson, my friendship with Bernie carried on, except it felt like a layer of dust had settled over it and neither of us could be bothered to sweep it away. The dust dulled our interaction, made it slightly fuzzy, so in my memory, very little stood out. I still went to discussion group, we still had a smoke together and played cards, and we even still showered together, though not side by side.

To make any serious alteration to the routine would've been to act as though something had happened, and I told myself I might've been mistaken. The stress of prison life had gotten to me. I was too sensitive and I'd snapped for no real reason. Bernie was affectionate, nothing more.

A few days later, I apologized.

"Forget it, this heat is making us all *meshuga*," he said, and smiled generously.

He didn't want to mention if there'd been a misunderstanding any more than I did, because that would've been to name it. I was grateful. Instead, we let that film collect over us. The next few weeks took on the quality of a dream, but not a nice one, or an interesting one either — just a very long and tiresome one in which so little happened that you began to pray you'd wake up, just to end it. I'd pass Bernie in the corridors or in the yard, and we'd say hi, politely, as if we were only acquaintances, but then later we'd make small talk, usually in a gathering of people out in the yard. Bernie would be his usual joking self but he wouldn't meet my eyes. We went to pottery class together, but Bernie spent time working on his projects and I took advantage of the instructor to better my skills. One day, our disaffected encounters frustrated me so much that I caught myself wishing for something to happen, just anything that would break the strain and the tedium.

I should've known better than to make wishes; they usually came to pass, only with some cruel twist. I'd wished my parents would stop thinking of me as stupid, but when they learned of my eidetic memory, they only saw it as a skill to be exploited, the way you might use a horse to pull a plough. I'd hoped for a girlfriend and I'd gotten Gussie, who'd then callously dumped me. I'd longed for my lip to be repaired ... that hadn't come true yet, but I was nervous of what might happen if it did.

By a few weeks into August, the summer already felt like it'd hung around too long, a supper guest that starts off amusing and then starts to grate. The heat hadn't let up any, and the work on the wharf wasn't much relief. I'd had to suffer a couple of encounters with Red Humphries along the way, and the prison-issued hats barely kept us this side of heatstroke. Later, in our cells, it was back to relentless sweating. At night, I'd taken to sleeping beside my bunk with only a blanket underneath me, preferring the cool of the hard floor to the heat of my lumpy mattress.

Bernie and I spent another listless Saturday together. Even his opening curse at discussion group was lacklustre: "*Baruch ata adonai*, may our captors know the scorching desert while we bathe in an oasis." Not up to par at all. Everybody just said, "Amen," but solemnly, no repressed smiles. We mumbled half-heartedly through group, then Bernie and I went to pottery class, where we prodded and tore at clay like Neanderthals hovering over fresh kill.

I couldn't stand it anymore. When we were washing up after class, I asked Bernie if he wanted to play a game of cards. He smiled and said sure, and so we decided to retire to the shade of his cell for a game of canasta.

We played cross-legged on his bunk, side by side, our backs to the wall with the cards between us. The afternoon sun shone into the cell from a window across the range and crept slowly up to the bunk, and then over it, as we inched farther and farther from its melting rays. When we reached the end of the mattress, Bernie got up to rig his blanket over the opening of the cell. A guard might remove it, but for now, it was worth taking a chance. It reminded me of a tree fort I'd made as a kid. With this rare privacy, we settled back into the game.

When we'd played two hands and I'd won them both, Bernie slapped my thigh and said, "Lucky we have nothing to bet on, or I'd be broke!"

I laughed with him, a rare thing these past weeks. Then, I noticed he'd casually left his hand on my leg, up above the knee. Palm up, but resting there nonetheless.

I felt the air in my lungs thicken. Holding it in my chest a moment, I vowed not to react like last time. Casually as I could, I gathered the cards and stretched my arms high above my head. I moved my thigh slightly, hoping it would dislodge the hand, but it didn't. Bernie was watching me, smiling. I sighed deeply, as though resting from the exhausting card game, and closed my eyes to work out how best to make an exit.

Then I felt his breath on my neck. I turned to find him leaning in, his own eyes closed, as if to kiss me, but he was frozen there, maybe waiting for me to meet him halfway, and now his breath was on my face, warm, moist but slightly sour. I pulled sharply away and stood up.

"Bernie..."

"It's okay," he said. "It's always scary at first."

I felt nauseated. I wasn't sure what would be worse — kissing him or the more sickening prospect, if I didn't, of the unravelling of our friendship. I looked down at my shoes.

"I ... I can't."

"Yes, you can, nobody can see us. We'll be quiet."

"No ... you ... you don't understand. I don't ... Bernie, I know there aren't any girls in here, and some guys ... because they don't have girls, they..." My words came out soupy and slurred — just about as muddled as the thoughts that produced them.

"It's not because we don't have girls." He barely shifted, but his body noticeably tightened, withdrew upon itself.

"I know how it is ... I've heard ... a few of the guys ... the ones down at the end of the row. I heard they have wives back home."

"Maybe they do. Doesn't mean shit. You hear guys saying, 'It's only while I'm in here,' or, 'Close your eyes and it doesn't matter.' I can tell you, it's all bull. It's just what those guys tell themselves."

He'd trounced on my last rationalization; I had no others. There was no accounting for what he was doing now, for who he was, except... "Then ... you mean you're really ... a..." I couldn't get the words out.

"...a homosexual pervert. You can say it. Only I'd prefer if you didn't." His voice was acidic, burning those two words into the air between us, and now it was as though I were seeing them on a page and would never get them out of my head.

"I'm sorry. I don't know what I'm…"

"It's okay. Listen, Toshy, it's real simple. I like guys — I have since before I got in here and I will when I get out." His voice, all at once, had risen to a crescendo.

"Sh! Someone will hear."

"Ach, nobody cares who doesn't already know. Anyway, I just figured you might feel the same way." There was lightness to his tone now; he spoke as if he were a balloon deflating, and his shoulders relaxed. "No harm in trying."

But of course there might be harm: how could he not be worried about what would happen now?

"I like you, Bernie. Really. But … it's just … you know…"

"As a friend." He leaned back against the wall. "Just tell me: is it me, or do you actually like girls?"

"Of course I do!" Now I'd shouted. Then more softly, "I mean, it's not you, Bernie. I really like girls." I squashed an old cigarette butt with the toe of my shoe. "Not that it's done me any good. They don't seem to like me back."

"Well, it's a cryin' shame," he said.

I remembered Gussie then, and how she'd appeared to like me well enough, but then she'd dumped me. Was she as uninterested in having sex with me as I was with Bernie? Then it occurred to me that this was the first time I'd ever been on the other side of rejection. What I'd done to Pearl might've been mean, but she wasn't actually interested in me. This had an unfamiliar taste, and I couldn't say if I liked it much better. I wasn't proud to admit it, but I swished that taste around in my mouth a little, as though it were a rare wine you might try at a party, and that you savoured just to see if you could tell the difference from the rotgut you were used to. A bit sweeter on the palate, I thought, but with a sour aftertaste.

I wasn't sure how to behave now that I was the one inflicting wounds, instead of receiving them, but when I looked at Bernie's face, he didn't appear wounded at all. I saw casual disappointment, and frankly, about as much as you might feel if you'd hoped for cake and instead gotten dried fruit. The kind that passes in about thirty seconds. For a moment, I was insulted; maybe to him, I'd been just any old fellow. Maybe his affections would have turned to anyone he happened to be alone with.

However, when I looked more closely, I saw that what I'd mistaken for disappointment was more like exhaustion. Maybe it was a romantic involvement he wanted, not just sex, and he'd pinned all his hopes on me. I became worried again; if all of the energy he'd put into spending time with me wasn't about friendship, he might be so embittered that he'd now pull away. He might feel the same as I had with Gussie, except unlike me, he wouldn't empty his stomach in a gutter and then retreat to solitude. Bernie was resilient. He'd invest time in another fellow who might turn out to be like him.

There was no way to tell, because I couldn't bring myself to ask. I thought of my sister Lil, how she faced challenges head-on, how brave she could be in uncomfortable situations. I remembered how she'd stood up to Emma and it had earned her respect, and how that respect had turned into friendship. I'd stood up but then retreated. I didn't have her kind of courage.

Something sure had happened, just as I'd wished, and once again, there'd been a cruel twist. Soon after, Bernie did get involved with someone else — a Metis guy named Gaétan, whose cell was on the lower range. I still went to discussion group and pottery class, but sporadically. Bernie and I didn't take showers together anymore, and I wasn't sure who was avoiding whom more.

I convinced myself there weren't many opportunities to deal with the situation directly. Bernie had moved on; it was hard to get him alone. I'd been right; he hadn't really been interested in my friendship. I began to notice that a couple of the other guys in the discussion group were that way too, and saw, from a distance, that they shared something with Bernie that I now never would: secrets, closeness, loyalty.

Sometimes, I paired up with Gaétan on our walks to the wharf. I found little ways to ask about Bernie, but it was difficult. I didn't want him to think I was moving in on his boyfriend. Bernie had told him I knew about their relationship. Gaétan was a man in his thirties from Clarence Creek, a farming community near Ottawa. He was in jail for robbing the Royal Bank branch in Plantagenet, a neighbouring town, but you would never have guessed it; he had skinny arms and legs and an honest face that suggested he might bring flowers to his grandmother on Sundays.

One Monday morning in early September, we set out at dawn to begin our last week of work down at the harbour. Our project was almost finished, and though we were experiencing an Indian summer, the water would soon be too cold to work in anyway. Some of the fellows had already been pulled back onto other crews, Bernie included. We were led into town double file, and I paired up with Gaétan again. While we walked, we shared stories from back home, kicking up damp fallen leaves that sweetened the air.

Red Humphries was walking two rows ahead of us and I noticed him turning around every now and then to glance our way. He strained to see us against the rising sun, and it accentuated the suspicion he was already exhibiting. I worried he could overhear us, he was that close. Nervous of what Gaétan might casually reveal about him and Bernie, I tried to steer the conversation towards safer topics. I told him about Bessie and Lil, about my parents' store, about escaping from the police through the alleys of Kensington. He told me about his sister Francine and her husband, Marc, and how they were preparing to take over the farm when his parents got too old.

"They were counted on me because I am the oldest, but then I tell them I am never to marry and have children. First, they tell themselves this is because I will becoming a priest and this make them very happy, but when I say that I just don't wanting to marry, they figure it out. They change all the attentions to Francine and Marc. Francine will producing many good little Catholics to help around the farm."

"Were they disappointed to find out ... you know...?"

"*Caaaalline*, what do you think? They almost don't talking to me. They are more disappointing at that time than later when I rob the bank. They always are writing to me letters to say, talk to the prison priest or else I go to hell. I write back and say, I am already here!" He started laughing, but then the laughter petered out. "They are afraid of what is different."

"I know that feeling."

"But Bernie, he say you were..."

"No, not like that. I'm talking about this." I pointed to my lip. "And I was born with the roof of my mouth split in half, too. That's why I sometimes talk funny." I had no idea why I was telling him all of this. We weren't even close.

"Oh, you are ... how do you say, *gueule-de-loup*."

"I'm what?"

"We say, 'mouth of the wolf.' But maybe yours is not mouth of the wolf — you only have one thing there." He pointed to my notch. "*Gueule-de-loup* is for when there are two, I think. I don't remember the other word when there's just one. Anyway, it make you look like, 'don't mess with me.' That's good here." He smiled.

Gaétan had no idea how ineffective that supposed warning had been. As if hearing my thoughts, Red looked back again.

"My sister Lillian once told me people thought I looked dangerous. I think I like that wolf thing of yours. Especially 'cause of my last name."

"My mother, she is Cree. She say the wolf is *courageux*. And strong. He can be independent, but then he always come back to the gang when he is ready."

I was pleased at this new way of looking at my condition, a new definition that I was disappointed to have lived all those years without knowing:

Wolf-mouth n. (wʊlfmaʊθ)
1. *A malformation of the lip such that instead of an adorable bunny rabbit, a devious serpent, or a stupid ape, people see a brave and ferocious wolf. Especially if they speak French.*

We reached the wharf, and the line reformed into a group surrounded by guards, while the foremen talked to one another, deciding how to best deploy us into work-groups. Humphries moved to the other side of Gaétan and whispered in his ear. He stared into my eyes as he did it.

The colour drained from Gaétan's face. "Go to mind your own business, Red," he said, but weakly.

"Why? Don't you want your retard friend here to know you're queer?"

"What about you, Red? You were sucking my cock last month and it don't bothering you then."

I didn't know if that was true, but it sure had the effect Gaétan wanted, no doubt about it. Red clenched and unclenched his fists at his sides, then clocked him so fast that I barely saw him raise his arm. Gaétan went down, and the men instantly formed a circle around them. I looked for the guards, but the only one I could see through the crowd was looking on, snickering. Red approached Gaétan, who lay on his back in the dirt, and he kicked him, then retracted his leg for another, and another.

I stood by, at first, while Red continued his assault. I was afraid if I helped, Red would think I was like Gaétan and Bernie. He'd make my life even more miserable. I even thought, maybe if I join in, Red'll stop bothering me. Could I actually *do* that? The temptation was blinding, almost sickening.

Then I saw the blood on Gaétan's face, saw him doubled up to protect himself from the assault. I saw his anguish, which might very well have been my anguish, had Red's whim blown another way.

I threw myself at Red in a football tackle, hard enough that when my shoulder hit his chest, I felt the thud reverberate down my spine, even as we toppled backwards onto the ground. I landed on top but didn't stay that way for long. We tumbled and flailed, and I remember getting in a few punches to his head, but I also remember blows hitting my sides and my neck, until I ended up on top again, with Red pinned underneath, his right arm under my left knee, his chest under the other. I felt a surge of power rising in my chest. Finally, I had him in a position of vulnerability. I didn't even care what happened next. That people saw us like this, me on top, Red squirming underneath — it was enough.

I didn't consider his free arm.

There must've been something sharp on the ground, a piece of glass or jagged metal, I couldn't see what it was, and he must've come upon it as he groped about for a way to regain the upper hand. I remember the chants around us, and in the corner of my eye, a guard pushing through the crowd. I turned towards the guard, and as I did, there was a blur much closer in my field of vision: Red's arm swinging up.

I don't know if turning to the guard saved me or not. Maybe if I'd turned the other way, Red would've missed. Or, maybe he would've stabbed me in the neck and it would've been the end of me. Instead, whatever he had in his hand sliced into my top lip and tore upwards. I fell off him and clutched at my mouth, the blood pouring through my fingers, and the last thing I remember was Red's foot coming towards my head.

I woke up minutes later to find people standing over me, a cloth pressed to my mouth, and one of the foremen shouting for help. The pain was searing; its intensity shocked me. I couldn't see Gaétan or Red. They took me to Kingston Pen and left me in the surgery with a guard posted at the door, as if I were in any condition to escape or had any notion to do myself more harm than had already been inflicted. I glanced about for a mirror but there wasn't one. A metal operating table dominated the room, and beside it a gleaming gas and oxygen apparatus that looked as though it had never been used. Most inmates had their medical needs taken care of on-site at Kingston, and they brought in outside specialists if required, but Lil had explained that, according to her research, the care was uncertain at best; to save money, they gave you the bare minimum treatment, and the quality of that treatment depended on which doctor you got.

The bandage on my face was enormous and weighty. Underneath, the throbbing was relentless. It felt as though whatever had cut me had either hooked on the notch in my lip and finished the job that had begun in the womb, giving me a full cleft now, or had made a second one, giving me a wolf-mouth. What would Gaétan think if he learned I had a real one now, from defending him. What had happened to him after the fight? Finally, the nurse came back to fuss at a cabinet off to the side, then gave me a needle that knocked me out again. I was grateful; I'd barely felt the cut when it had happened, but it was now excruciating, and I wanted a smoke more than life itself.

When I woke up from my operation, Nurse Grace was looking down, smiling. I felt her hand stroking mine and she got up to adjust the blankets. I blinked a few times, and looked about, expecting to see the room I remembered from the Hospital for Sick Children in Toronto, the gurgling radiator by the window, the roof tiles that I had counted over and over again. Maybe Ma and Pop would be coming in the door for a visit.

Nurse Grace said, "You're a lucky man, Toshy Wolfman. You have people who care about you very much."

My eyes cleared, and I saw that her greying hair was completely white now, and that I wasn't in the Hospital for

Sick Children at all, nor was I in the surgery at Kingston Pen either. I remembered that Pop was dead and I was in jail. I remembered Gaétan and Red Humphries, and the fight. I didn't recognize my hospital room, and Nurse Grace was not wearing her nurse's cap or uniform.

I tried to say something, but only a muffled squawk escaped, and it hurt like hell. Bandages covered my whole mouth and my lip felt gargantuan underneath them.

"Hush hush, love. You shouldn't try to speak just yet."

And then I drifted off again. When I awoke next, Nurse Grace was arranging flowers in the corner. I shifted under the covers, and she saw me stirring.

"Well, good morning, young man. Here, let me help you." She went to the foot of the bed and cranked a lever that tilted the back upright until I was facing her. The lines around her eyes and mouth made her seem even kinder than I remembered. She wore an elegant jacket and skirt.

"I expect you're wondering where you are, and who I am. I don't expect you'll recognize me, but I remember you."

I tried to mumble a response. She was a guardian angel, that's who she was — appearing at the most desperate moments of my life to protect me, care for me. I wanted to tell her I did remember, that I could never forget.

"Shh. Just be still and don't try to speak or the stitches will come out, and we wouldn't want that, would we? You are in Kingston General Hospital and my name is Mrs. Grace Fister. I was your nurse when you were a small child, back in Toronto." I knew that part, I knew much more than that. I knew that she was a Lady, even though she didn't say so. I knew she'd auctioned her wedding gift, the brooch containing the magnificent Orange Sunset, to help her husband save his company, that the diamond had been purchased by Rupert MacNabb, and that I was in jail now because of it.

"I'm friends with your sister Lillian now. We are colleagues in the Prisoners Support Guild. I told you that you're a lucky man, and it's true. I have been meeting with the prison warden about the state of his medical facilities — my pet cause these days — and he is a very accommodating man. I told him that if anything ever happened to you, I wanted to hear about it immediately. I told him if your family and I weren't both notified right away, there'd be hell to pay."

She laughed at that. "I haven't the faintest idea what I could do to him, but people are quite afraid of a woman with a title. Stick 'Lady' in front of your name and they very nearly shiver when you walk in the room! Anyway, when he wired me to say what had happened, I wired back to say he'd better get the best surgeon and that I'd pay for the operation to close the cleft you were born with, as long as they were repairing the other tear. I came straight to Kingston on the next train. Your mother and sisters will be arriving on the weekend — they're closing the store to come; that's how worried they are about you."

There had been a second tear, after all.

"You'll find, when you take those bandages off and everything's healed up nicely, that your lip is good as new. Apart from a bit of scarring, which I'm afraid is unavoidable, you'll be just like anyone else now."

I had to see it to believe it, and even so, I doubted I'd be like everyone else. Still, I couldn't help feeling hopeful.

She squeezed my hand.

I couldn't speak, I couldn't smile, I couldn't do anything, but what did it matter? Even if I'd been able to, no words would've been adequate thanks, no smile broad enough to express my joy.

No act of gratitude was grand enough to repay her, or at least none that I had the nerve to carry out until all these years later, when, sadly, Lady Fister would be long dead, and her kindness forgotten by everyone but Bessie, me, and no doubt the granddaughter who took after her in so many ways.

§

Letter from Lil to Emma Goldman, from the Berkeley archives:

Toronto, September 12th 36

Mrs. E.G. Colton,
St. Tropez (Var)
France

Dearest Emma,

Great sadness filled me when I read your letter. I have written separately to Emmy, who I imagine these days must be hanging on by a thread. When I was there visiting you, it was evident your dear Sasha was not well, but none of us could have predicted that he would be so depressed as to take his own life. No wonder you did not believe it at first.

His suicide has left me pondering this subject: life must be difficult for people like you and Sasha, who have spent your lives giving to others, and who have been hounded every step of the way. You at least have taken joy in the simple pleasures such as friendship, good food and wine, and the appreciation of art and poetry. These have sustained you, but what did Sasha have, apart from Emmy? Perhaps love isn't enough, when declining health and age weaken a person's defences against his old demons. Please know that I am there in spirit, and were it not for school and financial constraints, I would be there again in a heartbeat.

As I write this letter, I am staring out the window in the general direction of the Atlantic Ocean and France, but you'll forgive me if my mind lingers, as it travels that distance, on my poor brother, still locked up in Kingston. I worry he will emerge from prison as haunted by his time there as Sasha was. Will he end up a cynical old man, bitter and inconsolable? How will he face sickness and the march of years?

I should really be concerned with what sustains him now through the long nights in his cell. He was in a terrible fight not long ago, in which another inmate sliced his lip open in the most horrible way. Thanks to the kindness and generosity of Lady Fister, they have repaired it and also fixed his harelip, but the incident has left us terribly frightened for him. When we visited him in the hospital, he was thinner and more withdrawn than I've ever seen him. There was almost no trace of the cheerful little boy I remember, the one who collected pennies and trinkets to hide in the wall behind our local pharmacy, who would sit in the alley with me, surveying the treasures we would spread out between our legs, his eyes glinting with excitement and possibility. On a previous visit, he had told me he has made a friend, but while we were there, they transferred Toshy back from the hospital to the infirmary at the prison, and nobody came by to see him. Maybe it's nothing. Maybe they don't even allow him to have visitors. All I know is that this has reaffirmed my work with the Prisoners Support Guild.

As I write these things, I am certain they must be of no concern to you, with your heart breaking for poor Sasha, and your ears burning with the news of the Spanish Civil War. We had such hope when the Popular Front was elected, do you remember? Now to hear of the terrible military uprising, the world feels quite bleak these days. I was glad to hear that your comrade Mr. Souchy has offered you a chance to help with the resistance efforts, but it is not fair of him to keep you waiting to find out whether or not you will be going to London or Barcelona. Are you still in St-Tropez or have you left already? Wherever you are, I hope you won't forget our little project. It is of great importance to me and you are the only person I knew to turn to. You have to help us if anything good is to come of this whole tragedy.

I know that eventually I will hear from you regardless of where you are. It will be a wonderful letter telling me of your latest adventure. Nothing can stop the indomitable Emma Goldman, not grief, not prison, not war, not thousands of miles of ocean.

With condolences, ardent affection, and loyal friendship.
Lil.

break of day

The ocean wasn't odourless after all — it smelled fresh and alive. The scent of undersea growth and wriggling fish must find its way to the surface in minuscule bubbles or carried by the insistent, churning currents. It was briny, too, not like pickles but with a nose-tickling pungency to it, sea salt nourishing and preserving an ageless shifting mass stretching down and down for millennia.

For the first time since I couldn't remember when, I felt a lucky man.

I'd long ago given up on ever seeing France, and had pushed aside my curiosity about the ocean, dismissing it as foolish yearning born of youthful dissatisfaction. And yet, here I was, a man nearing the end of his life, standing in actual salt water of the Mediterranean and immersed in the sun's gentle morning rays. Its heat bathed me from every direction, even from below as it reflected off the water's surface.

The shoreline of the Côte d'Azur stretched out across the bay, a beautiful panorama of rolling green, peppered with white and brown villas. Tiny mushrooms in a bed of moss. This was better than the best postcard, which could never compete with the wondrous expanse of human vision. A picture couldn't bestow this same long, curved caress, one so tender I had to close my eyes and hum.

A cry attracted my attention, followed by the thud of a beach ball against the back of my leg. I turned around just as a mother called out an apology on behalf of her nearly naked four-year-old, and the child waded up to me to retrieve his ball. Sunbathers covered every inch of the beach behind me. Some of them had brought blue-and-white-striped chairs or brightly coloured parasols that they'd spiked into the sand.

I tried not to stare at a few topless women with buttery skin lying to my right. They'd applied lipstick and rouge to their taut faces and wore large movie-star sunglasses. Glittering sandals and skimpy metallic bikini bottoms were their only clothing, and two of them had very round, oddly shaped breasts that topped their chests like hardened Jell-O moulds. One of them had her legs tucked under her and was becoming badly burned, making me think of prawns in a buffet. It was all far from an unspoiled paradise, but if this was decay, who could complain? I only wished Ellen were alive to see this. As waves lapped at me, so did memories of her, and though I welcomed them, I tried not to let bitterness at how few years we had together spoil the moment.

I was already forty-nine when Ellen and I met, and had assumed my chances at love had come and gone. If you're forty-nine and the only women you've ever been with are the ones who wouldn't sleep with you, or the hookers who had to, it's a reasonable assumption. I was still working for Kagan's then, as operations manager for Eastern Canada, but to occupy as much of my free time as I could, I'd joined a pottery studio just off Laird Drive. I'd gone every weekend since it had opened and I was good, though better on the dishes and bowls than the few sculptures of seal pups that I did from time to time. One day, I arrived to find a new member had joined, and she was there at the second wheel, which faced the one I took.

Ellen Clarke was the daughter of a Jamaican politician, a majestic, broad-shouldered woman with smooth, deep brown skin and gorgeous, thick, nappy hair with flecks of grey in it, a beautiful silver cobweb running through a dark weave she kept pulled back in an intricate ponytail. When her family moved to Chicago in the 1950s, she came to Toronto to do an accounting degree at U of T and stayed on. A Bay Street firm hired her and she bought a small townhouse in Parkdale, purchased with family money and diligent saving. She'd never married, and her parents feared she never would. She told me she'd resigned herself to it too — she'd never met anyone who could see past her six-foot, two-hundred-pound frame to see the person inside. Then she hastily added, "Well, never anyone I would touch with a ten-foot pole — not until you."

With a throaty laugh, she loved to tease me about how we met, whenever she found an audience for the story: For the first three weeks after she joined the studio, she'd sit at that wheel and engage me in conversation, try to get me to raise my eyes away from the pot I was throwing. I grunted answers, and if I dared to give a full sentence, I'd remove both hands from the pot, leaving an index finger to trace circles on the outer edge of the wheel while the other hand tried subtly to cover my mouth. There was the scarring. I could barely meet her gaze.

Finally, she said to me one day, speaking over me as I mumbled through my fingers, "Toshy. This wheel is noisy, and I can barely hear you. If it's your lip you're trying to cover, don't bother. I've already seen it and it's very handsome. Besides, you're getting wet clay all over your face."

My hand fell to the bowl I was throwing and my creation became twisted, Daliesque. I took my foot off the pedal and stood to wipe my face clean at the mirror.

Emboldened, she added, "Those scars are nothing — you should see my brother Christopher. His are huge."

Wolf-mouth. I didn't feel quite so brave then, dabbing at my face with a cloth.

"How old were you when you had your operation? Christopher was just a baby."

"Nineteen," I said, my back turned to her still.

Slowly, I stopped struggling and Ellen gently reeled me in. I'd been watching her. For weeks, I'd admired her figure when she walked to the fridge to get more clay, or when she bent over to stack unfired pots in the top-loading kiln. As with most women I found attractive, I never once considered she'd feel the same about me.

We were married a year later in the Unitarian Church, with Ellen's family driving up from Chicago. With her friends from Toronto, there were almost as many people on their side of the church as on ours. I could barely believe the numbers that came that day. They'd shown up to make sure it was true.

Black and white pictures captured the wedding. There was one of me and Ellen standing next to the minister, an apple-cheeked man with black hair swooped back and streaked white up the middle. Ellen is to my right, towering above me despite my platform shoes, wearing a silk white strapless dress, majestic, proud, holding a flower arrangement handed to her by the photographer. Lil and Gerry were there with their daughters, who'd come up from Yale and Vasser, where they were students. One composition showed the girls as bridesmaids along with Ellen's four older sisters, all six of them with flower wreaths in their hair and wearing satin dresses with cantilevered bras. Ma was there, and Bessie and Abe, with Warren, of course, pre-Susan, pre-Ari.

Another photo was of me and my groomsmen, all guys from work. We're lined up in a row, wearing ill-fitting tuxedos, and the lot of them are standing expressionless, hands rigid at their sides as though they're having mug shots taken. The only ones with grins are me and Ellen's brother Christopher, at the end of the row, who is towering above the rest of us at six foot four. Various frames show people from the pottery studio and the old neighbourhood.

There was one portrait of me, Lil, and Bessie standing in front of a flower arrangement — me with a small boutonniere on my lapel and Bessie and Lil flanking me. They're both in stiff, elegant dresses, Lil's slightly shorter than Bessie's and with a sort of Dracula collar, but Bessie is wearing a pillbox hat and Lil has on horn-rimmed glasses.

I could almost see the relief on their faces.

Ellen and I were married for twenty-two years before she was diagnosed with late-stage breast cancer, and she died eight months later, within three weeks of the second anniversary of Lil's death from the same illness. Gerry, Lil's widower, used his connections to get Ellen the best oncologists and they tried everything — sent her to the Mayo Clinic for chemo, radiation, a double mastectomy — but in the end, same as with Lil, and now with Bessie, there was nothing to be done.

MADAME BORDUAS SHOWED UP ten minutes late, her skirt flapping in a light breeze coming off the bay. She wore her hair in two braids that hung down her back, a style very young for a woman her age.

"I am very sorry I am late. I have been painting an abstract — how do you say, *toile* — capturing the conflict between poetry and the modern novel," she explained, out of breath. "I'm sure you will agree with me that today's novels show no literary merit whatsoever and yet they are getting all the attention that poetry deserves."

"I suppose I haven't paid much attention to the publicity," I said. I wasn't certain I agreed, but I sure as hell wasn't going to contradict a retired poetry professor on the subject. I stood up and offered my arm.

"Oh yes! I don't know about English literature; I confess I do not read it very often. As for French, one only has to look at what they have on the shelves today, and you will see what I mean. Give me Hugo, give me Stendhal, then I would not argue. Give me Colette, ah Colette — have you read *La naissance du jour*?"

"I'm sorry, I haven't."

"I didn't think so, so I took the liberty of buying it for you. I saw it in English translation in one of our bookshops yesterday." She took it out of her satchel and handed it to me. "You must read it. The title is badly translated as *Break of Day*; it should really be 'Birth of Day' in my opinion, but no matter, it is magnificent. Written right here in St-Tropez after her second marriage failed."

"Thank you, that's very kind," I said, and tucked it away in my knapsack.

"It is nothing. In any case, I am sorry for being late. The canvas so captured my passions that I lost track of the time. I am depicting poetry as a Christ figure, besieged by the ... besieged, is that the word?" I tensed my shoulders. Was she going to say the Jews? "Yes, I think it is ... besieged by the Romans."

"I'd like to see your paintings, Madame Borduas."

"I'd be very pleased to show them to you later, Mister Wolfman."

"Please, call me Toshy."

"Very well, Tushie." This was a mispronunciation I'd heard many times, but it had never before been made innocently, without malice. "But then you must agree to call me Véronique."

"Véronique it is."

"Do you paint, Tushie?"

"No, I do pottery."

She clapped her hands. "I knew you were an artist!" she said. "It is the eyes. They show you have the soul of an artist."

"You're seeing jetlag."

"Nonsense. People can tell when you are an artist. People are always saying to me, 'Véronique, when will you be exhibiting your paintings?' I am flattered, but I am not ready yet. Perhaps in a year or two." She shook her head and waved a hand in front of her face, as though shooing away flies. "Never mind. Let us proceed on our journey. We can first go to my car and drive to see Colette's house. Very beautiful. Then we will go to see the Chapelle Ste-Anne, and after that we can go back to my apartment for some tea and you can see my paintings."

"Sounds nice," I said. "I especially like the part about going in your car."

She laughed loudly at that. "Oh, come now, we are still young, are we not?"

Véronique had joined me because we'd made a sightseeing date while Ari was hiking in the surrounding hills. He'd spoken to Lucien Sanschagrin, the old man François had found for us. It turned out Mr. Sanschagrin had worked at a notary's office for almost fifty years, and he remembered drawing up the documents when Emma's house was sold. He remembered it because Emma was a foreigner, not because he knew who she was. He told Ari that if he was to find Bon Esprit, we'd need to see the bill of sale because it would refer to the lot number. He offered to take us to his old office but was busy for the next few days, leaving us with time to kill until Thursday.

Meanwhile, we'd gone together to see the granddaughter of the man to whom Emma had entrusted the sale of her house, the one Pascaline had mentioned. The woman was in her late sixties now and didn't have much useful to say, except that it had taken her grandfather almost a year to sell the place and that in the end it had been a bit of a burden. That, I knew already, but Ari hadn't trusted my memory, both because it didn't fit with his research and because I couldn't exactly tell him why I would remember such a detail. At least this woman had confirmed my story, because it was the extent of what we would find out from her.

Today, I was going to spend with Véronique, and tomorrow, Ari and I would go together on the bus to the small town in the mountains that we'd seen on the way into St-Tropez. I'd come to the seaside early in the morning, after Ari had set off on his hike.

Véronique led me off the beach. "You appear to be a very vigorous man, Tushie, but Colette's house is too far to walk. Also, the *chapelle* is up on a hill; we can easily pass by there in the car on the way back, no?"

We made our way through town to the garage where she said her car was parked. We stuffed ourselves into a tiny Citroën and lurched off through the narrow streets; Véronique struggled with her stick shift as though it were a shovel caught on a tree root. Side streets gave way to wider two-lane roads that took us uphill and past the citadel to the outskirts. Gradually, a succession of side-by-side houses thinned out, until we saw vineyards interspersed with the occasional estate.

We stopped on a country road with tall grass and trees on each side blocking the view of the fields. Across from the car was a wrought-iron fence painted sky blue and bordered by rounded cement walls — two flaps bracketing the gate. The cement was painted bright red, and on the right-hand side there was an ochre sign that read, "La Treille Muscate."

"This is Colette's house. A relative of hers still lives here. And you can see the sign. The house was not named after the novel, but rather the other way around."

We walked up to the gate and peered through. Through it, we could see three arbours, one of them with vines growing up one side and over the top. They were perfect, simple arches leading the way into the property and marking the division between the short walk and the careless beauty of the rest of the yard. The unassuming two-storey structure at the end of the walk was more of a country cottage than a house, and it was painted the same red as the fence, but with a lavender-coloured door.

"A pity we cannot see the other side," said Véronique. "It was here that she wrote *La naissance du jour*, the novel I gave you. It is about a middle-aged woman who gives up on love in favour of independence and the beauty of her surroundings. I have seen pictures of Colette on the balcony on the other side, overlooking the sea, and I'm sure it must be a lovely view. "

"This is lovely enough," I said, and truthfully, I'd never seen such a peaceful-looking house. I wondered, did Véronique think I needed to give up on love? Is that what she concluded from looking at me? Was that why she'd chosen that particular novel to get me, or was it the only one she could find in English? I looked again at the house. I imagined what my life might've been like if I'd lived in La Treille Muscate, how that beauty might have affected me. How would I feel about my remaining time on this earth if I could live now in a place like that, instead of at The Terrace? Maybe giving up on love would have been less painful had I lived with the beauty of these surroundings. A person's home became a part of him — and I should know. I realized this in my fifth year at Collins Bay, when in my dreams, the walls and bars of my cell had replaced my childhood bedroom on St. Patrick Street. They'd become as natural as the uniform I wore day in and day out.

After several minutes of standing in front of Colette's house, it became too much. It was only reminding me of what I didn't have, and I didn't like to be reminded of it, not when I'd hoped the day would be an escape.

"Let's go see the chapel, Véronique."

We drove to the Chapelle Ste-Anne but found it closed. Still, the view from there was impressive. We were at the top of a hill overlooking the town, further away than the citadel, and much higher up. It was a more candid view of St-Tropez, from its rear end. For a town that was accustomed to strutting and showing off for the cameras, the vantage point felt like catching it with its hair in curlers, eating in front of the television.

I took a few pictures and then we set off for Véronique's apartment. She had a modest two-bedroom on the Place de l'Ormeau, with a small study where her easel was set up and canvases were stacked against the wall. She showed me her paintings, and I feigned admiration even though they were mostly terrible. The one representing poetry as Christ besieged by the Roman novel was technically poor. She characterized it as abstract, but the poem, with words laid out on the page in the shape of a cross, reminded me of the childlike chicken and duck paintings on Nesker's storefront windows way back when. The colour choices were odd, too. The evil novel, depicted as a hardcover book floating in the air and wearing a Roman helmet, was red and yellow with the helmet coloured purple for no apparent reason. I was no great art critic, but I knew enough to tell that Véronique was not an undiscovered genius.

We sat on her couch, upholstered an almost fluorescent green and covered with ornately embroidered pillows that might've been from somewhere in Asia. She disappeared into the kitchen to make tea but talked the whole time about the apartment, when she'd moved there, where she'd purchased the furniture or how she'd inherited it. I realized she hadn't asked me very much, except when it was an entry point to talk more about herself. Was she self-absorbed or just nervous?

A short while later, she emerged with tea and thin, flaky, cylindrical cookies she called Russian cigars, and sat next to me on the couch, even though there was enough space for her to sit farther down, near the end, or on a wingback chair beside the coffee table. Maybe this was a cultural thing; I'd read somewhere that people in other societies had a different sense of personal space.

We drank our tea, and I listened to Véronique explain her artwork. She drank quickly, and in between gulps rested the cup on the coffee table. Several times, she got up to point out a painting. I'd originally seated myself to the left of the centre, and each time she stood, I discreetly scooted over, but when she sat down, she'd seat herself right by me again, until I was pressed against the armrest.

I made an attempt to follow her to the painting she was discussing, my idea being that I'd then take the wingback chair when I sat down again. When I began to stand up with her, she pushed me back and said, "Please, sit, it is better if you admire them from far away — then you cannot see the flaws."

Véronique laughed at her own comment — the first true indication that she might be aware of her limitations and not simply modest.

"I'm that way too," I said. "Better from far away."

"Nonsense!" She laughed again. "Now tell me, do you like the tea, Tushie?" She sat next to me, even closer this time. "It is a blend from a small shop here in town. They sell a lot of it to the English tourists."

"Yes, it's nice, thanks." I took another sip, and then placed my cup beside hers on the table.

I was about to reach for another Russian cigar, when, well, I'm not sure exactly how it happened, but all at once Véronique was on top of me, pressing her lips to mine, and the armrest was digging into my back. I hadn't even seen her leap, she moved that quickly. One moment we were talking pleasantly about tea, and the next, I was underneath her, feeling the breath from her nostrils on my cheek.

My first reflex was to try to throw her off — a primitive response to being attacked — but that proved difficult. By the way she'd hurled her body, my arms were immobilized, one pinned against the back of the couch, the other sandwiched between her breasts. Véronique was a heavy woman and she'd taken me off guard. It must've felt as if she were kissing knotty pine: stiff, scratchy, scarred.

As soon as I realized what was happening and that my initial struggle had failed to move her, I made a decision. Not wanting to offend, I relaxed my body slightly, to respond to her kiss. The problem was that I wasn't feeling the slightest passion. They say you have to give women time to get in the mood — what a laugh. Véronique had gone from zero to a hundred in one second flat, while I was still stuck in neutral. I hadn't kissed a woman since Ellen had died, and this wasn't the one I wanted to take up with after all that time. Weren't we supposed to be talking about art?

I was quickly getting a cramp in my back. Thankfully, I was able to shift an inch or two and move one of my arms.

Not the one between her breasts, unfortunately; that one was firmly wedged and not moving unless she did. Now, with one arm free and my circulation being restored, I began to feel faintly aroused, probably just because it'd been so damn long. I was encouraged that, at seventy-seven, the plumbing still responded to a live female stimulus and not just to fantasy conjured from my mind or from the pages of a magazine.

I became briefly worried about wasting the opportunity — it would probably be my last, so I kissed her for a few seconds longer. I put my hand on the soft rise of her hip and leaned in, felt her tongue searching its way through my lips. I tasted cherry in her lipstick, smelled floral perfume on her neck, and as suddenly as it had arrived, the passion drained from my loins. After a moment, I used the free arm to gently push her away. I loosened my lips from hers, and it was as tricky as pulling a suction cup from ceramic tile without ending up on your keester.

"Véronique," I said, catching my breath. "I'm ... I'm only here a few days."

"Oh, Tushie, I do not want to marry you. We are adults, are we not?" she said, her voice smoky.

"Sure we are. It's just... Please don't be offended. I do find you attractive," I lied. She pulled off me and turned away. She smoothed her blouse. "I'm still in mourning for my late wife," I continued. That wasn't necessarily relevant, and she knew it. It'd been four years, and if Ellen was watching, she was probably cheering me on.

Véronique fixed her hair. "Please," she said. We could barely look at one another.

I stood. "I'm very sorry. I should go; I've offended you."

"No, it is I who should apologize. I am a silly woman to think you would be interested in me."

"Why is that silly?"

"You are such a handsome man. A man as ... as sexy as you, what would you want with a fat old Frenchwoman? I have been charmed by a dashing foreigner and I created a fiction for myself that you would be interested."

Now she stood too, and hastily gathered the teacups onto the tray and left for the kitchen. I made my way to the door, retrieved my knapsack, and waited for her there. When she came out, she'd composed herself and was standing tall. In that posture, I saw that she was really quite an attractive woman.

I took her hands in mine. "Thank you for showing me your beautiful town today."

I WALKED BACK TO LES RÉSIDENCES SOLEIL, but I was distracted and had to consult my map twice. I was only a few streets off, but I felt far from St-Tropez. My mind was casting itself about, here and there, from that couch in Véronique's apartment to across the sea, and back through my life.

My mother and sisters had always *said* I was attractive, but I never really trusted them, particularly after Bessie and Lil tried to set me up with Pearl. They'd have had to be monsters not to tell me I was handsome, but it only convinced me that love could blind a person or help her see past the physical. At the very least, it could motivate someone to tell a kindly lie.

I was a kid again back on Baldwin Avenue, standing across the street waiting for something — anything — and homely enough not to question a girl's motives or press her about the future. When things went sour and I came to my senses, I realized what I was to Gussie Kander: an experiment in which she proved to herself she was broad-minded enough to date a guy from the other side of the tracks. She never asked about my lip and I never told her. I was sure she thought it had split in a fight and healed that way, and that excited her. Though it smarted to admit it, I knew she never once considered staying with me. If ever someone accused her of snobbery, I was the experience she could recall to comfort herself, though she probably wouldn't dare to mention it.

My thoughts alighted on Bernie's prison cell. Although the incident had repelled me, I could be honest about it now: I'd also been a little flattered to think he'd found me attractive. When our friendship disintegrated, I began to take note of the physicality of the fellows he ended up with — Gaétan and then, later, others. I wasn't at all his type. I concluded that I'd guessed right after all: his interest had been primarily romantic and not sexual. Furthermore, with limited options, I'd been a convenient object for his affection.

Eventually, I ended up back in my wedding bed. Ellen's passion left no doubt about her attraction, but I was certain it had been socialized into her, then amplified by love. From an early age, she'd grown up with a brother whose face was like mine; she was conditioned to homeliness. It didn't matter to me; I adored her and counted myself lucky to have been with her. I'd never admitted that to a soul, not because I was ashamed, but because it was what everyone was thinking anyway, and why state the obvious, especially when it wasn't flattering and would only make people uncomfortable.

Then there was Pearl. I didn't know what to make of Pearl Feffer. From her behaviour and her verbal jabs, she clearly found me ridiculous, yet she was relentless in finding ways for us to spend time together. I'd assumed, because of her blemish, she simply felt more comfortable with someone like me.

But Véronique... Here was a woman I'd met only briefly, not long enough for love to take hold, with no apparent attraction to the criminal type and no known history of being around people with a cleft lip. She knew I was leaving in a few days and she admitted she didn't have romance on the mind. She didn't want anything from me, except a quick roll in the hay. Because she found me handsome and sexy.

As sexy as you, she'd said.

a salve, spread thickly

About seven months prior to my arrest, there was a change in Bessie. Irv's death was slowly receding into the past, so I assumed that grief's heavy cloak was slipping gently from her shoulders. Colour bloomed on her grey skin and she took greater care in her grooming, fussing with her hair before work, wearing lipstick, things like that. I'm not sure if Lil noticed except when Bessie took longer in the bathroom.

"What the heck are you doing in there? Hurry up, for God's sake!"

Ma would come by and knock on the door. "If you don't hurry, you'll make your sister late for class, and you'll be late too. If I didn't know you beter, I'd think you were trying to see how close you can cut it and still make it to the MacNabbs' on time."

There were conflicting signs of Bessie's recovery. She'd started slouching when her husband died, but now, strangely, she slouched more than ever. When she did emerge from the bathroom, Lil pushing past and slamming the door behind, Bessie still looked careworn; the lipstick and carefully pinned hair couldn't compete with her terrible posture and sad eyes. The patches of colour on her skin were more mottling than healthy glow, as though she'd been pinching her cheeks but the blood flow was resistant. She'd shuffle to the hall mirror and briefly straighten her back. She'd stand at various angles, suck in her tummy, pull at her hem, and smooth any wrinkles gathering over her bum, but then she'd slump down again, exhaling. Her dress would gather shapelessly, as if she were purposefully hiding her bosom, as if she had second thoughts about making herself pretty.

She began to talk about the MacNabbs more than she'd done when she first started working for them. She didn't have much good to say about Oonagh — "I've never seen a woman that vain and self-absorbed" — but she talked about Rupert as if he was an okay sort of guy. "People don't realize how hard that man works. It's amazing he can be civil at the end of his day."

This irked Lil. "The man is exploiting your labour, Bessie, and yet he's somehow brainwashed you."

"I'm not brainwashed. All I'm saying is he's nice to me. As usual, you don't know what you're talking about."

"I know what I see."

"And what's that?"

"That you've been duped by his charm, and you're falling for it hook, line, and sinker. Don't you know that behind his back, they call him the Friendly Executioner? People emerge from his office bleeding to death and don't even realize it. You're being suckered in, just like all the rest."

"Whatever you say."

Bessie didn't talk much about Rupert after that, but it didn't stop her from mentioning the MacNabbs as a couple, from going on about their extravagant lifestyle and beautiful home.

One morning, we opened the papers to find another mention of the Orange Sunset. Lil said, "Listen to this — 'Orange Sunset at Auction' — 'Lord Emmet Fister is putting up for auction the Orange Sunset, a thirty-six-carat diamond,' etcetera etcetera… 'After settling in Toronto, Lord Fister built a successful import-export business, but twenty-seven years on, Lord Fister's business has taken a downturn and there are reports that he is deeply in debt. Sources say that industrialist Rupert MacNabb'" — Lil looked to Bessie and raised her eyebrows — "'has been advising Lord Fister on how to recover his business assets. Now that Lord Fister has brought his son into the business, he is trying to secure a profitable future for his heir and a newly arrived grand-daughter.'"

We looked to Bessie, not sure why, but certain she'd have something to say about it.

"I know. Mrs. MacNabb was talking about it the other day. I told her she should get her husband to buy that diamond."

"Why on earth would you say such a thing?" asked Ma. "Didn't she think it presumptuous?"

"I don't know. I remembered that was the nurse who took care of Toshy. I thought it might help them to have the extra money. I'm sure Rupert will buy it for a good price."

"Rupert, is it?" said Lil.

"Mr. MacNabb, I mean."

"It's an auction," said Pop. "You can't be sure of anything. Besides, that man will do everything he can to get it for as little as possible."

"You have the wrong impression of him, Pop."

Ma said, "Read the rest of the article, Lil."

"'The auction will take place next Saturday at two in the afternoon, and interest in the diamond is already growing, despite its reported curse.'"

"What curse?" said Bessie. "That's nonsense."

"It says, 'A rumour has been spreading recently that if the owner of the diamond makes profit from its sale, both he and the new owner are doomed to poverty and torment for the rest of their days. Some say the curse was fabricated to scare off bidders, and if true, it is having the desired effect.'"

Pop said, "Fabricated by Rupert MacNabb; I'd wager our savings on it. They say that man will do anything to get what he wants. You mark my words; he'll buy that diamond for a song, when barely anybody bids on it."

Nobody ever found out who started the rumour, but my father was right about the auction, and Bessie felt awful for suggesting to Oonagh that they buy the diamond. There were only two bidders, and one of them dropped out after two rounds, leaving MacNabb to scoop up the Orange Sunset for a price that left Lord Fister with too little to revive his business to its former glory.

I'm sure people waited for the curse to take hold of the MacNabbs, but it never did. Of course, the Orange Sunset didn't stay with them long, which kept the idea of the curse alive. It was the Fisters who people say suffered its effects. Though they didn't live out their days in poverty, they landed in the middle class, and to the once-wealthy, that might as well be the same thing. As for torment, I couldn't say, but Bessie wasn't the only one who'd been pondering that question all these years. I had my own reasons, as had Lil before she passed away.

ONE SUNDAY AFTERNOON, a few weeks after we learned that MacNabb had snagged the Orange Sunset, Bessie, Lil, and I were all three helping our parents in the store, putting things in order because we were closed and it was the only day they had any time. Ma hadn't kept her promise of not making Bessie work on her day off, but Bessie didn't complain — we usually put in only an hour or two.

Lately, I'd been even more bored than usual, and found myself thinking about that diamond, about its curse, about how much it was worth, about what it would feel like to hold it in my hand. An idea took shape, and it was like discovering treasure somewhere you've looked a thousand times. You wonder how come you've never noticed it before. When Ma and Pop were out of earshot, I said to Bessie, "How 'bout you take us to see the MacNabb mansion some time!"

"Take *you* two?" She laughed. "I don't think so."

Lil had just joined us, having finished a chore in the stockroom. Her expression brightened at my suggestion. "Why not? We just want to look." After all of MacNabb's behind-the-scenes manoeuvring against Emma, this small violation must've been achingly enticing. While some were charmed by Rupert MacNabb, Lil wasn't fooled. MacNabb was concerned with cultivating an image of amiability — he was the sort of man who might have a chat with the door-man of his country club or talk about sports scores with his driver, and he probably thought people respected him for it. But those who only read about him in the papers weren't subject to his spell, and the spell wore off after a time with those who knew him well enough.

Those people saw the real man. He came from money, but not old money, so he used the humble family roots to draw people in. The story he told was that his father, Magnus, had been a Scottish immigrant who came to Canada as a teenager, alone and with five dollars in his pocket. He'd landed a job near Hamilton working for an old man who manufactured cast-iron wood-burning stoves. Lucky for Magnus, the owner didn't have any heirs; when the old man died, he inherited the business, expanded it to gas appliances, and eventually branched out to make coal furnaces.

Magnus's wealth and holdings increased when he married Mary Coombs, whose father manufactured wireless sets and gramophones. Mary had a younger brother, but the man had no business acumen and eventually Magnus took over his father-in-law's company too. Magnus and Mary had two girls and then a boy — Rupert — and by the time Rupert was fifteen, his father had turned two businesses into seven and built them up to such a profitable level that he was profiled in the *Globe* as one of Canada's leading entrepreneurs.

Magnus was said to be tough, but also kind. They said he could have had twice as much as he ended up with, had he had the stomach for it. Apparently, he didn't have the heart either; he died of a massive coronary at the age of fifty-two, when his son was in his early twenties. Rupert stepped in to run the business, with his mother as a more or less silent partner.

Rupert trotted out the memory of his father often, and especially when it served his interests. He talked about how the working man could rise from poverty and become a millionaire if he worked hard enough and was prepared to follow his dreams. I could believe that his tastes ran more to beer and crackers than they did to champagne and caviar, but beyond that, the man-of-the-people persona was an illusion. He was the heir to the estate of one of the country's leading industrialists. His father was one of the first men in Toronto to get a motor car. Rupert was head boy at Lakehead College and went on to get an economics degree from the University of Toronto. In addition to the businesses and the money, he had inherited a house in Rosedale and an enormous summer place on Lake Muskoka.

When Rupert took over, he proved himself more ruthless than a Manitoba winter. In public, he was all backslapping and "how are you doing, old fellow," but behind closed doors his ambition and brutality emerged.

He married Oonagh Vanstone, a former debutante, seven years later, in early 1930. She was a patrician beauty, with short curly reddish-brown hair, high cheekbones, and a statuesque figure. She'd even done runway modelling before she got married. Oonagh was the daughter of Carston Vanstone, the vice-president of the Dominion Bank, meaning she already moved in fancy circles.

Or maybe it would be more accurate to say that fancy circles moved around her. Women didn't dare throw a party and not invite Oonagh MacNabb. She could be vicious, and if she heard someone had left her off her social calendar, she could bring that occasion and its organizer to their knees. Her temperament was unpredictable, one minute warm and gracious, and the next, lashing out in anger. I heard a person say once that Oonagh MacNabb was like a candle flame — barely giving off any warmth but drawing you to the light, and if you were brave enough to pass your finger through, you'd better do it quickly or it would sure as hell burn you.

While people were sifting through the rubble of the stock market crash, Rupert and Oonagh were throwing one of the most lavish weddings Toronto had ever seen. Magnus had distrusted stocks and emerged from the crisis unscathed. When the papers announced that Rupert would be marrying Oonagh Vanstone, the joke was that if we were lucky, they might accidentally stab each other in the back while embracing at the alter. It was hard to say if they were ever in love, but they suited and complemented one another, which might be the only thing that people like that were really searching for in a marriage.

Bessie considered our request to take us to the MacNabb mansion, but then shook her head. "I can't just ... It wouldn't be right."

"We'd never tell anyone, would we, Lil? And we wouldn't stay long."

Lil took a moment before agreeing, straining under the agony of the imagined secret. "I swear," she finally said. "I wouldn't tell a soul, even though it would kill me."

Bessie hesitated.

"C'mon, take us," I pleaded. "I'm going crazy. We all are. We need a little excitement, Bessie."

"Take you where?" Ma hollered from the stockroom.

"Nowhere. A new shop on Spadina." Then, in a hush: "Will you guys calm down? I'll think about it, but there aren't that many opportunities."

About a month later, in mid-December, one presented itself. The MacNabbs were going out of town for a long weekend at her sister's country home near Stratford, leaving on a Friday and coming back Monday. Bessie felt that four days was a wide enough window to comfortably sneak us in early Sunday morning, well enough in advance of the MacNabbs' return that even if they cut their weekend short and came back Sunday night, we'd be well out of there. She told us to prepare for a visit.

I'd never seen houses as big as the ones we walked by that day. Rosedale after a fresh snowfall was sparkling, and there was a quiet on Glen Road that gave the neighbourhood a smugness, a self-satisfied calm. I saw it in a couple that strolled by silently, elegantly, arm in arm; in the fat squirrels that clambered up maple trees guarding front yards; in the stiff back and smirk of a man who drove by in a fancy car.

Bessie had made us put on our best clothes so that we wouldn't stand out, but we sure felt different, especially as we walked past the Rosedale United Church, where people streamed in for morning service. Down at the end of Roxborough, looming above the trees in Chorley Park with its turrets and sharply peaked roof, was Government House, the mansion where Colonel Bruce, the lieutenant-governor, lived with his family. Its size reminded me of Queen's Park itself, where the provincial legislature sat, but this building housed a single family — and their servants, of course.

"Holy smokes!" I cried.

"What? Oh, that," said Bessie, nonplussed.

"It's like a fairy castle!" said Lil, which was an unusually romantic comment, for her.

We continued on to the right, where Roxborough edged the Moore Park Ravine. The MacNabbs' home was a substantial one, even when compared to the mansion a few doors down. Three storeys, red brick covered in denuded vine, columns framing the front door, marble urns wearing toques of snow. We walked around back to the servants' entrance, stepping in Bessie's footsteps so we wouldn't raise suspicion. The backyard was a wedge of perfect white, bordered on one side by a low masonry fence, and behind it, widely spaced trees and shrubs adhering to the steep slope of the ravine. Snow still clumped on a few branches. We took our boots off outside and pulled them up behind us to place on a mat in the back hall.

Bessie showed us the laundry area first, because it was near the back entrance, and then she led us through the first floor, through the galley kitchen into the dining room, into a sitting area at the front of the house, and finally to the two-storey foyer. A spiral staircase faced the large carved-wood front door and led up to a balconied hall. Off this second-floor hallway was the master bedroom, which lined up with the front door. You could see its door as soon as you entered the house, without even looking up. There were two other rooms on each side of the master bedroom, and a narrow staircase at the end of the hall led up to the third floor, more small guest rooms, and a storage area.

Lil said, "Show us their bedroom, Bessie."

"Okay, but let's not stay long."

The bedroom's French doors opened outwards and I imagined Oonagh MacNabb bursting forth through them each morning in a fluffy nightgown, like women did in the movies. Maybe she stretched, surveyed the foyer, and called down to Bessie to fetch her tea.

Inside the room, there were armoires flanking the door. On the left side of the room, a large four-poster bed abutted the wall.

"Holy smokes, will you feel these?" Lil had run straight to it, flopped onto the mattress, and pulled back the covers to run her hand over the sheets.

"Lil, stop that!"

"They're silk. Can you imagine how well you'd sleep in this bed, Toshy?"

I went to feel the sheets too. They were almost slippery, made of the very finest material we sold in our store, not dull and fuzzy like the flannel covering our mattresses. Bessie came over, pulled Lil to her feet, and remade the bed. I went to the window and saw that it gave onto the backyard. I could see down the ravine through the barren trees. At the bottom, there was a footpath, and I wondered where it led.

"Nice, isn't it?" said Bessie, at my side.

"I'll say," said Lil. We turned to see her on the other side of the room now, where there was a large vanity. She was sitting in its chair and running a finger along the edge of the gilded mirror. She opened the top left-hand drawer and pulled out a jewellery box.

"Lil, I swear, you're gonna get me in trouble."

"I just wanna look. We'll put it back exactly how we found it. Hey, it's locked. Do you know where she puts the key?"

"Yes." Bessie didn't budge.

"Oh, c'mon. Don't be a spoilsport. We're not gonna take anything."

"I'm not opening it."

"Do it or I'll tell Ma and Pop you brought us here."

Bessie frowned but went to the windowsill. "I knew this was a mistake." She felt under the ledge and came back with a small key.

Lil gasped when she saw what was inside: an enormous brooch, with emeralds surrounding a very large, amber-coloured jewel. She grabbed it. "Holy moly! Is this what I think it is?"

"Lil, please. Put that back."

"It's the Orange Sunset," I said.

"Yes, and it's very expensive so please don't touch it."

I couldn't help myself. I reached out and ran my finger over the edges of the diamond, feeling its cool, smooth then sharp surface. I leaned in close and saw my reflection a dozen times over, each one of them distorting my face even more than it already was. The sunlight caught the edges, giving it a magical sparkle, and I felt giddy from the thought of that much wealth. I wondered how many dollars it would take to pay for it. Then I wondered how many dollar bills you would have to burn and then compress over millennia to make such a small object. So easy to slip into a pocket. I could walk around with thousands of dollars knocking into my hip, and nobody would know it.

Bessie took the brooch from Lil, locked it in the box, and placed it back in the drawer.

We examined the items on the vanity, while out of the corner of my eye I took note of where Bessie replaced the key under the windowsill. Alongside brushes, combs, and perfume bottles, there was a clock and a porcelain bowl and pitcher. Next to them were two framed photographs. One was of an elderly couple, probably Oonagh's parents, and the other was Rupert and Oonagh's wedding portrait.

Lil said, "He's a handsome sonofagun, isn't he, Bessie? I'll give him that."

"Yes, he is."

In the silence that followed, I stared at Bessie, her eyes locked on Rupert's image.

I knew then why she'd been acting so strangely; it wasn't about getting over Irv's death after all. I knew because in her face, I saw myself. While I was in Gussie's thrall, at the height of my infatuation, I'd seen in the mirror a kind of lustful desperation. It was a resignation to something stronger than pride, more powerful than resolve. What I'd given in to was dazzling, more so than a thousand glittering diamonds, and much more so than dull, thankless good sense. There was no competing with it.

Bessie turned away when she saw me watching, but it was too late. She said, "Let's get out of here. My nerves can't take it anymore."

We left the house, careful to put everything back just as we'd found it, and walked home.

I debated whether or not to say anything. I was worried about Bessie, but this really was none of my business. Then I remembered what she'd told me when I'd been sulking about Gussie. How sometimes we did silly things when we were lonely. Maybe she'd wanted to confide in me, but I hadn't taken the bait.

Later that day, while Lil was at a political meeting and our parents were visiting friends, I found a minute alone with her. I went to my sisters' room, where Bessie was lying on her bed, reading. From the doorway, I said, "I know about you and MacNabb."

She pretended not to hear.

"It's crazy, Bessie. He's taking advantage of you, and plus, it's dangerous."

From behind her book, she said, "It's not like that. I'm not in love with him and I know what I've gotten into."

"But you told me yourself: these kind of people, they might make us feel better for a short time, but in the long run, they make us feel worse."

"Did I say that? Jesus, you do remember everything."

"You were right. And you're gonna feel much worse than I did with Gussie." I didn't know if that was true, but I thought, even if she didn't *feel* worse, she could be fired, and then we'd have lost the income we needed for Lil's tuition.

She put her book down and fixed me in the eye. "Lil can never know. She'd say I was sleeping with the enemy." She did care after all, but for a different reason. "It's just ... I've been so lonely since Irv died, and Rupert..."

"I know. But you're gonna end it, right Bessie?"

"Of course I am," she said, reading her book again.

She wasn't convincing at all, but I decided to let her be. If only I'd known then just how badly things would turn out, I would've pressed her for details. Soon, I would've urged. I would've made her promise.

§

The heat broke late that year, in mid-September, blasting into my cell cool, damp St. Lawrence air that cleared out my woolly summer brain. By October, the stitches had come out, and by November, the scars felt smoother, less prominent. Still red and lumpy, and very noticeable, as I'd feared, but I marvelled at the unbroken line of my top lip. I'd stand at the mirror and rub my finger over it, and over the scars, again and again. I looked for any signs the swelling might be going down further or the redness fading. It was happening so slowly I feared one disfigurement might be replaced by another, as the doctors had warned my parents.

In the mornings, I shivered under the blankets, teeth chattering, but my mind was sharpened. The cold, and my new mouth, gave me an energy I hadn't had in months. Maybe I was desperate to stay warm, but I felt anxious to do something more than just sit around and smoke or play cards. The discussion group no longer held the same appeal, nor did the radio programs I'd used to listen to religiously. After the fight, they'd transferred Red back to Kingston, so I didn't even have *fear* to occupy myself anymore. I hadn't realized how much energy I'd spent avoiding him.

One day, in the courtyard, I saw someone writing in a notebook. It looked like arithmetic. I looked over to Bernie, across the yard, talking to some new fellow he might've been getting ready to make the moves on. I chuckled. I wondered if that guy suspected anything. I wished I could've gone over and asked Bernie how he was making out but knew that was out of the question. Aside from what had happened between us, I sensed he blamed me for Gaétan. He'd been transferred back to Kingston Pen, along with Red.

I turned back to the fellow writing in his notebook.

"What are you looking at?" he asked.

"Nothing … I was just wondering, can anyone sign up for those classes, or do you have to take a test or something?"

"No test, you just go. Next one is tomorrow and the teacher's a knockout, trust me."

I looked back at Bernie. He'd struck out; he was leaving the yard alone. Or maybe he'd just arranged to meet the guy later, I couldn't tell. I knew I wouldn't be going back to the group; it'd become too uncomfortable. Bernie'd stopped going to pottery altogether, and I took it as a sign he wanted us to stake out separate territory. I had a lot of time on my hands now, and no friend to fill it.

The next day, I enrolled in classes. We met in the same room we used for our discussion group, and the teacher *was* a knockout. She was a beautiful young woman from Belleville named Miss Carstairs and I quickly developed a crush on her. She smelled of lavender and wore bright dresses that showed off a terrific body: bust, hips, she had it all. The classroom was packed and it was clear why. She would roll a slate into the room and turn sideways to hold onto it while she wrote out her lesson. I'd stare, mesmerized by her figure, but more so her jawline, how it emerged dramatically from her long neck, angling perfectly forward. I watched her pink lips as she enunciated for us.

I attended class once a week at first, on Mondays just to try, even though they were also offered on Wednesdays and Fridays. On the third week there, Miss Carstairs brought in a projector and screen and showed us a film she'd borrowed from a friend in Ottawa. It was the documentary *Nanook of the North*, and after we'd viewed it, she assigned me a book to read, a study of the Eskimos and their hunting and fishing culture in the Arctic. I was to write a short assignment summarizing the book in two pages, drawing out the major themes and highlighting the author's perspective.

It was a very thick volume. She'd given me two weeks, but I finished it in nine days, devouring it during every spare moment, imagining myself spear-fishing for seals on the ice floes, kayaking in a fur coat, or tearing at raw meat with my teeth. I imagined that their guttural language was somehow easier for me than English or Yiddish, though it probably would've been more difficult. It was pure fancy, but a delicious escape, and I was sad when I turned the last page.

I wrote my two-page summary, but then on Friday, when I still had three days left before class, I somehow got it in my head that I wanted to do something else. I decided to write a story about a baby seal who goes off on his own to hunt fish for his sister. He's trapped under the arctic ice, can't get back to his family, is desperate for an air hole, and every time he finds one, shadows of hunters loom above, waiting to throw their harpoons. At the end of the story, the baby seal doesn't find his family, but he's led away by new friends, away to the open sea where no ice can form, far from where hunters can reach them. One day, he finds his friends have gone off to mate, and he realizes that although he's safe from harm, he has nobody.

Miss Carstairs asked me to read my story out in class.

"I'd prefer not to," I said. I was sure I'd be laughed at, as much for my story as for how my words would slur from being nervous. I didn't want Miss Carstairs to hear me like that.

"Oh, please, Mr. Wolfman; it's such a lovely and poignant story. Won't you let the other students hear it?" Her voice carried such excitement that I found I couldn't refuse her.

When I'd finished the reading, I realized that nobody had laughed, and I looked up at Miss Carstairs. There were tears in her eyes.

Later, she came to me privately and said, "Has anyone ever told you, Mr. Wolfman, that you are a very bright young man?"

"No, ma'am," I answered. It was kind of her to say so, but silly to think that someone could tell intelligence from a story that you made up. "Actually, they say I'm slightly retarded."

"No, miss," she corrected, but in such a gentle way and with a smile that made my neck flush. "And who says you're retarded?"

"Most people."

"Well, in my opinion, Mr. Wolfman, and in life generally, I've found that most people are fools. You have been greatly underestimated."

I had such a stupid grin on my face that I worried Miss Carstairs would revise her opinion. To my great relief, she didn't, and instead took the class to the prison library, where she showed us the catalogue, how to borrow books, how to request them if the library didn't have them. She encouraged me to write more stories, but once I found that others did it much better than I could, all I wanted to do was read. She said that was fine, that reading would expand my mind in wonderful ways. Then she asked me if

I wanted to get my high school diploma and I told her I did, very much.

I don't know what made the difference. Maybe it was having a good teacher. Maybe it was having a good-*looking* teacher. Or maybe I was just more interested in school that time around. I was older and not belligerent and mischievous, as I'd been in Toronto. Whatever it was, the world had opened up, and much wider than it had in discussion group, where I suddenly realized we'd been limited by the opinions of the more forceful participants. I couldn't turn my eyes away. I stared at it greedily, and not just through prison bars, but through literature and textbooks and Miss Carstairs's own lessons. Every once in a while, I had the giddy, dizzying realization that I was even forming ideas and opinions that were entirely my own, that I couldn't attribute to anyone or anything more than a spontaneous burst of creativity or analysis emerging from my very own brain. I started going to class three times a week, studied hard, and earned my high school diploma, getting A-minuses in every subject but two — mathematics, where I got an A-plus, and French, where I got a C.

I even continued to take classes with Miss Carstairs afterwards, until she got married, changed her name to Appleby, and moved away to Smiths Falls. They replaced her with an ugly gnome of a man who told me I had no place in his class since he wasn't qualified to teach university-level subjects. It didn't matter. By then, I didn't need him anymore.

le mas des sources

The bus to Grimaud hummed forward along the shore-line of the Côte d'Azur, rolling towards the hills in the near distance. But outside of Ramatuelle, we got ensnared in a traffic jam that stopped us dead for fifteen minutes.

With nothing to see out the window, Ari turned to me and said, "You haven't told me yet how you made out with Madame Borduas."

Almost made out, I had an urge to say. "It was fine. We went to see Colette's house, then an old chapel, and then we went back to her place for tea."

"And?"

"And nothing. Then I went back to our apartment. What are you getting at?"

"I meant how was it spending time with her, but if there's anything else you'd like to tell me…"

"What else would there be? That's all — Véronique has a very nice flat filled with her horrible paintings."

"Oh, so it's *Véronique* now, is it?" Out of the corner of my eye, I saw him studying me. "You sly old dog; did you two get into some hanky-panky?"

"No! What kind of question is that to ask your old uncle? Anyhow, if I *did* sleep with her, it would be my business, no one else's."

"You *slept* with her?"

"I did *not*. Contrary to popular opinion, I do not have women fighting to go to bed with me."

"Hmmm. I guess you're right. Only Véronique ... and Pearl," he counted on his fingers. "Coincidentally, the only two women your age you've met since Aunt Ellen died. I'd say that's a pretty good batting average."

"Pearl Feffer? Now you're just being ridiculous." Unfortunately, the word came out *ridiculush*, thus turning the tables on my comment. "Pearl is a pain in the ass. For the sake of your grandmother, I put up with her, and she puts up with me. In any case, she'd never be interested in a person like me. Too stuck up, hoity-toity."

"Yeah, okay, I'm being silly," he said.

"Let's talk about something else. Tell me, have you thought any more about my request?" That wiped the grin off his face and temporarily brought the conversation to a screeching halt. Just then, the bus lurched forward, the traffic briefly un-jammed.

"You wanna know something? You're relentless. How could I not be thinking about something like that?"

"I don't know. You haven't said anything."

"We agreed you would give me 'til the end of summer."

"Who said anything about the end of summer? You said a few weeks. It's already been more than a few weeks, and anyway, it *is* already pretty much the end of summer, if you hadn't noticed. Next week we'll be into September."

He was sitting next to the window and staring out at the cars, and beyond them, the hills in the distance.

"Look over there, Uncle Toshy. The countryside is bursting with life, and here we are discussing death in a bus full of strangers."

"You're avoiding the subject."

"I want to know what's so bad about your life. You can travel, you're in a beautiful place ... I mean, not now, of course; we're stuck on the ugliest stretch of road in France. My point is you're not even sick anymore. You know, my friend who died of AIDS, he was suffering badly. He had Kaposi's sarcoma lesions on the inside of his mouth and down oesophagus. Do you know how awful that is? He was skeletal, with peripheral neuropathy in his hands and feet. The pain was unbearable and treatments weren't working, but his heart was strong and he just kept hanging on. That's not the situation you're in. I know you're unhappy, but physically, you're in a different place than he was. Why can't you see all the good things in your life?"

I sat there a minute, staring at the vinyl seat back in front of him. There was no way to make him understand. Not without sharing what I couldn't bring myself to tell him. I *had* to do this, and my afternoon with Véronique hadn't changed a thing.

"I need you, Ari. I can't ask anyone else. If your aunt Lil were alive, she'd do it in a cold second."

"That's a crock of shit and you know it. Aunt Lil loved you more than anyone."

"That's why she'd help."

"You can't say that for sure."

"What do you know about what Lil was capable of?"

"I'm just saying, she'd be sad about this too."

There had to be something I could tell him, without giving away too much. I turned to him for the first time.

"A person shouldn't be a prisoner to their life, just because their body happens to be holding out too long. You should know that from what happened to your friend."

"A prisoner? Uncle Toshy, look around — you're not in jail anymore!" He'd raised his voice and a man in the seat in front of us turned around.

"Jail isn't what people think it is, Ari."

"Okay, I get it. You're a prisoner. You're a prisoner in your apartment. You're a prisoner to old age. You're a prisoner to cancer. Life is imprisoning you," he said, and I nodded each time. "Except you aren't any of those things. You aren't sick right now. You aren't even that old. Hell, one of my professors at the university brought in a guest lecturer who was seventy-six — the man still works and travels all the time."

I wasn't listening anymore. My mind was on Ellen, and how we used to go for walks every day to the park near our house, until her illness got worse and all she could do was stare out the window, be attended to by nurses, and sleep. *That's* prison. Ari didn't get it. I was talking about *staying* out, not *getting* out.

"Fine," he said, to get my attention again, "you want to move the hell out of The Terrace, move the hell out. You've got the money. Stand up to Mom and Dad — I'll support you."

"Hmph."

"I will."

We stared at the hills ahead of us. We'd finally pulled out of the valley and were heading up to Grimaud. Outside the bus, trees hugged the road protectively, sheltered it with their branches, and drew us up the hillside. To the left, there were openings through which we saw the valley down below, and beyond it, the sea. Prime real estate dotted each hill, every house with its own 7-million-franc view.

"Where can I go?" I said, very quietly into the window and as pathetically as I could, even though I knew that where I was living had nothing to do with the problem. Fortunately, Ari thought it did, and if this would convince him, I'd go with it. "You spent all this time helping me move out of my apartment. I'm not going to ask for help to move again, and then in two years have to move back. I'm not going to be a burden."

"You're not a burden," he said, but half-heartedly, confirming that I was. "You can go anywhere you like. Uncle Toshy, if you don't mind my saying so, it sounds like you need to talk to someone. Have you ever seen a therapist? There are social workers at The Terrace."

"I'm not going to see some woman half my age and talk about my *feelings* with her. What's this obsession your generation has with counselling? In my day, we just dealt with our problems on our own and we managed just fine."

"Okay, forget I said anything. Just consider the other stuff, about moving."

"And you consider my stuff. You're not off the hook."

I crossed my arms, he crossed his, and we turned away from one another until the bus let us off.

We'd been dropped near the post office at the most downhill part of town, and we meandered slowly up a series of switchbacking streets, zigzagging here and there, ducking under awnings to seek shade from the scorching sun. Two local churches with thick walls and tiny stained glass windows provided cool respite along the way. When we reached the top, we visited the scattered ruins of an old castle that once protected the town. Despite our conversation on the bus, the day was turning out quite pleasant. I decided to give Ari a reprieve, even though I was annoyed at him for waffling and didn't really feel that he deserved one.

I pulled out my camera. "For your grandmother," I said, and took a half-dozen shots, making him stand on the perimeter, overlooking the valley. After we'd finished with the ruins, we stopped for a late lunch on the way down. Afterwards, we bought almond cookies and takeout coffee from a patisserie and spent an hour reading in a park, sitting next to one another absorbed in our books. When we caught the bus back to St-Tropez, it was four o'clock and I was looking forward to a nap. I wanted to be ready, sharp, and alert for the next day.

IN THE MORNING, Ari and I walked to Monsieur Sanschagrin's old workplace, where he greeted us at the front door with a big smile. He was a man as short as I was, and I could see he was used to smiling; his laugh lines were deep, his cheeks were firm with well-exercised muscle, and his face was generally a little padded with the rewards of good eating. He shook our hands warmly and opened the door for us to pass through before him. The daughter of his former employer was now the head of the notarial firm, and because of the connection, the staff accorded him privileges others would never have had. Armed with Ari's extensive research and our recent confirmation, thanks to Pascaline's lead, that Emma's neighbour had sold the house a full year after Emma left town, we were able to locate a filing card that pointed us to the original bill of sale, bound in a thick leather volume. I've never seen Ari that excited. This was a primary historical discovery, and possibly the subject of an article that would help him get tenure one day.

The bill of sale described Emma as a "woman of letters." It said she bought the property from an Alexandre and Louise Blanche Mussier in February 1929, and then another adjacent piece of property from a Monsieur Stein in 1931. She paid a total of 54,000 francs for about twenty-five acres, including "a house with a top floor atop the main floor and basement, with various side buildings — a chicken coop, a covered shed, a well with motors, a wash basin and water faucets." The document went on to note that the yard was planted with vines, fruit trees, and a vegetable garden. In August 1936, she entrusted Sandstrom with the sale of both properties, including Bon Esprit, and it took until September of the next year to find a buyer.

French law didn't permit us to copy the document, but we only discovered this after Ari had taken copious notes and an officious clerk came into the room in a panic and kicked us out. By then, we had the key information, which was the lot numbers: 216, 217, and 218 of Section B of the old *cadastres*. Turned out a *cadastre* was like a survey map, showing lot numbers and building shapes. Monsieur Sanschagrin said he had a lunch appointment with his granddaughter, but that with the information we had, the town archivist would be able to help us pinpoint the house's current location.

We went to see the archivist immediately. She was a cheery woman who spoke English, thank God, and she got us an appointment straight away at the town hall, where a civil servant brought out two huge rolls that he superimposed on a light table. Over top of the old lot number 218, we saw an outline drawn on the modern *cadastre*. It was more or less the same shape as the 1930s building. We'd located Bon Esprit, and it was only two o'clock. Still time to get there before the end of the day.

DESPITE ITS BEING QUITE CLOSE to where we were staying, we hadn't yet been up to the Chemin St-Antoine. In searching for the house, we'd been so preoccupied with finding documents and first-hand accounts that we'd somehow put off the most basic research technique — direct observation. We trudged up the winding hill on the Chemin des Amoureux, which ended in a *T* at the Chemin St-Antoine. To the left, the road slanted to the south, towards the citadel, and to the right, it curved up a gentle slope and around a corner, leading out of town. We took the uphill part and began to count plots.

The road was a one-way, and with good reason — it was just wide enough to fit a car with about an extra two feet of wiggle room. We walked in the direction of traffic on the left side, in case a car came barrelling by, which it did in less than a minute. In fact, cars roared through there steadily every thirty seconds, at an amazing speed given the width and that you couldn't see around the corner.

Over the roar of an engine, I yelled to Ari, "This wasn't the way I wanted to die!"

He turned and glared.

In between cars, I took out my camera. Stone walls lined both sides of the road, but the downhill one was shorter, and despite overgrown vines and thicket growing atop of it, we could see the vineyards and ocean beyond it. Most of the houses were on the uphill side and I could catch only a glimpse of them from the road. This appeared to be a wealthy neighbourhood now, where locals probably never went out except in their Mercedes Benzes or Jaguars. The traffic made being a pedestrian treacherous business, and we didn't see a single soul on foot except us, no tourists, no residents, nobody. It was frustrating; the houses were hidden behind the wall, behind trees and hedges and driveways blocked by wrought-iron gates monitored by security cameras.

Though we couldn't see it clearly, the third house along on the uphill side was the one. It had a sign grafted to the wall near the gate — it said "Le Mas des Sources." Ari explained that *source* meant either a spring or a well, and he'd read in our guidebook that *mas* was the Provençal word for a small farm. On our tiptoes, we could see that the house behind the gate was painted salmon, with light blue shutters covering rounded second-floor windows. I couldn't see the first floor. I took a deep breath, amazed that I might actually be close to my goal after all this time.

We discussed what Ari would say to the owner. We'd given no advance warning we were coming, and there was no time to do so either. We only had two days left in St-Tropez. Ari pressed the buzzer and took a breath.

A few seconds later, I saw the security camera move, and a woman's voice crackled. "*Oui, hallô?*"

In French, Ari gave his prepared speech about our being Canadian researchers and how we discovered that the historical house we'd been searching for was hers. He also mentioned that his great-aunt had once stayed there.

A pause. The voice asked several brief questions, which Ari answered in turn.

Lastly, she asked how she could be certain we weren't robbers. I smiled into the security camera. She was nervous about Ari, though I was the one with the record. Ari mentioned we were friends of Lucien Sanschagrin, and after his name was spoken, it took only a few seconds until the intercom crackled again, and she said, "*Entrez.*"

The latch clicked, and the gate slowly swung ajar. The driveway led to the left and separated manicured lawns.

There were still a few of the fruit trees mentioned in the old bill of sale. On the right side was an old stone retaining wall dividing an upper and lower level of the lawn, about chest-high, I gauged. Tufts of grass sprouted from the spaces between the masonry. This was the division between the Mussier and the Stein properties. They'd been sold together and had obviously been passed on with each successive sale. There was no sign of a chicken coop, but maybe it was on the other side of the house.

Bon Esprit — now Le Mas des Sources — was built on a gentle slope, and we followed the driveway uphill to the front door. An elegant, middle-aged woman with jet black hair pulled into a bun was waiting for us.

"*Bonjour*. I am Nadine Letour. You are English speakers, no?" she said in a thick accent. She wore neatly pressed tan slacks and a blouse so smooth and stiff that when she extended her hand, the wrinkles on her skin stood out in sharp contrast. Long nails crowned fingers laden with various precious stones. She smiled, her face taut.

"Yes, we are," said Ari. "This is my great-uncle, Herman Wolfman, and I'm Ari Kagan." He gave her a business card he'd had made up so that she wouldn't think we were there to see what we could take.

"I am happy to have a chance to speak English. My husband was a banker. He is dead now, but we used to spend a lot of time in London."

"Thank you for letting us in," I said, taking the woman's hand.

She ushered us through the front door. Her blouse barely rippled as she extended her arm. "I am sorry for being suspicious. Occasionally we have people coming around to ask us to sell our property. It is very bothersome. May I offer you coffee? I have just made a full pot."

"We don't want to impose," I said. "We only wanted to take a look around." And I did just that, scanning the first floor, or what we could see of it.

"This woman you mentioned who lived here. She was your great-aunt?"

"No. My sister only visited that woman here, many years ago."

"There's really nothing to see from those years."

Madame Letour led us in through a simple foyer past stairs that led to the lower level and pointed us to a floral couch in a room that stretched from the front to the back of the house. The broadloom still had vacuum cleaner streaks on it. "I don't keep very much. I don't like to have clutter; I am like my mother that way." She left us to get the coffee, calling out, "You're from Canada, you said? I have a sister who lives in Quebec City!"

"This house looks very modern," said Ari, when she was gone. "It's hard to imagine Emma ever being here. I wonder where Aunt Lil slept when she visited?"

I went to the windows at the back of the house, which opened onto the stepped lawn and the retaining wall that divided it. Ari sat down on the couch, pulled out his notebook, and started furiously scribbling details while we waited for our hostess. I knew it didn't matter very much that the house was vastly changed. He'd have all he needed for the paper he'd write. Finding Emma's Bon Esprit would earn him points with his academic colleagues.

Madame Letour returned with a tray, poured us cups, and sat on the edge of the armchair with her back utterly straight. "Tell me about your research," she said.

I took my coffee and returned to the back window. Ari must've sensed I didn't feel like talking, so he carried the ball. He explained who Emma was and brought out his notes taken from the bill of sale. He showed Madame Letour one of the books he'd brought, and the pictures in it.

She said her parents had bought the house in the late '40s from Belgians, and then retired in the '60s to Toulouse, leaving the house to her and her husband. They'd made substantial renovations in 1969, redesigning most of the interior. The exterior was re-stuccoed and painted, the shutters replaced, and the yard landscaped.

"And the old chicken coop?" I asked, turning my back to the window to face them.

"Destroyed along with the shed. The only things that remain of the grounds are the fruit trees, the old brick walls in the yard, and the well, which is only for decoration now."

After we'd exhausted the subject of how we'd located Bon Esprit, there was a silence, and Ari looked to me; maybe he was waiting for me to ask more questions. When I didn't, he said, "Would it be too much of an imposition if you showed us the rest of the house now? I'd love to take some pictures."

"Yes, but I must warn you, it is very messy…"

"Your place is beautiful," he said, and it was true. There wasn't a thing out of place. "We won't photograph anything you don't want us to."

She smiled and extended her arm towards the other room.

I wasn't interested in the tour. "You go, Ari. I don't feel so well. I think a little air might help. Madame, is it all right if I take a walk outside in the yard while you show my nephew around?"

"Of course. Be my guest."

I was sure she wasn't the sort of person who liked to have people walking on her lawn, but she was a gracious host. She pointed me to a path leading around to the back of the house.

A half-hour later, when we were heading down the Chemin des Amoureux, Ari turned to me and said, "Are you feeling okay?"

"Oh, sure, I'm fine. You don't have to worry about me."

"Suppose not," he said, and started humming.

It'd been a good day, for both of us. I tightened the straps on my knapsack, pulling it snugly against my back.

parole

a sharp intake of breath

People believed I was caught with my hand in the cookie jar, simple as that. After all, the story had been repeated for nearly sixty years: Bessie had gone to work as the maid of nasty Rupert MacNabb and his vain wife, Oonagh. I broke into their house; they came home early and caught me climbing out their second-storey window. I had a priceless diamond brooch in my hand, and when I saw Rupert, I threw it down the ravine out of spite, and it was never found again. They interrogated Bessie, Lil, our parents, and me, and with the evidence, they had enough to convict me. Because I'd thrown the diamond down the ravine when I could've handed it over to its owner, the judge sent me away for eleven years. When people told this very short story, my very long sentence was its ending.

Of course, a story looks different depending on the perspective and whether or not you consider all of its essentials: context and character, setting and set-up, motivation and movement. Whether or not you consider its beginning and its ending. A story travels in a full and continuous arc, like a ball pitched forward by the teller. From my perspective, my figure in that windowsill was only one frozen moment in the arc. The ball had been tossed when I was ten, when we heard Emma Goldman talk for the first time, and its apex was reached in that frozen moment, with no-good Toshy Wolfman caught in that compromising position.

Without all the story's elements, that one picture was worth a thousand lies.

Here was the truth: In the spring of 1935, I was a nine-teen-year-old staring at a bleak future, but my sisters still had hope. Nothing was going to mess with their chance at happiness. Nothing and nobody, not if I could help it.

In February, Bessie's situation, already complicated, tightened, like a Chinese finger puzzle being pulled from both ends. She met Abe Kagan, a shop owner ten years her senior. She went on a Sunday outing to go skating on Grenadier Pond, and Abe was there playing hockey with friends. He accidentally flicked the puck out of bounds and Bessie stopped it against her blade. She handed it to him and he smiled. After their game, he invited her and her friends to have hot chocolate with him and his teammates.

Her feelings for Abe developed rapidly, and it was mutual. All that was missing in her affair with Rupert crystalized in Abe, but the promise of a future with him was like a beautiful snowflake that seemed to be fluttering to the ground, where she would be helpless to stop it from melting. Poor, proper Bessie now considered herself a tramp, a woman sleeping around on a man she hoped would ask for her hand in marriage, cheating on him, really, even though the affair had started before they met. She was working up the courage to tell Rupert she wanted to break it off but she didn't have the nerve. She was afraid of what he might do if he didn't want the affair to end. Occasionally, what others knew of him revealed itself from behind his charm and passion. There was a tinge of ruthlessness, carefully suppressed until he released it in swift, punishing blows. I suspected that there was something attractive to her about that ruthlessness, a kind of sexual energy that powerful men harnessed and dispensed to lovers like a kind of opiate.

One Saturday in April — the twenty-seventh, to be precise — Oonagh called Bessie into her room to ask her opinion about an outfit for a gala theatre opening she and her husband would be attending that evening. She asked Bessie to fetch the key to the blue velvet case that she brought out of the top drawer of her vanity. She told her it was under the windowsill, but Bessie already knew that.

As she opened the box, she said, "This case is filled with all of my most precious pieces of jewellery. Most of them are too formal to wear to any occasions Toronto has to offer." Then she said, "It's been ages since I last looked in here."

She brought out the Orange Sunset and asked Bessie's opinion on the appropriateness of the brooch to the cream evening gown she had on.

The jewel glinted. "It's stunning, truly," Bessie said.

"You know what this is, of course. It's thanks to you I have it, really. You suggested to me that Rupert buy it, remember? Such a terribly romantic story. Lord Fister bought it for his wife as a wedding gift. I've since learned it's one of the rarest diamonds in the world." She didn't mention the part about the supposed curse. Or that her husband had taken Bessie's suggestion and run with it, how he'd bought it for a shamefully low price despite pretending to be Lord Fister's friend.

Bessie said she remembered. She didn't mention that she'd brought me and Lil into the bedroom a few months before, and that we'd all seen the Orange Sunset first-hand.

Ultimately, after trying on a few more pieces, Oonagh decided she wouldn't wear the brooch after all. She locked the jewellery case, returned it to the drawer, and asked Bessie to place the key back under the window.

An hour after the MacNabbs went out, Bessie began to prepare to leave for the evening. She had two sets of work clothes, French maid uniforms supplied by Oonagh when she'd started her job. She'd wear one from Monday to Wednesday and the other from Thursday to Saturday. She'd place her soiled uniforms into a bag in the laundry room but wouldn't launder them there. The MacNabbs' laundry schedule didn't correspond to when she needed to do her wash, and Oonagh didn't like Bessie to waste her time washing a single garment. She'd launder her uniforms at home late on Saturday nights and iron them Sunday once they'd dried.

That night, Bessie took off her uniform as usual and stuffed it in her bag on top of the other one, deposited there mid-week. She changed into street clothes and went home. Later, in our laundry nook, she dumped her uniforms into a pile. There was a rat-a-tat of a hard object skipping and rolling, and a flash from the corner of the room.

She flicked on the light. There, on the floor beside the laundry, was the Orange Sunset.

Bessie was a pretty smart girl, despite being overshadowed by Lil's brilliance. She knew right away what had happened. She bolted upstairs and saw me sitting in my bedroom reading a comic book I'd nicked.

She had something clasped in her hands. "Where's Lil?" she said. Her voice was shaky, and the next moment she started to cry.

"In your room," I said, pointing down the hall. "What's wrong?"

Lil had heard the commotion and came running. "What's going on?"

"Shhh!" I said. "Close the door." I didn't know what had happened, but I had a sense it had to do with her affair.

We sat in a row on the bed, Lil and me on either side of Bessie, and we watched her hands. She opened them slowly. The Orange Sunset sat in her palms and stared up at us, enormous.

"Bessie!" I grabbed it from her. "What have you done?" It refracted the light from the bedside lamp, making me blink. In contrast, the twelve emeralds that hugged it were tiny and dark.

"I didn't take it! Mrs. MacNabb planted it in my bag. I don't think she meant me to find it until tomorrow."

"Why would she do such a thing?" Lil asked. She took the brooch from me and fingered the pin on the back, as if it would give a clue to Oonagh MacNabb's behaviour, or our sister's. "My God, this thing is hideous. Green and orange: how can rich people waste money on such bad taste?"

I knew why Oonagh had planted it, and Bessie did too. If Bessie were caught stealing, Rupert would have to fire her, even if they didn't lay charges. To keep her, after such an apparent betrayal, would be too conspicuous.

Bessie turned to me for help.

"You have to tell her, Bessie."

"Tell me what?"

There was a long silence, and then softly, Bessie said, "I'm sleeping with her husband."

"You're doing *what*?" Then she looked at me.

"I tried to warn her, believe me! Bessie, we can't let Abe find out about this," I added. My caution seemed out of place, hardly the time to be mentioning it, and it embarrassed me as soon as I'd said it.

"You knew and didn't tell me?"

"I made him promise. It's not his fault."

"I don't believe this. What on earth are you doing sleeping with your boss? Bessie, do you know how stupid that is?"

"Don't yell at me. I've been trying to end it, okay?"

"But your boss!"

"I was lonely. It started before I met Abe." We stared at her. "I'm sorry, but I'm not perfect. I'm sorry if that shatters your image of me."

Lil never believed Bessie was perfect, but at least that once, she was kind enough not to say so. "You've been going with Abe for two months now. Does he know about this affair?" It was a stupid question, but I was relieved she was thinking about it too. Still, I don't know why either of us was concerned about Abe at a time like that. Maybe because he was such a nice guy and didn't deserve to be cheated on.

"Of course not! Are you insane? And he can't find out. Ever. Oh my God, what am I gonna do?" She threw herself forward and sobbed, her back rising in deep heaves.

If Lil was as upset as I was, she sure as hell hid it well. Her voice evened quickly, the way a bubbling pot does when you've taken it off the stove. She said, "Bessie, never mind about Abe for now. You have to go put that back, and then you have to quit first thing Monday — before she does something else."

"I can't go back there now. I can't. Mrs. MacNabb knows."

"Are they at home?"

"They're at the theatre, but I can't go back there again. Don't make me go." The tears came more quickly down her face. "My life is ruined. Abe'll never marry me now. No one will; who'll want a girl who's done something this disgraceful?"

In all her life, that was the closest Bessie's ever been to unravelling. Closer than when her first husband was killed or when, years later, Abe died. Grief might cut deeply, but shame slashed in wide, sweeping arcs and left us with ragged wounds that were harder to heal, more permanent, maybe.

And despite it all, Bessie never thought of jail. Not then. She believed she was being framed for theft but that it was only a ploy to fire her, one that Rupert couldn't contest. She was a more trusting person in those days and her mind was preoccupied with her tarnished integrity.

I knew jail was a possibility, even if I realized it too late, after I'd put my grubby prints all over that damned brooch. Lil and I both knew we had to do something with it, and fast.

Lil stood up to check the clock. "It's nine-thirty and the theatre started at eight. There's still time, if we hurry. Is there a party afterwards?"

"Probably," Bessie said, through her sobs. "Mrs. MacNabb said it was a gala."

"Perfect!" I said. "Now let's put our heads together."

"We should make it look like a break-in and *keep* the brooch," said Lil, "but we'll hide it somewhere safe. She'll never be able to prove it was us. Those buggers deserve to lose their stupid diamond. Do you know how much this could fetch on the black market?"

"No, and neither do you," I said. "It's too risky. Who do you think you are, Al Capone, all of a sudden? Since when are *you* the criminal in the family?"

"You're not a criminal," said Bessie, raising her head. She was speaking to Lil, not me. As an afterthought, she put her hand on my leg and said, "Neither of you is." Still the big sister, despite her predicament. "You're just hanging around with the wrong people, and getting into trouble sometimes."

My chest constricted, hearing her say it. "I thought you didn't know."

"We know enough."

"Yeah, well, you're in no position to be giving lectures about getting into trouble, Bessie," I said.

"I know, but what Lil is proposing *is* too risky. I'm agreeing with you, for once."

"C'mon!" Lil pleaded. "Can't we take advantage of this opportunity and play Robin Hood? That man has cost my comrades a lot of money. I say it's time for payback. Emma left Toronto last week — someone's gotta stick it to him now that she's gone."

"Lil, will you forget your stupid politics for one minute?" Bessie snapped. "This is a serious situation. I need your support."

"Then we'll have to go and return it ourselves," I said. "Bessie, give us the house key."

"No, it's too dangerous."

Lil said, "Do you want your life to be ruined?" She put her hand out. "Think of Abe, what he'd say if you were charged with theft, or if he found out about your affair."

It was a calculated blow. Though she couldn't be sure of it, Lil probably suspected, as I did, that Abe would stand by his girl.

Bessie fished the key out of her dress pocket and dropped it into Lil's palm. "Promise you'll be careful," she said. "They have snoopy neighbours. Rich people are completely paranoid. Get in and get out. You remember where it goes — in that blue velvet case in the top left-hand drawer of the vanity in the bedroom. The key is under the..."

"I remember," I said, closing my eyes and retrieving the image.

We stood up to leave. We were halfway to the staircase when Bessie called out. "Wait a minute!"

We turned around.

"Thank you," she whispered.

Lil made me put on my nicest clothes, and I grabbed a cigarette lighter from the dining room and slipped it into my coat pocket. We told our parents we were going out with friends, and left the house.

All the way to the MacNabbs, we reviewed the plan, whispering even when there was nobody in earshot. We argued about who'd go into the house and who'd stand watch. In the end, I won because of my experience as a thief, and because I was wearing pants — easier if I were in a tight spot. What was unspoken was the other reason: Lil had more to lose than I did. We decided on the details: I'd go in, and Lil would hide in the bushes around the back of the house, in case someone arrived.

Rosedale was different at night. It had the feel of a grave-yard. The street lamps cast sinister, haunting shadows over the sidewalks. Front windows and porch lights cast their rays upwards, making the houses like faces when you put a lantern under your chin. The air was unnerving, even stiller than it had been that snow-covered day, and that seemed almost impossible. Hardly any cars, even on the larger bridge above the Moore Park Ravine. Nobody was outside, save one woman walking her dog, and she had a Grim Reaper–like cloak over her head. A shiver slid up the back of my neck. When we passed into North Rosedale and out of the wind on the bridge, the air got even quieter. It was as though the neighbourhood were placed under nightly curfew, one reserved only for people who had enough money to be robbed. This was lucky for us, because we would be able to slip up to the house without being spotted.

The MacNabbs' place was completely dark, which was what we'd hoped for. First, we cased the joint, observing different things than the first time we'd seen it, when it was covered in snow. There was a granite footpath to the front door that branched off to the side and around the house. Large hedges hugged the walls, but there was a clear view of the front windows.

We followed the footpath around to the backyard, to remind ourselves of what lay below the bedroom. The window was near the wide point of the wedge-shaped lawn. From the house to the edge of the ravine was a depth of maybe a hundred yards, and depth was an appropriate descriptor. In winter, it had been white; now it was a murky pool. We reviewed the plan once more, and while Lil stood guard, I slipped the key into the lock in the back door. I wiped my feet outside, checked the soles to make sure there wasn't any dirt or mud or dog poop, but took my shoes off anyway.

I didn't turn on any lights as I made my way through the house. Lil and I had discussed that — we didn't want any neighbours seeing a lit house in case any of them knew the McNabbs were supposed to be out that night.

I crept through the kitchen, around through the dining room to the foyer. I tiptoed up the spiral staircase to the master bedroom, which I'd remembered overlooked the front door. I opened the French doors, and when I stepped inside, I saw the vanity to the right. I went to it and pulled the top drawer open, but remembered there was something I was supposed to do first. The clock on the vanity said 10:15.

I went to the bedroom window, unlatched it, and heaved it upwards. The air smelled of the first blossoms of spring — there must have been a fruit tree or a magnolia in the backyard, but it was too dark to tell.

Funny that I remember the smell of spring blossoms, given all that happened next.

I saw Lil's outline. She was standing about thirty feet back. I could've seen her from inside, but I craned my neck out the window anyway. There was a clicking down below and then I saw the tiny flame from our parents' lighter. A few feet behind Lil, past the knee-high fence, the yard fell away into the ravine.

I waved to her. She waved back. I was about to pull inside to return the brooch to its jewellery box, but her waving got more vigorous and she pointed to the front of the house. Then she jumped up and down and finally yelled hoarsely, "*Toshy!*" — as loud a whisper as she dared.

It took me too long to realize that something was wrong. This was not our test; this was the real thing.

The next thing I heard was the front door latch, behind me, at the bottom of the stairs.

"Shit! There's someone coming into the house!" I whispered back.

"They're home early!"

I felt a mass in my throat and blood rushed to my head, making me dizzy. My first instinct was to hide. I closed the window and searched the room. I wouldn't fit under their bed — the sideboards came down too low. There were no closets — what kind of stupid bedroom had no closets? Instead, there were the two large armoires. I'd left the French doors slightly ajar but I certainly couldn't leave through them. They opened straight onto the foyer, where Rupert and Oonagh were probably taking off their coats. What about their gala? Bessie'd said there'd be a party, hadn't she? Even then, it didn't occur to me that there was no gala that night. Oonagh had invented it as an excuse to show Bessie the diamond. She'd planned to tell the police Bessie had seen it earlier in the evening.

I ran to one of the armoires and opened it. Goddammit if there weren't shelves running halfway up, with pants and socks and underwear folded neatly on them. The available open space, containing shirts and suits, was far too small, and besides, the shelving wouldn't have been sturdy enough to hold my weight. I tiptoed to the other side, jumping past the open doors, and trying to land as soundlessly as possible. I opened the other armoire. Same thing. Oonagh's dresses hung neatly in rows.

Then I felt real panic clog my lungs. I'd been in lots of sticky situations, running from police down Kensington alleys, that time the Neskers almost caught me stealing, but I'd never been trapped in a corner, not ever. I went back to the window and pushed it up again. It squeaked. Lil was still in the backyard but had come up closer to the house, just under the window.

"I don't know what to do!" I said. "I'm gonna have to put the brooch back and jump!"

"Toshy, listen to me. Throw that brooch down here."

"What are you talking about?"

"There's no way to return it," she said firmly. "They'll know someone was in the house, they'll test the brooch for fingerprints and find yours and mine and Bessie's all over it. Throw it down now and jump! There's at least a chance they'll just think it was a regular break-in."

They would never believe it was a regular break-in. How could they? The back door was opened with a key and then locked again and the window had been opened from the inside by flipping the latch, not by breaking it. Who would think there was an unknown robber?

It did cross my mind that we might shatter the window from the outside, but then I realized that the timing of the shattered glass would be all wrong, and I remembered my shoes sitting by the back door. Any detective would figure it out in no time, even if we weren't caught running away.

In spite of all the evidence telling me Lil was wrong, when it boiled down to it, I didn't trust my instincts. And there she was, calling to me from below with her hand outstretched, very sure of herself.

Rupert called from the foyer, "Who's there?" There was murmuring, and Oonagh said, "Careful!"

I heard footsteps coming up the staircase.

Lil caught my eye, waving her arms.

"Throw it, dammit, and jump!" She stepped backwards in long strides from the edge of the house and held out her hands, half crouching, as though she might catch me as well as the diamond.

I threw one leg over the windowsill and felt my heart race. It was a long way to the ground. Long enough that I might break my legs. How would I get away if that happened?

Just then, I saw Rupert, backlit, his legs slightly apart, standing in the doorway.

There was a moment when we stared at one another's faces, and though I couldn't see his features, I'm sure I was more frightened. Nothing was said for that long second. I sat rigid in the window frame, and he stood frozen in the doorway. He held in his hand a long cane, to bash me with, I supposed, if he got close enough. Then his head turned to the open vanity drawer.

"Don't make a terrible mistake, young man, or you'll regret it forever. You'll injure yourself if you jump and you'll never get away. My wife is at this very moment calling the police. If you know what's good for you, you'll drop whatever you have in your hand and climb back in the window."

I inhaled, and the air cut like knives. Even so, I held it there, painfully, for three seconds. The Orange Sunset was hot and its edges dug into my sweaty palms. Then, I exhaled, and with that same breath flung my arm out the window. I felt the brooch sailing from my fingers into the darkness. My eyes didn't leave Rupert's, but I heard a faint thud on the ground and then, just barely, the soft padding of Lil's feet. From where he was standing, Rupert never heard a thing.

In my dreams, I can remember the gorgeous, exhilarating arc of my leap from that window. I can remember the fall: its slow-motion glide, my arms swan wings, and then my nimble cat-landing, all fours into a tumble roll and then into a dead run. Not a moment of hesitation. I can remember the soft branches licking my sides and closing behind me as Lil and I sank into the ravine, as we plunged to safety.

But those are just dreams. I never did jump.

§

During the eleven years I spent in Collins Bay, I received news of world events with an odd detachment. Those events were so improbable, so far removed from my life that they felt unreal, as if part of a serial I listened to on the wireless set in my cell. A *second* world war? How derivative. The Soviet Union, our wartime ally, was now our *enemy*? A preposterous plot device to keep us hooked for the next episode.

It didn't help that the war only grazed the people I knew. Thousands had apparently died on the battlefields and in the camps, but incarceration, sex, age, or disability exempted my entire family from duty. In our circles, the person most affected was Emma, who hopped about Europe in the late '30s as things started to heat up. Even she got out in time. After brief stays in London, Amsterdam, Paris, and Barcelona, she returned to Toronto in 1939. Less than a year later, a stroke paralyzed one side of her face and left her unable to speak. *Old age has silenced her*, Lil wrote me. *It did what no government ever could.* A month later, Emma returned home from hospital, but she never did regain her speech. Being unable to communicate was too much; any other form of persecution she could bear, but not that one. After two months of convalescence at her Vaughn Road apartment, Emma died at the age of seventy-two.

Lil's final medical school exams came on the heels of Emma's death. We feared she'd spent too much time visiting her friend and not enough studying. She even considered going to Chicago, where Emma was to be buried, but Ma and Bessie talked her out of it. Fortunately, they helped her pull herself together in time to write her exams and graduate with honours in May 1940.

Without Emma alive to warn her about the traps of marriage, Lil decided to accept Gerry Dunkelman's proposal. They moved to Montreal after the wedding, where Gerry trained in obstetrics at the Jewish General, exempt from military duty because of a hearing problem. Lil didn't practise at first because she became pregnant right away and gave birth to their first daughter, whom they named after Emma. But she couldn't be held back long. When baby Emma was one, they found a nanny and Lil did her internship in obstetrics too. By the end of the war, she was one of the first female gynaecologists in Canada. Slowly, she drifted away from anarchism, but not from activism and civil disobedience. From the mid-1940s until they amended the laws in '69, she and Gerry helped women obtain birth control and performed clandestine abortions in their medical offices.

Bessie got married too, to Abe Kagan, in '37. His business did so well that he eventually bought Ma's fabric store, saving her from having to carry it on her own. Fortunately, Abe was also exempt from military service, in his case for being too old. Buoyed by his mother-in-law's business sense and his wife's support, he parlayed the two stores into a chain that became Kagan's Discount Clothing and Fabric, then Kagan's Discount Clothing when they got out of textiles, and eventually just Kagan's when they expanded into housewares in the '50s.

Bessie was only twenty-six when she remarried but she had trouble carrying a child to term. Over the next seven years, she had three miscarriages. Self-recrimination and despair filled her letters; she was certain this was punishment for her affair with MacNabb, and, as she put it, for letting me go to prison. Even though I wrote consoling letters back, I wondered if she might not be right, if the affair might not have cursed her in some way. In those days, we believed things like that.

Lil told us this was all superstitious nonsense but, tactless as ever, illustrated her point with the example that evil Nazi women were having children left, right, and centre. Bessie was stung by the comparison and was never fully convinced this meant she could have children. Maybe those women were too wicked to have a conscience, so God didn't bother tormenting them. Why punish their innocent babies, after all? She, on the other hand, had been consciously wicked, she wrote. In the eyes of God, maybe this was worse, she reasoned. When she did eventually have a baby, she couldn't concede that Lil was right. She'd finally been punished enough, she concluded, though I wonder if she ever believed it. Warren was born, healthy and plump at eight pounds even, just in time for the European peace treaty in May 1945.

Over the years I spent in jail, Lil worked tirelessly for my early release, but her appeals weren't successful. By July 1946, I'd served my full sentence.

As the day of my release approached, I had no great plans, no big dreams concocted during idle afternoons, beyond what I wanted for my first home-cooked meal — brisket and mashed potatoes — and the longing for a door without bars that I could close at night. Some of the guys urged me to think of how I'd earn my living. I had my high school diploma now, and I was still young enough to apprentice with a tradesman, or even go back to school, if my family could afford to pay. I listened to their advice, but any ideas I came up with just floated like feathers in the air that would blow out of reach if I tried to grab them. I had no experience with responsibility. Formulating a goal struck me as wishful thinking; the goal was unlikely to stick even if I did land on a decision.

Fortunately, Bessie had a plan, and she wrote me about it a month before I got out. Her husband, Abe, wanted to hire me to help with his books. A few years before, I'd proudly written home with my final marks from Miss Carstairs' classes. Bessie had tucked that information away, especially my A-plus in mathematics, alongside her knowledge of my photographic memory. At the right moment, she sat down with her husband and with Ma, and they worked out a solution. Ma would slowly pull back from her bookkeeping duties and move into the storefront. This was charity, but I was in no position to refuse it. Besides, numbers made sense to me; they were comforting somehow. If we human beings sometimes lost our way, or lost control, numbers never did. They could always be found, predictably, on the other side of the equation, dutifully resting beyond the equal sign, always willing to be balanced.

With Ma picking me up and a job waiting at home, I walked out of Collins Bay one bright summer day. I gripped the handles of a carpet bag filled with pottery and letters from home, the only possessions worth taking away. I didn't know if the worst was behind me or in front, but that morning, when the wind swept at me from the east, I turned to meet it head on. It pulsed, hot and resolute. I puffed out my chest to resist its pressure and, without much thought, started whistling. My free hand made a visor, and if the sun hadn't been shining in my face, you might have wondered if I was trying to see all the way to France.

a long time to be hidden away

Just when the summer heat had steamed us all into wilted spinach, flattened us, and drained our juices, September arrived and the mercury dropped. For most Torontonians, who slowed down during July and August, the cool air sharpened the edges they'd let dull, getting them ready again for when the city started making its fall breakaway. People hustled more urgently towards their bus stops, teeth set, eyes forward. They squeezed coffee cups just a little more tightly. Their faces lost their summer tans within days of the Labour Day weekend.

I, on the other hand, had spent much of the summer both fretful and purposeful, so the cooler temperatures allowed me a few decent nights' rest. I'd always found September to be Toronto's kindest month, at least in terms of the weather. I could go for walks without shvitzing. I could sleep without air conditioning. The summer air, thick from urban smog, thinned out and made it easier to breathe.

I watched the nightly news for any updates on Sue Rodriguez's appeal to the Supreme Court. She'd given several recent interviews about her right to die, and though her speech was more slurred now by Lou Gehrig's disease than mine had ever been by my cleft palate, I understood her perfectly. She'd made a private and painful decision because she now found her life to be intolerable. The court decision was due at the end of the month, but her eyes showed a determination I'd seen before. I knew what she'd do, either way.

In my world, instead of the Supreme Court, I had Ari, who all summer had been reserving judgement. He'd dragged it out so long that I was beginning to think I'd learn the Rodriguez decision first. Nonetheless, he'd come home for Rosh Hashanah, and when it was over, he'd called to say he'd made up his mind. He offered to take me for Saturday brunch, so I suggested a dim sum place on Dundas, because Pearl and I had tickets to a Pollack exhibit at the Art Gallery of Ontario.

"Where's Grandma?" he said, when we met in front of the gallery. He peered through the glass doors to see if she might be waiting inside in her wheelchair.

"She's not feeling well today. We decided to come on our own," said Pearl.

"No sense in wasting the tickets," I added.

"Toshy, you stay here with Ari, I'll just go in and get our coats."

"Is she coming with us?" said Ari, as soon as Pearl was out of earshot.

"No, no. She has a hair appointment." He didn't want to have our discussion in front of her, any more than I did.

"I was right about Pearl, wasn't I?" he said, raising his eyebrows a few times like Groucho Marx.

"Will you stop it? Nothing is going on."

We walked Pearl to the subway and then doubled back a few blocks to Lung Fung, a place where the food was good enough that I overlooked the rat I once saw scurrying across the floor. Prison had been crawling with them and I never got sick there; why should I worry now? There were only four other people in the restaurant, and we took a seat near the back, near the kitchen where the carts came out. Ari chose for us — fragrant bamboo steamer pots of shrimp and beef dumplings, tin trays of barbequed pork wrapped in long flat rice noodles, a tray of almond cookies, and two tiny dishes, one with deep-fried yams and the other with curls of tripe in salty-sweet sauce. We ate noisily and made small talk, slurping noodles and tea, clacking our chopsticks against china bowls. I asked about school and we exchanged reports on Bessie's health from our separate visits.

When I returned from a visit to the men's room, Ari said, "I've been meaning to ask you something."

"Oh?"

"Ever since you told me the real story of how you got sent to jail. Is it okay if we talk about this?"

"Why not," I said, "as long as we get to the other topic you've been avoiding."

"We will, I promise. It's just been bugging me ... not knowing what Grandma thinks about what happened."

"Why don't you ask her yourself?"

"I couldn't. She and I don't have that kind of relationship. Besides, you took the fall for her. I'm not sure how I feel about that. I'd be worried it'd come out all judgemental."

"Maybe you *should* be worried."

"How can you forgive her, after all that happened? Not to mention Aunt Lil."

"Why wouldn't I?"

"Aunt Lil manipulated you. She convinced you to throw her the diamond and then she stood by while you took the rap. She got away with everything and you went to jail. And Grandma? She had nobody to blame but herself for the mess she got herself into, but you saved her butt by perjuring yourself in court. And how did they reward your sacrifice? Neither of them confessed in order to save you."

I swallowed and lowered my head, suppressing the urge to slap him. "Ari, I don't want to be unkind here, but sometimes you can be a real horse's ass, do you know that?" My voice was level, but his expression showed that it had been a slap after all.

"What do you mean?"

"You have such a rigid idea about right and wrong. One act does not define a person."

"I know that."

o you? You're only upset because none of us is who
ought we were. If you didn't try to fit people into little packages, you'd be much happier."

"That's not fair. I was only..."

"So and so is smart, so and so is stupid, this one is strong,
that one is a weak — people aren't like that." I was talking to
him as one would a child, and it worked. He sat meekly,
rebuked. "The problem is you've never faced a situation of
real courage, one where you're tested because doing the
courageous thing might mean disgrace. You might be thinking
it would be a sacrifice if you gave me those drugs, but there are
many, many people who believe in assisted suicide. You won't
be facing humiliation — not like I have. Like Lil was. Like
your grandma did."

I paused. I had to find a way to soften the message, or he
wouldn't hear it.

"We can't all be like your hero, Emma Goldman, certain
what's right and wrong, strong enough to do the right thing
straight away, no matter how it might make us look. All I
know is that when most of us common folk come face to
face with a terrible choice, we have the same gut reflex, so it
means we all have the same potential — to do the right
thing, or the wrong thing, depending on the choice."

He met my remarks with a blank stare.

"Maybe I'm not explaining this right. I'm trying to say I
know why it's been so hard for you to understand what my
sisters and I went through. Why you don't seem to understand me now, at all."

He shook his head slightly, his mouth hanging open. "I
don't understand you."

"Let me put it this way: I realized something straddling
that window in the MacNabbs' house. Do you know what
it was?"

"No. What."

"That faced with a terrible dilemma, there always comes
a pivotal moment when we know we have to act. We have a

sharp intake of breath" — and I inhaled to illustrate my point — "and as sure as we have to expel that air, we know that no matter what, someone's going to suffer. I think you know what I mean."

He pondered this a moment, dragging his chopsticks through the remains of some sauce in his bowl. "What if we don't make the right choice?"

"Some of us don't. Not the first time, anyway, but there will almost always be another breath. Take Lil, for instance. She paid for her decisions by *not* going to jail. Her guilt over seeing me in prison, while she went free, was in many ways more punishment than I had. You know how powerful guilt can be. I shouldn't have to tell you that. And she made it up to me."

"You didn't deserve any punishment at all."

"Jail wasn't all bad for me, you know. Before I was sent there, I was a little shit. That place gave me time to think. I developed a political analysis, I finished high school…" I wanted to say I'd made a friend, but I couldn't admit to Ari how badly I'd messed that up, and more to the point, how. Besides, thinking about Bernie was still painful, even all these years later.

"You should've been given the chance to do all of that, without being locked up for eleven years."

"Maybe. But maybe that's how it had to be. It might look like I took the fall for my sisters, but I don't see it that way anymore. Through that whole ordeal, we were all selfish and we were all selfless. Two things can be true at the same time. Lil really did want to help Bessie when we went to the MacNabbs' that night, but when she convinced me to throw her the Orange Sunset, fundamentally, she knew it was about greed. She told herself it was revenge against Rupert MacNabb for what he did to Emma and to Bessie, but she didn't believe it for long. As for me, I was no better."

"How so?"

"I had years and years to tell the police where that brooch was, but I never did."

"I thought it was lost in the ravine. You knew where it was?"

"Of course we did; Lil and I both knew. And if I kept my mouth shut, it wasn't just to protect Lil. We grew up poor. The MacNabbs had so much money; I assumed they wouldn't miss one piece of jewellery. Same with Lil. Later, she convinced herself that selling the Orange Sunset was her chance at redemption. If she could sell it and invest the money for me, she'd assuage the guilt she felt seeing me in prison. She was still focused on money as the solution, and don't think she didn't suffer for it."

"What about Grandma?"

"She never knew anything about it. She had enough to deal with, what with her affair with her boss. Your grandma had lost a husband. How can either of us know what it was like for a woman in those days to find herself a widow at twenty-two? She didn't deserve to be framed for theft. That was no sweet, loving couple she was coming between. They each had their thing on the side."

"I can understand that. But what I don't understand is how she could sit back and let you take the blame for her, no matter what she'd gone through."

"But she didn't sit back. She did try to take the blame."

"Well, you see? How am I supposed to know that? You never told me *that!*"

"You want I should give you a complete transcript of the trial? It was on the second day, when she was called to the stand. The Crown asked his first question, but she ignored it and blurted out '*I* took it! I took the Orange Sunset and then I told my brother about it. He was only trying to return it when he was caught!' It was sweet, but ridiculous. She was nearly hyperventilating, and the tears started flowing. She was a mess. She left Lil out of the story altogether, because what reason would there have been to include her? She didn't even know Lil had the brooch."

"What did the judge say?"

"As you can imagine, her confession created a stir in the courtroom, especially when Oonagh MacNabb jumped up and shouted, 'I knew it!' The judge shushed Oonagh and told the Crown to continue. When he began to ask your grandma questions, it was clear the confession was too little and came too late to be believed. If she'd told the whole truth and nothing but the truth, there might have been a chance. The Crown was no dummy. He asked her, 'How can you explain that your brother was caught holding the brooch, climbing out a window that had been opened from the inside? If he was returning the brooch, why wasn't he empty-handed? And why would he throw it down the ravine?' Your grandma couldn't answer. And there was Abe, sitting in the courtroom gazing at his girlfriend with even more love than he normally did, same as our parents, and Bessie was still too ashamed to admit she'd had an affair with Rupert. You see, it's complicated."

"The judge dismissed her confession?"

"Which suspects did he have after that crazy outburst? First, they had a young anarchist girl. The Crown used up a great deal of time questioning Lil, mostly about her political activity and hardly at all about the theft. Our defence attorney objected repeatedly. He painted Lil's politics as a passing fad of youth, which as you can imagine infuriated her. Her medical school acceptance was all the proof the court needed that she was on her way to becoming a serious and contributing member of society. Being a doctor counted for even more then than it does today, and a woman doctor — she must've been very serious about her career, they'd have been thinking.

"Then you had your grandma, and when they heard her confession, everyone just assumed she was being heroic, which she was, in a way. Foolish, but heroic. They might've been prepared to believe that a young woman working as a maid to help her sister through school could've stolen from her employers, but not when your grandma's story was so implausible. Not when what you had left was me, a young punk who'd already seen the backside of the law and was caught red-handed. The Crown, the police, the press, my parents, they were all too ready to believe I was stupid, incompetent, and criminally minded.

"You see, Ari, you have your story of courage, but truth is in the nuance. Most people aren't tested by facing stark and blatant evil. They're thrown into situations that are muddled. The truth is I could never get the Orange Sunset out of my mind. It caused our family so much trouble, and yet where did it end up? In the South of France where we couldn't get it. Sitting there waiting for who knows who to find it. No chance to profit from it. And no chance to return it."

"Did you say the South of France? You mean it was…"

"In St-Tropez." I brought my teacup to my lips and gulped a mouthful down. I reached down to the floor where my knapsack lay, unzipped the front pocket, and took out a small canvas pouch with a drawstring.

Ari's eyes widened. "Oh, you can't be serious…"

I opened the pouch and placed its contents on the table. "The Orange Sunset. In all its splendour."

"How the hell?" He covered it with his hand as a dim sum cart wheeled by.

"You don't need to cover it here. Besides, it's been hidden away from the world for such a long time; it deserves to be out in the open."

"You know … you are *such* a devious little man!" He drew his hand back tentatively.

"I retrieved it when you were being shown around Bon Esprit. Remember how I went for a walk in the garden?"

"Sonofagun. I thought you were acting strangely. You kept staring out the window and couldn't wait to get outside. I just thought your visit with Véronique had spooked you."

"It was in the retaining wall. You remember how your aunt Lil and I used to hide things when we were kids? In the wall behind Mr. Rothbart's pharmacy? Well, she stuck to what she knew best. I didn't have to memorize a thing — it was the same configuration we used back home. Ten bricks in from the end and five rows up from the ground. While that woman gave you a tour of Bon Esprit, I took a pocket knife out of my pack and worked the brick loose. The brooch was wrapped in cheesecloth in a small bag that had almost rotted away." We both stared at it now, all shiny. "I cleaned it up. She looks pretty good, doesn't she?"

"But how the hell did it end up in France in the first place?"

I told him how, and to explain it, I had to bring myself back to 1935, to that windowsill in the MacNabb bedroom. So many things came back to that place, to that moment of decision when one of two very bad options had to be chosen. At least this time I went intentionally, instead of being pulled there by some random event or stray thought percolating through my subconscious.

When Rupert caught me in that window, I'd stepped back into the room, and like a coward, I'd put my arms up, even though he didn't have a gun. He brought me downstairs, where Oonagh was skulking at the edge of the dining room. She held a crystal vase, probably to bash me with, just as her husband meant to with his cane. Rupert asked my name and I told them, and then Oonagh said, "Bessie's brother?" She said something about how Bessie had probably given me the key, and I said no, that I'd stolen it from her. I took the key slowly out of my pocket and handed it to Rupert, while he watched carefully to make sure I wasn't pulling out a weapon.

Rupert said, "Oonagh, go outside in the backyard and try to find whatever he threw down there."

I said, "Good luck. I threw it down the ravine."

The police showed up fifteen minutes later and took me down to the station. My confession went like this: I'd seen the Orange Sunset when Bessie'd showed me the house a few months before, and then and there, I'd decided to pinch it. I'd stolen Bessie's key, I said. Why had I thrown the diamond down the ravine? Because I felt like it, I said. One policeman mentioned to another about my being an idiot, that he could tell from the way I was talking, and then he brought in a file. Constable Richards, who walked the beat in Kensington, had been keeping tabs on me, he said.

They searched the ravine extensively but they never found the Orange Sunset. That's because Lil had seen it land on the grass and, in a clean pass, had swept it up, hopped over the masonry fence, and shot off down the ravine. She made her way carefully through the trees, down the steep slope, and along the path she found there, until she reached the Don Valley Brickworks at the bottom, where she hid behind one of the buildings until she was sure nobody had followed her. Then she walked the west bank of the river until she found the old Don Mills Road. It's no longer there, but it used to run up into Cabbagetown at the south end of the Toronto Necropolis, where it connected to Winchester Avenue. Calmly, she strolled out to Parliament Street and grabbed the Carlton streetcar.

She didn't go home, at first. She went to Mr. Rothbart's pharmacy and into the alleyway behind it. Tapping along the wall, she found the loose brick that concealed our childhood hiding place: ten columns from the end and five rows up. She removed the brick, placed the brooch there, and only then did she go home to find the house empty. She had just enough time to change and throw her clothes in a bucket of soapy water before a police constable showed up. They'd already taken Bessie and our parents to the station and now he'd returned to take Lil in for questioning too.

It was just as well. Lil was right. Just as well that she have the brooch if I was to go to jail anyway. What I didn't realize was how angry the judge would be when he heard I'd thrown it out the window. Eleven years was almost unheard of for break, enter, and theft. That didn't matter to me by then. Even without jail, I couldn't see hope or possibility on the horizon of my life. If I wasn't at all nervous on the stand, if my words came out clear and unslurred in the courthouse that day, it was because I was an actor who'd finally remembered his lines. I'd heard of actors being nervous wrecks if they had to address an audience as themselves, but give them a role to play and their butterflies disappeared.

We each had our role. Lil had to go to medical school, which would give her a legitimate profession that would sustain her in her life of political dissent that might otherwise scare away a husband. Bessie had to find a safe way out of an imprudent affair and a dead-end job in order to have her second chance at love, at marriage, and at children. As for me, that night in my holding cell, I realized that being locked up was where I was meant to be. It was the perfect and logical conclusion to an ignominious youth.

If I was to convince people I'd thrown the Orange Sunset down the ravine, if I was to divert them from suspecting Lil or Bessie, I had to act stupid, even if it meant risking being committed to an asylum. It was easy, really; it's not hard to act dumb when people are looking for it. I simply amplified their expectations.

The trial was swift and brutal for everyone except me, and at its conclusion, they led me willingly away to the Toronto Jail, and later to Kingston. Lil, meanwhile, had more than guilt and grief to occupy her. She had to figure out what to do with the diamond. The publicity surrounding the trial made it impossible, with her few connections to the criminal underworld, for her to sell it locally. She remembered Emma, newly arrived in France. She didn't even dare write her about it, so paranoid was she that the police were watching her.

The next year, when Emma presented Lil with the opportunity to visit, she seized it. Seeing France would've been enough of an incentive on its own; getting the chance to finally sell the brooch, well, that was just gravy. She retrieved the Orange Sunset from behind Mr. Rothbart's pharmacy, packed it up deep in her suitcase, and took it to Europe. There, she left it with Emma, who promised to try to find a buyer. Emma was angry that Lil was implicating her in our crime, but Lil knew she wouldn't tell anyone. Though she grudgingly agreed to help, Emma asked Lil, while she looked for a buyer, to put the brooch somewhere safe, always worried that police might search her house without warning, as they had on many occasions throughout her life.

Things didn't go according to plan — nothing did in this whole venture — and it wasn't really Emma's fault. She had trouble finding an appropriate person who would also pay a decent price, and her attentions were legitimately pulled elsewhere — first in June with the death of her lifelong friend Sasha Berkman, and then in July with the outbreak of the Spanish Civil War. In September, she left St-Tropez hastily for Barcelona, deciding to sell Bon Esprit and leaving the Orange Sunset in its new hiding place until she was in London later in the fall. She'd intended to come back one last time, and again, with the constant threat of arrest, it wasn't safe for her to travel with the diamond.

In London, she continued to grieve for Berkman, and became caught up in her new fight for a free Spain. Nevertheless, she sent a message to a former neighbour that he should alert her when someone was interested in purchasing the house, and that he should contact her before the sale closed. Unfortunately, when Bon Esprit was finally sold after a full year of being on the market, the transaction took only days. The move-in date was tight and Emma wasn't able to get back in time.

She wrote to the Belgian doctor who'd bought the place to say she'd forgotten something and could she retrieve it, but he replied that the house had been left in a deplorable state, that they'd had to hire someone to clear out her junk, and that she wouldn't be welcome back. The doctor knew of

Emma. He was opposed to her politics and was therefore not inclined in any way to do her favours. She even tried to get a friend who was passing through St-Tropez to snoop around, to see if he could retrieve the brooch when the Belgians were away, but he discovered they'd erected a tall fence, that they had a guard dog, and that one of them was almost always at home.

When Emma came back to Toronto nearly three years later, she tried to console Lil, saying that they'd both done everything they could and that the Orange Sunset was, after all, ill-gotten and only of monetary value, not sentimental. Emma tried to convince Lil to think of the diamond as lost and therefore best forgotten, but Lil couldn't get it out of her mind, and neither could I.

Because it wasn't lost, only hidden, and we knew exactly where. For my part, I knew, if I could ever find Bon Esprit and get access to the grounds, that retrieving it would be relatively simple, provided that wall was still intact. Lil had tried once in the '70s, but the heavy iron gate had prevented her from entering, and unlike me, she had no Ari to provide a convenient excuse.

Ari sat back and shook his head. "Why didn't you tell me any of this when we were in France?"

"Because I try not to let other people in on my crimes until after they're committed. Not unless I absolutely have to. I couldn't risk that Madame Letour would place a claim on the brooch, seeing as it was found on her property. If she did, how would I counter it? According to police records, I'd stolen it. What would I have said at the airport if I'd been questioned? Nobody'd believe I'd brought a priceless piece of women's jewellery with me to France. Or that I purchased it there; I'm a single man living on a fixed income. There might've been trouble, Ari. If they'd done some digging, things might've turned out badly." I pushed the brooch towards him. "I'm giving you this to return it to the people it really belongs with."

"The MacNabbs?"

"No, it was never rightfully theirs and they have no descendants anyway. I'm talking about the Fisters, its first owner. Grace Fister was swindled out of her wedding gift. Lord and Lady Fister aren't alive anymore, but their granddaughter is." I brought the newspaper clipping out of my pocket and passed it to him too. "For so many reasons, she deserves it more than any of us. I told your grandma all of this yesterday. She agrees it's the right thing to do."

He sat, silent for a moment, covering the diamond with his hands. "I promise I'll get it to her," he said. "I'm so sorry, Uncle Toshy. I really have been a horse's ass. I've kept you waiting so long for … you know what. It's just that I don't want what I do to eat away at me my whole life. The problem I've had is deciding what'll eat at me more, helping you, or not helping."

He reached into his pocket, brought out a bottle of pills, and rolled it across the table.

I smiled at him and reached over to pat his hand. "Good boy." I rocked the bottle in my palm. "What you're doing is a mitzvah."

"I hardly think the rabbis would consider it a mitzvah to be participating in a suicide, but I'm doing it anyway."

I could've just taken the pills and not said anything. I could've walked out of there and dealt with the consequences later.

I looked into Ari's face and found I couldn't lie anymore. I was finished with keeping secrets from my family. I gave him back the bottle.

"What are you doing?"

"Hold onto these for a second, until you've heard me out. If, afterwards, you haven't changed your mind, you can give them back. There's something I need to say, something else I need you to do for me. I wasn't going to ask, but it's time I started trusting you."

"You can trust me, I promise."

I pulled out of my pocket a small, sealed envelope and handed it to him. "There are two notes in there, both written by your grandma, but they're not for you to read — hopefully nobody will ever have to read them. One was written a few months ago, and the other, just yesterday — to confirm she hasn't changed her mind. I need you to keep them for us. Bessie can't have them in her room because they would be found and they're only meant as a safeguard. I could keep them myself, but I'm afraid to be the only one who knows about this. With my criminal record, they might not believe me; they might accuse me of forgery or some damn thing. Pearl doesn't know about this and I don't want her to."

"I don't understand."

I leaned in and lowered my voice to a whisper.

"Don't you see? Those drugs you're holding, I'm not the one who wants them."

learn the new

This morning I went to Bessie's room and sat in a chair beside her bed. It was achingly familiar. Years before, I'd visited Lil, sat by her cot set up in their front room on Strathallen. And later, I'd spent days, hours, minutes, small eternities by Ellen's side. Both of my sisters and my wife have ended up in that place of silent touch and shallow breath, with my gentle stroking the signal that they could finally take their release. They say letting go isn't easy, but I realized today that with the right catalyst and a firm decision, there's no controlling the force of it.

In my shirt pocket was a magazine clipping I found in a box of Lil's belongings just after I moved here. It was from *Harper's*, and across the top edge it said December 1934. It was Emma Goldman's essay "Was My Life Worth Living?" — the one we helped her type. Lil had underlined the following sentences:

Those who insist that human nature remains the same at all times have learned nothing and forgotten nothing.

Human nature is by no means a fixed quantity. Rather, it is fluid and responsive to new conditions.

If only we can first learn the new and forget the old.

WHEN BESSIE FOUND HERSELF a childless widow at twenty-two, she adapted to her new circumstances. She seemed so conservative to us in those days, but in retrospect, she made bold moves. A Jewish woman working as a domestic instead of a garment worker? And then let's not forget her affair with a married man. It was a salve spread thickly over her loneliness, when other women might have retreated to black scarves, crochet, or romance novels.

Lil was the more predictable one; although she was the most radical, she was also more consistent. Prompt her with an opening and I could mouth the response along with her. She had a keen sense of right and wrong but it was nearly always driven by political analysis, instead of vice versa. She wasn't hard and unfeeling; people who didn't know activists often drew this faulty conclusion. Yes, Lil developed her analysis using her keen mind, but the concepts were supported by a good heart. She planned and debated her actions in terms that stirred passion into a bubbling brew of ideas. She was rarely rash, but, like the rest of us, she had her lapses. And when she did something questionable, oh, the loops and twists she would make to rationalize her decision! She would apply a precise logical framework to what was essentially a question of poor judgement, and she fooled a surprising number of people.

It took me longer to see through her rationalizations when it came to the incident at the MacNabbs', but eventually, over many nights in a jail cell, I figured out that her obsession with keeping the Orange Sunset was fuelled by longing. The longing was an ache that betrayed her from the marrow of her resolve. It throbbed against politics and rational decisions and logic. Deep in her bones, she was tired of sacrifice and duty and she was angry at the lengthy road to a comfortable, just existence. She was weary for herself, yes, but also for her whole family, and especially for me. She knew the money from that diamond would've given me a security and independence she was unsure I could achieve on my own.

When I came to that conclusion, I forgave her for her lack of faith in me and chose to love her for her sense of duty. She left me straddling that windowsill to face the police on my own, but because she saw herself as my protector, I forgave her for that too. Eventually, I embraced her even more — for her failures and for her humanity.

Lil died first, as we somehow assumed she would. Maybe because she had such fire, we expected she'd burn out long before the rest of us. I knew that was silly; it wasn't passion that consumed her but cancer — same as with my Ellen, just as it had started to eat away at me and was nearly finished with poor Bessie.

Bessie was tougher than cancer expected her to be, and in the end, that's what frustrated her enough to want to end her life. She surprised me with that, Bessie did. Strange that it had taken me this long to realize it was the conservative ones you had to keep an eye on, for what they might be concocting. Or repressing.

Or slowly becoming.

Bessie was always a smart girl — maybe not as skilled academically as Lil was, but she learned quietly, absorbed facts and truths imperceptibly, and in that way acquired something more precious, in my opinion: wisdom. For a long time, I turned to Lil for moral guidance, but it was Bessie whose hand was steadier when it came to questions of personal integrity and loyalty and intimate kindness.

Lil was better with the big picture, the greater good, and sure, Bessie could've learned a thing or two from her younger sister about the downtrodden. But Lil? One person could be a blur in the corner of her eye. Worse, she could sometimes trample you as she rushed headlong at justice. Bessie was slower, more observant, and despite a certain crustiness that we all developed as the years hardened over us, she'd nurtured an unerring sense of goodness within her. Those of us who'd had the privilege of her company had been fortunate for her generosity. Twice now, she'd come to me for help, asked me to take enormous risks for her, but she'd more than earned the right.

Back in jail, when Gaétan told me about the wolf and his essential nature, I realized that Bessie, Lil, and I were a pack. We'd each spent time alone, hunting, and I would certainly wander off again from time to time, but one thing was certain: We always came back to one another.

I raised my eyes from the bedside to the wall. Our family's phone numbers were listed in oversized type: Warren and Susan's, then mine, then Ari's, then Lil's daughters' in the United States. A slight twitch in Bessie's wrist brought me back to her hand, warm and slack in mine. I stroked her fingers, touching the loose skin above her knuckles, and considered what those hands had held in their eighty-plus years. A mother's breast and a baby's bottom. A husband's casket and a lover's back.

An amber diamond and an empty pill bottle.

I brought my free hand up and moved a lock of hair off Bessie's forehead. As I did, my wrist passed before her mouth, and I felt her breath, so faint now that I wasn't sure if there'd be much left. She stirred and her eyelids parted slightly.

"Abe?" The question was a wisp that barely carried over her lips.

"No, Bessie. It's me, Toshy."

She stared, puzzled. I wasn't sure I should've disappointed her, but I didn't want to deceive.

She closed her eyes again. For a few minutes, I sat there, searching for something else to say. The silence stretched and yawned and then began to claw, slowly at first and then more insistently until I grew afraid this would be my last chance and I was wasting it. I drew myself stiffly upright and spoke loudly, to penetrate the fog that was gathering.

"Bessie! Look at me. Open your eyes, sweetie."

She opened them, one last time.

"Do you know who I am?" I asked, trying to sound cheerful, but hearing the desperation that escaped.

A pause, as she pondered my question.

She squinted, and I realized the sun from the window was in her eyes and she might not really be able to tell. When I moved my head so that her face was shaded, her eyes relaxed and she considered me for a moment.

Then, softly, so softly I almost didn't hear, she said, "You don't know?"

I laughed.

Such a stupid thing to do, to laugh, when your sister is dying by your side. Stupid, stupid, stupid.

I leaned into her and rested my cheek against hers.

I LEFT HER ROOM and went to join the new Recollections Group, just beginning over in the other building. Since moving into The Terrace, this was my first attempt at sociability and it surprised everyone, especially Pearl, who'd been trying to get me there for over a month. Her grin was so generous when she patted the chair beside her that, heaven help me, I actually sat down in it.

She smelled of lilac.

The instructor introduced the group's objective and asked us to put pen to paper, but before I did, I took the *Harper's* clipping out of my shirt pocket and spread it out carefully on the desk. The brittle paper crackled as it unfolded, much as I did these days.

Those who insist that human nature remains the same at all times have learned nothing and forgotten nothing.

Maybe it was perverse, but musing on a quote chiding us for hanging on to what we knew felt like the perfect way to start a recollections group.

Forgetting the old would've been hopeless, so I did the next best thing: I let my memories drain onto the foolscap, collecting in a stream that grew deeper and wider as its accumulated force tugged at the ink. It was the first time I'd written a story since prison, since my tale of the lost seal pup, which had made Miss Carstairs cry. Now my own tears were flowing, but I didn't care. There were so many years, so much to let go of, that it was a torrent. Of words, of grief, of confessions, of regrets. When the instructor came by to check on me, I waved him away. I wiped my cheeks with my free arm and carried on.

And when I'd finished, I rested the pen neatly across the top of the page, I leaned over to Pearl, and I kissed her.